REQUIEM

Jack Ross

WINDSOR
PARAGON

First published 2008
by Hutchinson
This Large Print edition published 2008
by BBC Audiobooks Ltd
by arrangement with
The Random House Group Ltd

Hardcover ISBN: 978 1 405 68678 5
Softcover ISBN: 978 1 405 68679 2

This novel is a work of fiction. Names and characters are the product of the author's imagination and any resemblance to actual persons, living or dead, is entirely coincidental

British Library Cataloguing in Publication Data available

Printed and bound in Great Britain by
Antony Rowe Ltd., Chippenham, Wiltshire

For my wife, Susan

Prologue

Death. It was the way of all flesh.

He gazed at the heavens, tears in his eyes, as blood seeped from his neck. Lightning bugs and insects buzzed around the gaping wound. He was staring into oblivion, all alone, just before dawn. Unable to summon help, prostrate on the clay basketball court within Flamingo Park. Every time he tried to shout he swallowed some more warm blood. He felt no pain and did not fear the darkness. Strange. Face to face with eternity and he began to wonder how the headline writers would report his death.

Perhaps, *Senator's Son Slain by Knifeman in Florida Park . . .*

He closed his eyes for a moment and smelled the cut grass in the steamy air—a hint of azaleas. The overhanging palm trees and sodden oaks partially obscured the billions of stars in the darkness. Then the sun winked across the horizon, throwing long shadows over the court. What a way to go.

He felt himself slipping away. The wail of a police siren in the distance split the sultry South Beach night and snapped him back for a few moments. Vivid images of his childhood seared through his fading mind.

Hauling in his first barracuda as a boy while deep-sea fishing with his dad and uncle in the Gulf of Mexico. He remembered the turquoise waters and the proud look on his father's face when he held the fish aloft for a photo. It was as if he had arrived.

Scoring his first touchdown as the quarterback for St Columba's Prep, his exclusive private school in West Palm Beach, his father roaring him on from the sidelines. He turned to salute him, and his dad saluted back.

That was the worst part. He'd never see him again. Or his mother who worshipped the ground he walked on. Waves of sadness threatened to drown him in grief.

His breathing grew shallower and his mind switched track. He remembered climbing the park's perimeter wall with the Cuban girl, less than half an hour ago.

It was strange. In Flamingo Park he felt free. No paparazzi or low-life tabloid reporters around to bug him, as they had for months after his appearance in court. The 'Playboy Frat Boy', they'd dubbed him. Just because he liked the girls and a few beers.

Then, all of a sudden, it changed. A man emerged out of the shadows and walked slowly towards them. Then he remembered a serrated knife blade pressed to his throat. Sour whiskey on the old man's breath. He ordered the Cuban girl to scram and she ran off in the direction of Espanola Way, screaming hysterically, hitching up her skirt and kicking off her high heels to run faster. The man then frogmarched him through the park.

The man was old, tall, and thickly built. He was also well dressed—very conservative, blue suit, white shirt, muted tie. Not like some tramp begging down the beach. That freaked him out.

He could see the man's face—lined, handsome. His hair was very short and gray.

He remembered being beaten senseless. Then

the man's cold staring eyes, clenched teeth, before he drew the blade across his throat, the blood spurting onto the man's white shirt. He froze with shock when he realized what had happened. He dropped to the ground, and the man turned on his heels. But he did not run. He strode out, head held high.

Suddenly, he was staring down at his own body. His eyes were closed. Pools of blood around his matted black hair. Red splatter on his polo shirt, chinos and Top-Siders. His face was swollen, battered black and blue.

Christ, it really was him—the only son of Senator Jack O'Neill.

He wanted to cry. But he could not. He thought of his father, hearing the news at their West Palm Beach home. The media descending on the park after the police tipped them off. He thought of his poor mother, realizing that her darling son lay cold in a Miami park.

He slipped away into a sea of darkness, wishing she was with him now.

1

Deborah Jones shifted in her seat, phone pressed to her ear, as ice-cold air blasted out of the new air-conditioning system. 'I'm sorry, ma'am, but I haven't got time to discuss the merits of Ricky Martin's music.' She gazed across the bright waters of Biscayne Bay from the fifth-floor offices of the *Miami Herald* and wondered how many other readers were so enthralled by the Latino heart-throb.

'Ma'am, I described him as flamboyant,' she said, drumming her newly manicured fingernails on her desk. She brushed away a loose thread off her honey-brown suit, which matched her skin tone. She noticed a few of her colleagues were even wearing sweaters. In Florida? 'I didn't insinuate anything about his sexuality.' She let out a long sigh. Why did she get stuck with the cranks? 'I understand you're a big fan.'

Deborah looked up and saw her managing editor, Sam Goldberg, standing outside his door. He smiled and cocked his head in the direction of his office, indicating that he wanted to speak to her in private. She wondered if there was a problem.

Was it about an article she had written? She feared the worst—he hadn't really spoken to her since she'd joined the paper, six months earlier.

'Ma'am, I gotta go.' She nodded back at her boss to acknowledge him. She paused briefly as the woman kept her tied up for several more seconds. 'Yes, if you want, call tomorrow.'

Deborah hung up and blew out her cheeks. It

was the third time that morning that the mad woman from Boca Raton had phoned about her stories. Talk about obsessive.

She followed Goldberg into his cluttered office. She ran her hand through her shoulder-length hair and hoped she didn't look too disheveled.

Goldberg's desk was a mess. Scraps of paper with shorthand notes, yellow Post-Its, empty mugs of old coffee, readers' letters, clippings from back issues—despite them being available on-line. She noticed that he kept a space for a color portrait of his late wife, a woman of remarkable beauty, almost Mediterranean in appearance, who had a carefree smile on her face.

Some people found such sentiment old-fashioned. She didn't. It seemed sweet to want to show others how much their loved ones still meant to them.

'Shut the door behind you,' Goldberg said. He slumped into his leather desk chair and loosened his tie.

He looked exhausted, dark rings around his eyes as if he hadn't slept in a month. Some of the reporters said he was hitting the liquor hard.

He pointed to the seat opposite. 'Please.'

Deborah sat down. 'Thank you.' Her smile was tight.

'This is just an informal chat, Deborah—nothing to worry about.'

'Sure.' So why was she feeling so tense?

'How are you settling in?' He sneaked a glance at a CNN live broadcast. Florida's governor was speaking to a rally of the faithful in Tallahassee ahead of the November 2002 mid-terms.

'Just fine, although it's not a place for the thin-skinned, especially when dealing with the public.'

'Any gripes?'

'Apart from the freezing temperatures in the newsroom, I guess the mailroom could be a bit more efficient bringing up letters or correspondence to the reporters.'

Goldberg nodded grimly. 'The air-conditioning company has people looking into the problem. As for the mail, well, it's been like that since I've been here.'

'Okay.'

'Anyway, down to business. I've been hearing some good reports about you, Miss Jones.'

Did he say 'good reports'?

'They tell me you're the most promising young reporter we've had in years, coming up with stories instead of relying on the features desk.' He smiled across at her. 'I've been keeping a close eye on your progress. That surprise you?'

'A bit.'

Truth be told, Deborah was shocked. She thought of Goldberg as a distant man who didn't take a keen interest in the young reporters. It didn't bother her as she assumed he would have far more important things to worry about.

Deborah took a good look at Goldberg close-up. She'd been told he was in his mid-forties and had enjoyed a meteoric career on the paper after a successful spell at the *Washington Post.* His hair was black, although gray at the sides. A small piece of bloodied tissue was stuck to his chin, as if he'd rushed while shaving. His white shirt was creased like he'd slept in it and his tie was loose.

Despite a reputation for seriousness, he was known as one of the good guys—a journalist's journalist. He wasn't the type of editor who shied away from controversy. He took on unfashionable stories and confronted vested interests—Miami police corruption or immigrants being used as cheap labor in trendy, overpriced South Beach restaurants. Goldberg backed his journalists to the hilt, despite pressure coming from above.

He was also known to encourage minority reporters like her and spoke out about journalism still being too much of a white preserve.

Goldberg cleared his throat. In the background, the governor droned on about lower taxes and better schools. 'Okay, down to business.' Goldberg fixed Deborah with his weary stare. 'Believe you've had a few run-ins with the features editor, Michelle Rodriguez, since you joined.'

'It's a difference of opinion.' Who'd told him? 'I promise it won't happen again.'

Goldberg smiled. 'I don't usually have to speak to our young reporters about badgering a senior journalist.'

Deborah stayed quiet.

'She mentioned that you've been pestering her to interview William Craig since you started working here.'

'That's right.' Why didn't she just leave it alone?

'Helluva brutal case.'

Deborah nodded, wondering where this was going.

'She also said that you've even shown her a dossier on his case, one that contains the court transcripts of his trial and every newspaper clipping. You wanna tell me why?'

'William Craig's story is remarkable and I think our readers would like to know a little about him.

He's being executed in their name, after all.'

'He can't have long now.'

'Five weeks and one day.'

'Is that right? Not a long time to find out about him.'

'I've been at Ms Rodriguez for a shot at this story since my first day on the job.' Should she come clean on why she really wanted to interview Craig? Should she tell him why, when she was at home in her Miami Beach condo, she watched and rewatched old news clips of Craig?

Goldberg gave a rueful smile. 'So she says. Look, there are many people you can interview up at the state pen. We've had Amnesty call us recently about two guys on death row up in Raiford, cast-iron innocent. Why Craig?'

'I think what William Craig did deserves closer examination.'

'How do you mean?'

'I mean his motivation for killing the only son of a Florida senator after the trial.'

'Young O'Neill was innocent.'

'He was acquitted—it's a different thing.'

Goldberg smiled as if he enjoyed her take on the case. 'Smart girl, but you haven't answered my question. Why Craig? Usually journalists try to prove a man is innocent and get him moved off death row. We know this guy's guilty.'

'Yes,' she said, a small frown creasing his forehead, 'but I think it'd be good journalism. What provoked Craig to exact such revenge for his granddaughter?' She paused and looked at Goldberg.

He picked up a pen and nibbled the end like he was uneasy. 'No one's interviewed him. What does that tell you?'

'No one wants to touch it with a ten-foot pole?'

Goldberg leaned forward, fixing her with his intense stare. He lowered his voice. 'I've been thinking over the ideas you suggested to Ms Rodriguez. I've gotta tell you, a couple of my colleagues said you're a bit inexperienced to tackle such a story.'

Deborah kept quiet. She had a good idea that Kathleen Klein, the veteran political writer—who used the senator as a source—was one of those who objected to her. Probably because it would jeopardize her relationship with O'Neill. Admittedly, she was a fine journalist but she seemed to despise any new female reporters. Ever since Deborah's first day in the newsroom, Klein's steely gaze had seemed to follow her round the room.

'But I decide.' Goldberg smiled. 'I think an interview with Craig is overdue—that's assuming he grants us one.'

The words skidded across her brain. 'You're kidding?'

Goldberg shook his head.

'And you want me to interview him?'

'You write clean, crisp copy and you've got an eye for a story.' His gaze seemed to linger.

'I appreciate your faith in me.' This was what she had waited for.

Her mind flashed news-footage images of seventy-one-year-old Craig being led away in chains after his trial in the summer of 1991—orange top, baggy pants, sneakers, and short hair.

'Don't let me down. Do a good job and the fixed-term contract you're on could become permanent.'

So he thought she was good enough?

'There's something you need to be aware of.' Goldberg paused for a beat and stared at her like her own father had as she headed off on prom night. 'You know Senator O'Neill's a powerful man?'

'Of course.'

'He's got influential allies throughout the country, not just the state. I've lost track of the number of times we've crossed swords.'

'Why?'

'Mostly, he was pissed that I didn't pull articles criticizing his close links to the big military contractors.'

Deborah knew that from her research. 'He's also well connected in the media, isn't he?'

'You've no idea how well connected that guy is. And he's fighting an election, too.'

Deborah nodded.

'The people who mix with him are important—movers, shakers, politicians, judges and movie moguls. Even the governor is close to the senator, and yes, even journalists. He's the establishment.'

'I understand.'

Goldberg leaned back in his seat and smiled benignly at her. 'Look, I don't want to come across as the hard ass, but you need to be street-smart for an assignment like this. Everyone says you're a very by-the-book kind of journalist. That's great. We need ethical people, but I'm looking for you to get underneath this story.'

'How do you mean?'

'Well, if Craig speaks I want to know if he's found God. Has he opted for the chair instead of the needle? Something interesting, something meaty.'

Deborah winced.

'Does he fear death?' Goldberg shrugged. 'That sort of thing.'

'I understand.'

'Don't get all idealistic and harp on about the unfairness of the death penalty—that's not what this is about. It's story, first and foremost.'

'Got you.'

Goldberg went quiet for a few moments as if thinking of something else to say. 'You gotta remember this is a helluva tough place you're going to.'

Deborah wondered if she was up to it. This was no fluffy feature on Ricky Martin. This was the real deal. Could she handle it?

She tried to imagine Craig. Would he be in the same room as her? Would he even want to be interviewed?

'One final thing.' Goldberg looked straight at her. 'I want you to communicate only with me on this story.'

Had she heard right?

'This is a potentially sensitive scenario. If you want to talk about your story, you phone me. You wanna e-mail the features desk, you e-mail me. Is that clear?'

Deborah nodded, unconvinced.

'Don't speak to anyone in the office until I say.'

'Anyone?'

Goldberg sighed. 'Look at it from my side of the fence. With the election nearly upon us, and you trying to interview the guy who killed a senator's son, we could be accused of bias. That's why only a few editors and a couple of senior journalists know about this.

'Look, this isn't some small-town paper in Mississippi, Deborah. The *Miami Herald* breaks major stories and occasionally runs into trouble with the rich and powerful. We've got to box clever and keep this under our hat, unless Craig speaks.'

Only now was the full magnitude of the story becoming clear.

Deborah understood the logic although it seemed slightly over the top. 'When do you want me to start?'

'Right away. I want you up at Raiford by tomorrow afternoon.'

'That might be a problem as I don't fly.'

'Well, you'll have to drive up overnight. I'll clear things with Michelle, and arrange things with the warden. Oh, before I forget—one final thing.'

'What?'

Goldberg stared across at her, his eyes dead. 'Be careful. Florida may be the Sunshine State to most people, but it's not. It's a swamp. Don't ever forget that.'

2

It was mile after mile of loblolly pines between the odd homestead as Deborah drove deeper and deeper into the backwoods of northern Florida.

She yawned as she sped on through another small town, her convertible eating up the miles. She'd driven through the night from Miami up I-95 and had stopped twice for gas. Her fear of flying was something that she had tried to conquer with hypnotism and special relaxation exercises devised by her therapist but, in a way, she was glad to take to the road.

Deborah looked out over the fields and wondered how people around here survived. This was cracker country. Poor white farmers tried to scratch a living from the barren sandy soil of Bradford County. Baseball caps pulled down low to shield their eyes from the fierce sun.

This was a tough part of the Sunshine State. Old Victorian towns like nearby Starke were rooted in the penal culture. Whole families worked in the state pen. She was a long way from her nice Miami condo.

In this piney swatch of redneck villages and towns, there were no chic restaurants, dazzling nightlife, or relaxed vibes like in South Beach. Here, people had to work hard for not much. People like her ex-boyfriend's parents, who ran a Seven-Eleven.

Deborah's thoughts turned to Brett, her one-time college sweetheart.

It was less than two years since she'd followed him back to Florida like a dutiful lapdog after they'd graduated from Berkeley. She'd just wanted to be near him. He got a job in a law firm and she got a job at the *Orlando Sentinel,* but she could see in his eyes that he didn't love her any more. He had changed. Sure enough, before long he dumped her, leaving Deborah all alone in a part of the country where she had few friends. She felt as though her world had collapsed around her.

She didn't tell anyone for a month. Not a soul. Her mother seemed glad that he'd left. Her father? Well, he never did much care for him. Thought she should hold out for a black lawyer or doctor. Brett, a handsome white boy from a poor background who won a football scholarship to Berkeley, didn't fit the bill. It was like she'd never please them. Her happiness seemed incidental.

Deborah sped on. She passed sodden fields of strawberries and sweet potatoes drying out in the sun after an overnight downpour. The area seemed to be stuck in another era. Life was agriculture-based and slow.

I-95 gave way to the old pre-Interstate federal highway. She was getting closer. An old country song—'Okie from Muskogee'—played on the radio.

Deborah looked to her right and saw dozens of mostly black and Hispanic inmates, heads down and all wearing blue prison-issue pants and tops. The men were bent double in the blistering sun as they picked vegetables. She wondered if they were from the nearby New River Correctional Institution—also known as the 'O' Unit—which housed minimum and medium security-risk inmates. Four white guards on horseback watched over them with shotguns at the ready. It was as if things hadn't changed since Civil War days.

It was common knowledge that black people made up a large percentage of all those incarcerated in penitentiaries across America. Were they far more likely to commit crimes than whites were? Why did black killers have a significantly higher chance of ending up on death row than white killers? Double standards, that was what it was. In many respects, Craig was the exception. The disparity was striking, especially in the South. Deborah remembered what her father had said about Florida: 'It isn't the Deep South. It is the *deep* Deep South.'

She gazed down the shimmering road as Hank Williams's 'Your Cheatin' Heart' played. She smiled at the irony of being a twenty-something African American woman who preferred country music to Destiny's Child, Jennifer Lopez, and the rappers favored by her peers.

What would she choose if she were a prisoner? Stuck in a concrete cell for twenty-three hours a day or back-breaking work in the sun? She figured that the open air was better than suffocating in a stifling cell like Mr Craig was.

Deborah drove on for around two hundred yards, turned a corner and there it was—Raiford. A metal archway proclaimed 'Florida State Prison'. It looked like the entrance to the TV ranch owned by the Ewings in *Dallas*—secure, comforting, and imposing. It could've been an entrance to a gated community.

Deborah took off her shades and drove on through. A chain-link fence topped with razor wire encircled Raiford. High up in towers at the four corners of the jail, armed guards stood watch. Behind the fence were a combination of old and new—mostly wooden—prison buildings. More prisoners tended the grounds. Some mowed lawns, while others hoed the gardens. Everyone's head was down.

She squinted as the concertinaed razor wire glistened in the sun and wondered how many men had ever left Raiford rehabilitated. Probably very few. The thought depressed her.

Deborah pulled up outside a red-brick administration building. She walked through a series of checkpoints, pat-downs—which she hated—and metal detectors. A uniformed guard examined her ID and passes, and her briefcase containing notepads and background notes. She lifted her arms and a female guard with peroxide hair patted all the angles for contraband.

The guard said, 'She's clean.' She chewed her gum and stepped back to allow Deborah through into the administration block. She fixed Deborah with a blank stare, arms folded, as if trying to intimidate her.

It worked.

Insides churning, Deborah walked on. She felt self-conscious wearing the overpriced black Versace suit she'd bought on Washington Avenue. She turned and saw that the peroxide guard had taken her shades off and was staring back, mouth tight. She knew how insular this part of Florida was. The fact that the prison was a major employer in the area probably heightened the effect.

Take it easy, Deborah.

A black officer escorted her into the building. He said nothing.

Deborah climbed several steps and walked through a shiny maze of corridors. The smell of bleach hung heavy and reminded her of public toilets. Inmates wore jumpsuits and mopped the shining halls as uniformed guards looked on. Occasionally, an inmate would wink at her. One whispered, 'Anytime you like, sister.'

Do not run.

Deborah resisted the instinct to do so and walked on in a businesslike manner. These prisoners were probably low-security and allowed to mingle near visitors. Nonetheless, she was glad to have the guard escort her to the warden's office. Deeper and deeper into the bowels of Raiford . . . The walls seemed to close in. The clanging of keys and doors and incessant noise threatened to overwhelm her.

Breathe in, Deborah. Breathe.

She recited the relaxation exercises her therapist had given her. She wondered if she should have told her editor about the occasional panic attack that stopped her from flying. Probably not. It would've killed her chances to meet Craig.

She moved down a wider corridor and felt the cold blast of an air-conditioning unit. It was a relief. She knew there were none on death row.

*   *   *

Harold Erhert, the warden of Raiford, was a huge man. He sat slumped in his seat like he'd just had a big lunch. His face was round, his eyes blue. He wore a brown suit and matching tie. He seemed stiff, as if he hadn't moved for hours. Nothing changed when Deborah entered his office. He just smirked.

He said, 'Wasn't expecting no lady journalist.' His stare crawled all over her and she felt her insides turn cold. 'Y'sure you're from the *Herald*?'

Deborah gave a tight smile, exhausted after her twelve-hour drive. 'Absolutely.'

'Mind if I see your credentials and pass?'

'Not at all.' She handed over her papers and ID. 'It's all there.'

'I'll be the judge of that.' Erhert's eyes scanned the papers in front of him.

Deborah could taste his hostility. She let it go,

remembering what her father had once said. ‘No need to pick fights when none need to be fought.’

She leaned back in her seat and looked around the office. A huge American flag was positioned behind Erhert’s desk. The walls were painted a muddy beige. They sported a couple of pictures—one of the warden shaking hands with Billy Graham, the other of him with the governor. The room smelled of mothballs and bad breath.

Erhert handed back her papers. ‘Okay, seems fine. First time in a penitentiary, miss?’

‘Yes.’

‘Thought so. Any idea what kind of place this is?’

‘Top-security jail.’

‘That’s right, and we ain’t got no fancy ways of doin’ things.’ That didn’t surprise her.

Deborah nodded.

‘Y’know, we never had no Negro reporter in here, neither.’

Don’t take the bait.

‘I think the term’s “black” or “African-American”, sir.’

Was that part of his strategy to teach her who was boss?

‘I see.’ The warden gave a tobacco-stained smile. ‘No offense, miss.’

‘None taken.’

‘Usually the only young Negroes we have coming in my office are the wives or girlfriends of guys on death row, pleading with me to save their man. Kinda sad.’

‘I graduated Berkeley, top of my class.’

‘Is that right?’ Erhert said, a sneer at the corner of his mouth.

Deborah stared back at him, unwilling to be

intimidated.

What a dinosaur. In the early 1960s Erhert had probably been the kind of young man that rode around nearby Starke in the back of his pick-up with his drunken friends, wearing Klan sheets and terrorizing black people.

She realized that she'd been fortunate. Having been educated in a private Baptist school in Jackson in the 1980s and 1990s, she'd been shielded from the racism of the street. The influence of the Klan in the South, or so it seemed to her, was on the wane. An internship at the *Jackson Advocate* was her wake-up call. The paper styled itself as the only defiant voice of poor Mississippi blacks, but it convinced her that things, in some ways, were as bad as ever. Firebomb attacks on the paper's offices—yards from where her parents still lived in the historic yet run-down Farish district—told their own story.

Deborah realized that the illusion and upbeat talk of progress being made was coming primarily from the black middle class, people like her. Meanwhile, in the South, the poor blacks stared into the economic and social abyss. Segregation and racism were far more discreet. Substandard education paved the way for a life of welfare, drugs, and no future.

Just what the warden would want.

Erhert smiled and pushed his tongue round the front of his yellowed teeth as if he was searching out bits of chicken. Then he looked up at the pictures on the wall and pointed at himself posing with the governor. 'Real proud of that. Y'know, that man came to speak at our local church out of the goodness of his heart. And him a Roman

Catholic. But he's a fine family man.' He nodded his head. 'Nice that us Christians can reach out and talk like that.'

Deborah smiled. Didn't he realize how mixed-up he sounded? 'Believe he's heading a trade delegation out to the Far East later today.'

'Is that so?' Erhert grinned back at her like a well-fed cat. He was around the two-hundred-and-fifty-pound mark, rolls of fat hanging over his thick brown belt. She glanced up at the picture of the governor.

He looked the part. A handsome, rugged white man with a far-right stance on everything from crime to homosexuals, from crack-addicted welfare mothers to tax cuts. He could usually be seen on election posters posing with wealthy white hunters—usually corporate donors to his campaign—out in the wilds of Florida, holding up any bird or animal they'd killed that day, highlighting his macho image. No wonder Erhert liked him. The world of simple choices without any shades of gray would suit him.

'Looka here, young lady.' More rolls of fat wobbled around his neck. 'Here's what we have. We've got the worst of the worst, y'understand?'

Deborah nodded and wished this self-important man would just let her see Craig.

'A pretty young Negro girl like you may not feel too comfortable with the Aryan Brotherhood jailbirds we have cooped up here.' Erhert paused and stared at her as if wanting the word 'Negro' to sink in and annoy her. Then he slowly licked his lips, like he was getting turned on by the thought. 'Would kill you soon as look at you. And we have Hispanic gangs. Real mean.'

Deborah nodded.

'That's just the bread and butter of the prison. To top it all, we've got the death-row inmates, caged up to twenty-three hours a day. Go everywhere in chains, for security—except the exercise yard and shower.'

'Seems a little excessive.'

'You wouldn't say that if you knew what these guys are like.'

'Is it really necessary, especially for Craig? He's in his early eighties.'

'Doesn't matter what age they are, miss—that's the way it is and that's the way it should be. They're evil people, don't ever forget that.'

Deborah stayed silent.

Erhert's eyes grew hooded. 'This ain't no Disney World. We don't pussyfoot around.'

Deborah nodded.

'Some people get the wrong idea of this place.' A beat. 'You know the name Valdes, Miss Jones?'

'Guy that was beaten to death?'

Erhert's face froze. Had she said the wrong thing? 'It was an accident.' He shifted in his seat. 'See, I say that guy's name and suddenly we've got misconceptions about a place like this and some of our officers. Beatings and violence are a daily occurrence, some say. Well, it ain't like that. We're professional. Tough but fair, just like the Bible says.'

Deborah stayed silent again. Mustn't jeopardize the interview with Craig. Wouldn't put it past Erhert to turn her down flat without good reason.

'You do believe in the Bible, Miss Jones?'

'My father's a Baptist minister, sir.'

'That's good to hear, but that wasn't my

question. Do you believe in the Bible?'

'Not any more.' She couldn't be bothered going into the reasons. Besides, it would take hours to explain.

'I see.' Erhert didn't seem surprised. 'Lot of non-believers these days. Guess that's free speech for you, huh?'

Deborah smiled and crossed her legs—and caught the warden's gaze on her crotch. She felt her insides move.

'Big-shot newspaper like the *Miami Herald* must get a lot of our guys writing in, complaining 'bout conditions, right?'

'A few . . .' That was a lie. The paper received dozens of letters each month from wives and girlfriends alleging torture and humiliation by guards. Some even claimed that they themselves had been sexually assaulted. She wondered if all the prisoners could be lying. 'Tell me about Mr Craig. How's he coping?'

'Keeps himself to himself.'

'Read somewhere that a guard lodged a complaint about the volume of the classical radio station he was listening to.'

'Yeah.'

'How else does he pass the time?'

'Reads and writes letters, mostly. Cell's like a library—every kinda book piled high. Think he's the only one on the "row" that can write a sentence.'

'What about the other prisoners on the "row?" How's he treated by them?' Deborah had found out from court transcripts, much to her amazement, that Craig had in fact been a senior policeman for many years in Scotland. 'Can't be too popular, him being an ex-cop after all.'

Erhert shook his head and pressed his tongue into his cheek. 'They like him. That surprise you?' He smiled and Deborah saw that he'd finally freed the small piece of food from between his two front teeth.

'Sure.' She tried hard not to look at his mouth. 'I've read many stories about bad experiences for ex-policemen in jail.'

'Let me tell you a story about Craig.' He pointed directly at her. 'And don't be quoting me on this, okay?'

'Sure.'

'In his first week here, way back in the early 1990s, an Aryan Brotherhood guy, notorious homosexual predator, tried it on with him near the showers.'

'With Mr Craig?'

'Oh yeah.'

'What happened?' Did she really want to know this?

'Craig strangled him unconscious with his chains and darn near killed him. Had to be dragged off by eight of my men.'

She was going to interview this guy? 'Were there any repercussions from the gang?'

'Not at all. Overnight the other white guys left him alone. Respected him for standing his ground. Never went near him again. The Negroes and Hispanics liked him for what they called "kickin' the shit out of a racist faggot".' Erhert showed his teeth again. 'Pardon my French. And the guards got the message to leave him alone. Some try and rile him.' He arched his eyebrows and showed his palms. 'I admit that, but this is a tough place to work in.'

Deborah said nothing.

'You're scared of meeting him face to face, aren't you?' He enjoyed making her feel uncomfortable.

'I'm slightly apprehensive.' Not true. Scared. Afraid of the unknown.

Erhert looked at her for several moments as if trying to gauge her suitability for the interview. 'Called him the "Butcher of South Beach", didn't they?'

'Yes.'

'Darn near took the senator's son's head off, they say.'

'Can I see him?' Deborah's tone was more edgy than she'd have liked.

Erhert stared at her. 'You'll need a guard to take you down.'

'I'd appreciate that.'

Deborah's mind flashed back to the news footage she had scrutinized over the years—Craig's defiant face, the staring eyes, the fixed mouth, the tattoos. She felt a shiver of fear run down her spine. She stood up and shook Erhert's sweaty hand. She tried hard not to recoil.

She sighed as she left the musty office. A stocky guard, bundles of keys hanging from his belt, escorted her down more corridors. She felt disoriented.

Closer and closer.

The sound of their steps echoed down the maze of passageways and sounded like an army on the move. Steel doors slammed, on and on. Feet hurting in her new shoes.

She was patted down, all the angles, and felt herself tense up automatically. More searches. She was made to shake out her hair, pull out her trouser pockets, remove her belt, and open her mouth.

When the guards were satisfied, Deborah was taken down into a bleak room. It was the room where visitors saw their loved ones—death-row prisoners—face to face.

At the far end of the room were partitioned booths, separated by Plexiglas. Phone contact. Deborah walked slowly to a middle booth, her legs like jelly.

3

Deborah stared through the scratched plastic at an empty booth as she waited for Craig. The smell of cheap perfume and stale sweat lingered—the odor of despair. It was as if all the dashed hopes and dreams of thousands of women and children who'd filed through the door had seeped into the bricks, Formica, and plastic seats.

She looked at her watch. He was ten minutes late. Was there a problem? Had he had second thoughts?

Since she'd started investigating Craig's case, this interview had been the thing uppermost in her mind. Even while doing the numerous features on Ricky Martin or whatever celebrity breezed through South Beach publicizing a record or a new fitness video, she'd still kept hold of the hope that it would happen. It seemed, with hindsight, as if she was being pulled towards Craig. Maybe her fate was tied up with his. Who knew?

Deborah shifted in her seat as she waited, wondering what he looked like now. She'd studied all the press clips over and over again. Occasionally she leafed through the file, gazing at the photos, including the stark black and white images of Craig as a detective—dark suit, sharply knotted tie, hair short, clean-shaven, face inscrutable—surveying a crime scene back in the 1960s in Glasgow, outside a run-down tenement. She'd read that he'd been in charge of dozens of the most high-profile murder investigations in the city. Feared hit man Alec Campbell whose specialty was garroting his victims; serial killer Jack Boyle who preyed on prostitutes in the city's East End, amassing at least twenty-four victims; and gangland enforcer Rab McGill, responsible, it was said, for the deaths of six of his deadliest rivals in a spate of killings in the late 1960s.

In addition, Deborah read that Glasgow had spawned deadly gangs like the Tongs, the Cumbie and the Toi who slashed and stabbed their way across the city, leaving a trail of bloodied and battered bodies in their wake.

So it seemed strange to her that a man like Craig, an upstanding detective whose record was virtually impeccable, should stoop to such a level, knifing O'Neill like the young gang members he used to put away.

But as Michael West, the DA at Craig's trial in July 1991, pointed out to devastating effect, it was not the first time that the Scottish detective had crossed the line between legality and street justice.

According to statements read out in the Miami courthouse, following an internal investigation it transpired that on the night of October 21, 1968,

Detective Chief Superintendent William Craig had been deemed responsible for a 'sickening attack' on a habitual thief, Paul Bain, in the basement of Govan police station on the city's south side. It happened after his team had discovered a ninety-year-old widow lying trussed up in her own home, following a break-in at her ground-floor flat in the affluent Kelvinside area in the city's West End. She'd suffocated after a sock had been shoved in her mouth, presumably to stop her from screaming while her home was ransacked.

When Craig's men raided Bain's run-down room in the Blackhill area of the city, they found jewelry that had been stolen from the old lady's house. Bain was sentenced to eleven years for manslaughter.

Craig's bosses wanted him demoted for the attack on Bain. But an outcry from rank-and-file officers fiercely loyal to Craig despite his aggressive style and unorthodox methods led to an informal rap on the knuckles instead.

The steel door on the other side of the transparent barrier opened and Deborah snapped out of her thoughts.

Don't be afraid. Breathe in, breathe out, like the therapist said.

Craig was led in by two guards. He was manacled at the waist, ankles and wrists. He was tall and his barrel chest nearly burst out of an orange prison top, but his blue penitentiary pants hung loose as if he'd lost weight. He wore shower slides on his feet. Deborah's gaze was drawn to his powerful arms—like lamb shanks—that had tattoos on both forearms. He looked at her long and hard, his face expressionless.

Just keep calm.

Craig, despite his advancing years, didn't look eighty-two. It was strange. He looked the same as in the news clips, except whiter, his face leaner.

Craig was locked into the booth on his side of the partition. He sat down slowly, restricted by the chains, and watched the two guards retreat behind the door. Then he faced her through the plastic.

Deborah picked up the phone in her booth and smiled. Craig reached out with both of his huge, manacled hands for his phone and raised it.

Well, here goes, girl. Give it your best shot.

'Afternoon, Mr Craig.' She gripped the phone tight. 'Good of you to see me.'

Silence.

Deborah cleared her throat. 'My name's Deborah Jones. I work for the *Miami Herald*.'

Craig smiled. 'Afternoon, Miss Jones.' His Scots accent was almost tender, his tone that of a patrician grandfather. As if sensing her apprehension, he said, 'Don't be afraid, I don't bite.'

'Sure.'

'So, to what do I owe this pleasure?'

'I'm trying to find out more about you.'

'Are you indeed? You took your time.' He cracked a smile. 'I've been in here more than eleven years.'

'I'm sorry, but I'm relatively new to the paper. I've only now been given the go-ahead.' Did he think she was some sort of death-row groupie?

Craig's icy stare fixed on her and he sighed. 'Look, I'm afraid you're going to be disappointed. I don't know how I can help you.' He shrugged his huge shoulders, a movement which rattled his chains. 'We're reaching the endgame here. My lawyers have told me to prepare for the worst. Next week they're moving me on to death watch.'

Deborah knew that meant round-the-clock surveillance for the final month of his life. She felt sick. 'I'd like to try and help you, Mr Craig.'

'Bit late in the day, my dear, don't you think?'

'It's never too late.' *Don't rush things*. She wanted him to settle before they got down to business. 'Before we go any further, do you mind me asking how your health is?'

'Apart from the heart murmur and insomnia, can't complain.'

'Are they treating you?'

'They do what they can. They've been giving me the same angina drugs since I came in here.'

'That's not right.'

'They're going to kill me soon enough. Why waste money on expensive new drugs for an old man on death row?'

'That's terrible.'

'You learn to deal with it.'

'Do you want me to take this up with the warden?'

'Absolutely not.'

Deborah stared at the old man opposite and thought of her own father. Expensive drugs treated his stroke and his progress was monitored weekly by his doctor.

'Okay, down to business. I'd like to ask some questions, if I may.'

'Let's take things slowly. I don't get too many visitors.'

Deborah curled some loose hair behind her ear. 'I'd like to learn a little more about your motivation for killing that boy.'

Craig arched his eyebrows. 'What else is there to say? To be frank, I'd rather forget about it, if you don't mind. I've accepted my fate.'

'Well, *I* haven't accepted your fate,' she said with false bravado. 'The trial of the senator's son was a farce.'

Craig said nothing.

'I've read a great deal about your case, but what I'm missing is your thoughts on what happened. In particular, what I can't get my head round is why did an esteemed former detective from Scotland like yourself—'

'You'll know perfectly well from the reporting of my trial that my reputation in the police was somewhat less than exemplary, Miss Jones.'

'Okay, I'll rephrase that. Why did a former Scottish detective—'

'Slice up that ratbag college brat?' The words weren't spoken with venom, just uttered in a matter-of-fact way.

'Well, I wouldn't have put it like that, but yes—what drove you to such lengths?'

'It was covered at my trial. You should know what happened and why.'

'Please, I want to hear it from you.'

Craig leaned back in his seat and grimaced as he adjusted his grip on the phone. He went quiet for a few moments, and deep lines in his forehead bunched tight. 'You're very persistent, Miss Jones.'

Deborah said nothing.

'You want to know what drove me to such lengths?'

Deborah nodded.

Craig smiled through the glass at her. 'This is not

a set-up job, Miss Jones, is it?'

'I'm here to help. I want to know more about you. And why you felt compelled to kill Senator O'Neill's son.'

He seemed mollified. 'Okay, well, it's important that you are clear how it all started. Everything which followed can be tracked back to that night when my granddaughter didn't come home.'

Good. He was finally talking. Deborah sat in silence, scribbling her notes in shorthand.

'I was staying with Jenny at her house in South Beach for a few weeks. One night she didn't return after going for a few drinks with her friends after work. As the night wore on, I got more and more agitated.'

'You went looking for her, didn't you?'

'Damn right I did. It wasn't like her. It was the middle of the night, and I was scouring every street, bar, club, you name it. Then I tried the park. I climbed over a perimeter fence. And it was there, on a basketball court in Flamingo Park, that I discovered my granddaughter.'

'That must have been awful.'

Craig shook his head. 'Awful? Words can't tell you what I felt. My granddaughter, a brilliant lawyer, lay naked and bleeding, unconscious.'

Deborah scribbled her shorthand, and saw his manacled hands shaking.

'Thankfully, we got her to hospital before she lost any more blood.'

'So, then Joe O'Neill stood trial, but he was acquitted. Was that the final straw? Is that what did it for you?'

'No. It was what came after.'

'I'm sorry, I don't understand.'

'O'Neill had returned to party in South Beach a few months after he was acquitted of raping my granddaughter, as if nothing had happened. I ran into him and his rich-kid college buddies in a bar one night. And they were laughing at me. I just turned and walked out . . .'

'That must've been difficult.'

'You have no idea. That was just the start of it. Did you know that he started cruising past her house, laughing and shouting and spouting obscenities?'

'Yes, I did.'

'Put yourself in my position. How would you feel if it was your granddaughter?'

Deborah said nothing.

'She'd been drugged and raped, and the boy who did it—and, make no mistake, he *did* do it—was goading her, night after night. I called the police repeatedly about it, gave them the license-plate number, but they said there was nothing they could do.'

'So you confronted him?'

Craig leaned forward, his ghostly face nearly pressed against the plastic. 'One night I followed him from a nightclub. He was heading into the park with some girl. I didn't know if he was going to do the same to her. The confrontation ended with me losing control.'

'Do you regret what happened?'

Craig went quiet and gazed at the floor.

'Look, I'm here trying to help you. I want to find out more about your case.'

'What's done is done.'

'With respect, Mr Craig, I don't believe it is. O'Neill's case was a travesty—DNA going missing, arguments among the jury, and, from what I've heard, pressure from local government as well. It stank.'

'Done your homework, haven't you?'

'Do you want to die?' *Damn, that was insensitive.*

'No one wants to die.'

'Well, why don't you open up and speak about this?'

Craig paused for a couple of beats. 'Deborah, I'm an old man. I don't want to open it all up again.'

Deborah did not respond.

'Look, I don't have the energy to fight on.'

'I want to help you.'

'Deborah, look at me.'

Deborah locked on to his gaze. He was not the tough guy in handcuffs outside the Miami courtroom in 1991, but an old man close to death eleven years later.

'Do you know what a place like this does to a man?'

Deborah shook her head.

'It destroys him from the inside. It eats away at your soul. You know how many men I've seen and heard go mad in here?' Craig's hands shook as he held the phone. Strangely, she wanted to hold his hand, to reassure him.

'There was a young man in the cell opposite me. His name was Billy Lee Drew, a functionally illiterate farm laborer from here in Bradford County.' The case rang a bell with Deborah. 'Killed his parents on his eighteenth birthday. A week ago, he took a home-made shank to his wrists.' Craig's eyes turned glassy. 'He had been babbling incessantly for the last few days. That boy, probably no older than you, was poor white trash. That's what he kept on telling me. "I'm just nothing, Mr Craig." His parents told him that. The kids at the school told him that. The guards laughed at him and told him that. The boy believed he was filth. And no one—not a soul, not me, not anyone—could persuade him otherwise. He died alone, drenched in his own blood, crying for his mother.'

Craig bowed his head low like a lame dog.

'I didn't mean to upset you.'

He looked up. 'You didn't upset me, my dear, but I don't have it in me anymore.' He reminded her of her father, two years after his stroke, unable to function properly. The life seemed to have seeped out of him as well.

'Without trying to belabor the point,' Deborah said, 'according to a juror I've spoken to, Joe O'Neill's trial was—to put it crudely—fixed.' She let the comment sink in for several seconds. Craig didn't blink.

'I don't know that for sure. There are other people who could put you in the picture.'

'I'm sorry—you've lost me. What other people are you talking about?'

'Look, Deborah, the trial of Joe O'Neill produced more questions than answers. But I'm not about to start whining. I'll face the consequences of my action.'

Despite Craig's physical presence and fearsome reputation, he seemed vulnerable, wrapped up in chains like a circus animal.

'I want to help you, Mr Craig, but you've got to try and help me as well. Is there something you're holding back?'

Craig didn't say a word for nearly a minute. Then he smiled. 'Have you ever considered why I haven't spoken to anyone until now, Miss Jones?'

'I've wondered.'

'It's to do with being closer to death. I do want to talk. And I feel I can trust you.'

'Thank you.'

Craig smiled. 'But there's something about you I can't figure out.' His gaze lingered on her face and Deborah felt her neck flush. 'This is about more than my story, isn't it, Miss Jones?'

'I don't know what you're talking about.'

He smiled again. 'I can look into your eyes and see everything there is to know about Miss Deborah Jones.'

'What is there to know about me?'

'You want this story bad, don't you? You want to make a name for yourself, don't you?'

'Every journalist does. But I want to help you as well.'

'I know you do.'

Craig went quiet again. When he spoke, his voice was barely a whisper. 'I know a man who knows something about Joe O'Neill's case.'

'Who is he?'

'A police officer. He may be able to help you.'

'In what way?'

'He was linked to the police inquiry. He kept in touch with Jenny and myself after O'Neill was acquitted.'

'I need to speak to him.'

'Look, this was nearly fourteen years ago, after Jenny was raped. I don't know if he is even alive.'

'Do you think he might still be in touch with Jenny?'

'Might be. I don't know.'

'Doesn't she say?'

'I don't want to talk about Jenny. She's suffered enough.' Suddenly Craig's tone was sharp.

'You got a name for this police officer?'

'I can't go telling you that. You're the journalist, aren't you? You should know all about keeping sources confidential.'

'I understand.'

Deborah made a mental note to track down Jenny Forbes. It was time.

She wondered if Jenny would put her in touch with the mysterious police officer. Was he sympathetic to Craig's cause? Why didn't Craig just give her the name? Was he scared that Erhert's men were listening in?

Craig leaned forward. 'I must warn you, my dear, that if you pursue this you have to be very careful.'

'Why?'

He just stared back at her, the blacks of his eyes now pinpricks. And Deborah remembered Goldberg's last words of warning.

'I understand,' she said.

'I wonder if you do. Anyway, you want to know how I spend my days? My conversion to the straight and narrow? Might be useful for a feature.'

Deborah ignored the new, cynical tone. 'I'd like to find out a bit more about your past. Tell me about your involvement in the war. Your lawyer just said you—'

'Miss Jones, I've got trouble remembering what I did yesterday, let alone remembering that long ago.'

'You were in the British army. Where did you

fight, for example?'

'I can't see the point in raking up that sort of stuff.'

The conversation ended as the siren wailed.

Craig spun around. Two burly guards came through the door behind him. 'What's all this about?'

Deborah heard one guard saying, 'Lockdown.'

Craig still had the phone pressed to his ear as he faced away from the plastic barrier. 'My interview's just started.' The guards hustled him away, and the receiver fell from his manacled hands and swung to and fro in the empty booth.

Craig turned round. He looked anxious. Deborah barely heard him say the word 'Careful' again, muffled as it was by the Plexiglas. Then he disappeared through the steel door.

The interview was over.

* * *

Erhert escorted Deborah back to her car, his hand briefly touching her back. She tensed up as soon as he did it.

'I'm sorry about that lockdown situation, miss, but you know how it is.'

'Not really.' She suspected that the whole thing had been orchestrated to interrupt her interview with Craig.

Erhert didn't shake her hand before he turned and walked away. 'Gimme a call if you need anything else,' he said, heading back into Raiford.

Deborah's heart was pounding as she got in her car and headed off. She felt angry with Erhert and with herself for not getting anything more precise from her interview.

Things had been going well until the interruption.

She pulled over to the side of the road outside the Raiford archway and took out her cell phone. She punched in Sam Goldberg's direct-line number at the office.

'Get anything from Craig?' He sounded tired.

'Not yet, although I think I made progress.' She watched a group of New River inmates coming back from the fields. A red Chevy cruised past heading north, driven by a scruffy white man. He wore shades and a baseball cap pulled low, elbow out of his window.

'He mentioned some police officer who kept in touch with Jenny Forbes and himself until O'Neill was acquitted. But he clammed up when I mentioned the war.'

'Sounds like you've got nothing more than a pile of dust.'

'I'd still like to follow it up.'

Silence. Deborah wondered if Goldberg was going to pull the plug on her story. She'd only have herself to blame.

'How do you plan to do that?'

'I need some help . . . I felt he was hinting at something important.'

Goldberg went quiet for several seconds. Then he let out a long, wheezy sigh. 'You mean you have a hunch?'

'Yeah, a hunch.'

'I like hunches. What do you need?'

'I need to find Jenny Forbes. Fast. A number, an address. She might be able to help if she's still in touch with this guy.'

'Why didn't you get the details from Craig?'

'Got kinda edgy when I mentioned her. Obviously it's a sensitive issue. I'm sure he doesn't want me interrupting her life. Also, I reckon Mr Craig didn't want to talk on the phone about this police officer.'

There was a short pause. Then Goldberg said, 'How about Larry Coen? He'd find her.'

Yeah, that would work, Deborah thought. She liked the *Herald* crime reporter. His contacts were legendary—from crime families in Little Cuba to senior FBI and CIA sources within Quantico and Langley. 'That'd be great.'

'Gimme a few minutes. I'll get back to you.'

Deborah killed the call and sped off. Her mind was racing. She was relieved that she hadn't screwed up. Goldberg was still on her side. Just.

Deborah accelerated off the old road and a warm breeze blew through her hair. She switched on a local radio station. It was the standard country music. It reminded her again of Brett's parents.

She headed south on 301 and wondered if her boss would call back.

Fifteen minutes later, he was on the line. 'You're in luck—Jenny Forbes lives in Key West. I'll phone through her full address when we get it, hopefully in the next thirty minutes.'

'I'm on my way,' she shouted above the traffic. 'I appreciate it, Mr Goldberg.'

'Okay. Remember, only speak to me.' He hung up and Deborah wondered why he was so reluctant to let anyone else know what she was working on. She hadn't heard of any other reporter being asked to follow such a procedure. Was he just being protective?

Deborah put her foot on the accelerator. She felt good despite the eight-hour drive ahead of her. She turned up the music and smiled at the corny lyrics. Above her, the northern Florida sky was blood red.

Her stomach rumbled and she realized that she hadn't eaten since breakfast.

She glanced in her mirror and saw the red Chevy again, crossing lanes, two cars behind her.

Her stomach knotted.

Hadn't it been headed in the opposite direction when she was outside Raiford?

4

Just before midnight, Senator Jack O'Neill sat at his huge mahogany desk in the wood-paneled first-floor study of his mansion in Naples, southwest Florida. He was jet-lagged and fatigued but was enjoying the balmy breeze, which blew through partially open French doors. The expensive silk drapes that his wife had bought billowed, while outside in the darkness pelicans fought over scraps. He wished he could just forget everything and stay where he was, but he couldn't stop preparing for the forthcoming election—strategy meetings, pollsters, and wall-to-wall business breakfasts.

He felt anxious, not getting enough sleep. His gaze was drawn to a FedEx parcel, which lay unopened amid a clutter of important papers on the desk, and he knew that the election and his workload—as chairman of the Senate Intelligence

Committee—wouldn't allow him to relax.

O'Neill sighed and adjusted a large table lamp on his desk. Then he gazed at a gold-leaf-framed photo of his dead son.

Confident eyes and a big grin—that was how he would be remembered. O'Neill couldn't believe that it had been over twelve years since his only son had been taken from them. July 18, 1990—the date was burned into his soul. It seemed like a matter of weeks, not a dozen years. Time meant nothing anymore.

O'Neill switched on his computer and lit up a cigarette, trying to focus again on work. His reflection in the monitor was frosty from the pale blue glow of his screensaver. His suit was creased after his overnight flight from Saudi Arabia.

He undid his waistcoat and exposed his paunch. He knew he'd let himself go since Joe died. But he was way past caring. He took off his tie and dropped it on the floor. He then ran his hands through his slicked-back gray hair and yawned, unable to remember the last time he had slept.

He looked again at his son's handsome face and slowly exhaled a stream of smoke.

Would Joe have made him a grandfather by now? He imagined his son playing basketball with his kids in their huge garden as he looked on, proud as any dad could be. His wife Rose would've loved that. She adored kids more than anyone. That would never happen. Not now. Not ever.

O'Neill gazed across the darkness of the bay and dragged heavily on his cigarette. Joe's death still haunted him. Every waking hour of every day, or so it seemed, he thought of him. The nights were the worst. Sometimes he didn't want to wake up . .

. Sometimes he didn't sleep, and walked around the huge gardens outside his home. In many ways he was a prisoner, locked away from the world.

He liked his privacy most of all. No one came knocking. And that was a small consolation.

His house was located in a nature preserve, part of an exclusive gated community, shrouded by mangrove and palm trees, and could not be viewed from land or sea. At night, infrared surveillance cameras swept the bay and the deserted, sleeping streets.

The seven-bedroom Mediterranean-style property with terracotta roof tiles and Moorish archways was the finest home in the enclave, which boasted a swanky golf and country club.

Some of his neighbors' homes also overlooked Cocohatchee Strand, a pristine nature preserve. Others had access to their own private beach and the Gulf of Mexico. The streets were quiet, which he liked, as he couldn't abide noise since Joe died.

O'Neill let his mind drift to another concern.

He'd heard that a *Miami Herald* reporter had interviewed William Craig, the man who'd killed his son. Hal Lomax, his director of media relations, had contacted him while he was in the Gulf. The specter of a story about Craig appearing in a respected newspaper brought back all the old memories. It was the last thing he needed. He just wanted to forget.

He wondered what sort of article she'd write. Would it be sympathetic to Craig? Would it try to resurrect the original allegations about Joe?

His mind flashed back to his son's rape trial. He remembered arriving outside the Richard Gerstein Justice Building in downtown Miami on the day

Joe was finally cleared. It was a flawless November morning in 1989 . . . blue skies and balmy temperatures, and he was flanked by his wife and Joe's lead counsel, Marty Sanderson, a silver-tongued top-drawer defense attorney he'd been advised by his old friend, John Richmond—who lived across the bay—to hire. TV cameras and microphones pressed in on them as police helped them push their way through. It was the trial of the year. Maybe the decade. The only son of Senator Jack O'Neill, charged with raping a high-profile Miami lawyer, Jenny Forbes. He sat loyally by his son's side throughout the three-week trial, feeling his every twitch during the evidence. But what bothered him most, what he still remembered vividly, was the look of rage and anger in the young woman's eyes as she was cross-examined, humiliated in front of the world.

What also bothered him was that Sanderson had made her out to be a woman with 'loose morals', implying that she was having sex with every man she encountered. She admitted she couldn't remember what happened the night she was in the bar with friends. Joe's lawyer went for the jugular. He wiped the floor with the prosecution team. He exposed mix-ups in the DNA evidence, the 'unfortunate' recollection of events by Ms Forbes and the shady nature of some of the witnesses—including a black transvestite who claimed he saw his son taking her from the bar, semi-conscious.

Jack O'Neill's son came across like any young man his age. He admitted he had a weakness for nightclubbing and drinking. This played well.

The controversial trial sparked headlines across America. Much navel-gazing and hand-wringing from civil-liberties groups on prime-time TV about the 'appalling suffering' of Joseph O'Neill. Right-wing shock jocks castigated the 'authori-tarian' elements within the police and legal establishment.

The last thing that Senator O'Neill remembered about that day was Jenny Forbes breaking down in court, and her grandfather William Craig—the man who killed Joe eight months later—wrapping a protective arm around her as she sobbed on his shoulder. He might even have glanced across at Joe.

O'Neill sighed. If only he had known what was to come.

He stubbed out his cigarette in an overflowing ashtray and looked at the paper mountain strewn across his desk. It was the last thing he wanted to see.

Where should he begin?

Briefings from the Pentagon and the NSA, national security meetings scheduled for the situation room at the White House, specially couriered memos from the president, strategy documents from his team ahead of the November elections—five weeks away—and letters from lobbyists working for NASA who invited him to 'discussions'. It seemed like a never-ending string of meetings, meetings about meetings, and more meetings.

He was sick of it. He logged on to his computer and checked his encrypted e-mails.

There was nothing of note, mostly briefings from his hard-working election team on tactics and strategy. That could all wait.

O'Neill gazed at the photo one more time. Such a precious time with Joe. He remembered the day the picture was taken like it was yesterday. A family barbecue on a perfect July day at their old home in West Palm Beach, less than forty-eight hours before he was murdered. Joe had been drinking down at Clematis with some buddies and had brought them all round. Great guys. Joe was swigging beer from the bottle. Center of attention, and didn't he know it. No wonder he made him so proud.

His mind flashed back to Joe as a child. Back in Brooklyn. He remembered the first time he smelled Joe's sweet, milky baby breath. Never felt happier. His career as a young Manhattan lawyer had taken off. Then he'd entered politics.

Long hours, sure, but great days.

He closed his eyes and the memories flooded back: the dirty diapers, Rose breastfeeding at all hours, her home-made bread, and the sleepless nights.

God, how he missed that time. It was the late 1960s and America was in turmoil. Rioting in all the big cities, civil-rights changes, and hippies. It seemed as though the world was going mad. It was as if he, Rose and baby Joe were the only sane people on the planet, content with their lives as America tore itself apart.

He stretched his arms and groaned. The long flight had taken its toll.

O'Neill closed his eyes for a moment and thought about the coming weeks. His heart sank. Re-election was stressful in the extreme—hitting the campaign trail across Florida. To compound matters, William Craig's execution was scheduled around the same time. His wife was against the death penalty, as he had been, until Joe was killed.

Now, well, he wasn't sure anymore. If he were honest with himself, he'd rather not have to confront the situation. He'd prefer to let it run its course.

O'Neill's mind flashed to the telephone call he had received more than a decade earlier. The hard voice of the desk sergeant in Miami Beach told him that Joe had been murdered. He drove alone, in a daze. He saw the bloody neck wound first when he arrived at the mortuary. His boy's blue-gray complexion. He remembered the shock he'd felt when he touched his cold skin and began sobbing, wishing he would wake up. He then stroked Joe's hair, matted with blood. It reminded him of washing his son's hair in the tiny plastic bath each evening when he returned from work. His beautiful hair . . .

Craig didn't just kill Joe that day. He'd also destroyed Jack's own will to live, and his wife Rose was now virtually a recluse.

O'Neill looked again at the FedEx package. Still there, untouched.

It'd been delivered an hour ago and left in a box outside his study as his mail always was. He'd been told to expect it from John Richmond, the man across the bay. He lifted it up and ran the tip of his index finger down the seal.

He opened the package—a video cassette.

He wondered what it was.

He slid the tape into the VCR beneath his desk and switched the volume off. He stared at the screen. It was amateur footage. His jet-lagged eyes tried to make sense of the scene.

It looked like the video clip had been taken in an upscale hotel room. The angle at which the footage was shot gave the impression that it was covert. Just then, a man in his late forties came into view, a white bath towel around his waist. He bent over and pulled out a bag of white powder from a bedside cabinet. He then placed a small vanity mirror on the bed, and started cutting up lines of the white powder—perhaps cocaine.

O'Neill was transfixed.

The man then snorted the powder and turned to face the camera, eyes closed in ecstasy.

O'Neill freeze-framed the picture, having seen enough. He picked up his cell phone and punched in Richmond's number. Five rings later Richmond answered. 'What in God's name did you send me that for?' O'Neill asked.

'Thought you'd want to know what he did in his spare time.' Richmond's accent was Brooklyn rough.

'Look, I've just got back from fucking Riyadh, and I—'

'He's been compromised. He needs to be told.'

The phone on O'Neill's study desk rang. 'Listen, I'll catch you later and we can talk some more about this . . .'

He ended the cell-phone conversation and reached over to take the landline call. It was Hal Lomax. 'Guess what, Jack?'

O'Neill groaned. 'You know what time it is?'

'Listen, I might be able to make the Craig story go away.'

'Hal, can't this wait?'

'Jack, I might have information which we can use to our advantage, to derail this story.'

O'Neill stared into the darkness of the bay, unwilling to enter into discussions in his state of mind. 'Hal, pull a few strings if you have to, but just keep the story out of the papers. Look, I'm dog-tired. I'll see you in Washington.'

He hung up, his mind craving sleep, but hoping that Hal could work his magic—whether by cajoling or browbeating editors—to make sure the story didn't see the light of day.

5

The small wooden conch house was painted indigo and could've come from a Key West brochure. It was located on a quiet street—lined by palms—five blocks from Duval in the city's Old Town. Azaleas and bougainvilleas in neat flower beds fringed a tiny lawn. The sun was low, sky burnt orange.

Deborah climbed the two steps onto a creaky porch, knocked on the door, and waited. It seemed strange to be standing outside Jenny Forbes's home, if indeed it was her home. She'd researched the case thoroughly but didn't know what Jenny looked like: her face had been electronically obscured during the trial on TV.

Often, when she was walking through Flamingo Park, she thought of Jenny Forbes, anesthetized by Rohypnol—a drug used to treat sleep disorders—on that notorious December night in 1988. Alone, drugged and at the mercy of a psychotic frat boy. It was just bad luck that he'd picked her. It could've been any woman in that bar. How she'd managed to rebuild her life and cope with her grandfather's incarceration on death row was beyond Deborah.

A minute passed, and still no answer. She

knocked again, harder this time, and heard padding footsteps on the other side.

The door opened and an attractive woman in her late thirties, with straggly mousy brown hair and a gentle face, stood before her. She was barefoot, wore a white tight-fitting T-shirt, and faded jeans.

'Jenny Forbes?'

The woman nodded, eyes wary. 'Yes.'

Deborah smiled. 'I need to speak to you.' She flashed her ID. 'I'm a reporter with the *Miami Herald*.'

There was no response.

'Look, I'm sorry for dropping in on you like this, but I'm investigating your grandfather's case. I spoke to him yesterday.'

Jenny Forbes folded her arms in a defensive pose. 'You've got some nerve.'

'Jenny, I'm new to the paper. I'm the first journalist who's interviewed him. Bottom line? I need your help.'

'I don't give interviews. My life's not public property.'

'Jenny, I hope—'

'Are you for real? I've been trying to highlight his case for years. Now you turn up on my doorstep when it's too late.'

'I'm not here to interview you.'

'Well, I don't believe you.'

'This is not about you. It's about your grandfather. I want to try and help him, that's all.' Deborah's voice was edgier than she wanted.

'I don't know. This doesn't feel right.'

'Jenny, I spoke to your grandfather. I know all about his case. And I know that he did this because Joe O'Neill wouldn't leave you alone after the trial. Your grandfather told me how he followed Joe from a nightclub. He's only got weeks to live. I beg you, I've just got a few questions, and then I'll be on my way.'

Tears filled Jenny's eyes as she shook her head. 'How is he?'

'He's a tough old man, all right. But he was complaining of heart murmurs and insomnia. And that's why I need to speak.'

Jenny sighed. 'I don't mean to be disrespectful, but I need your assurance that you won't use this as a pretext to interview me.'

Deborah lifted up her right hand. 'You have my word, Jenny. Just need a few more details about the police officer who kept in touch with you in Miami after the trial.'

Jenny's face softened like she understood what Deborah was talking about. She opened the door wide. 'You better come in.'

Deborah followed her along the polished wooden floors of the hallway into a bright yellow living room. Jenny's scent was like a rose.

Dozens of candles cast a soft glow around the small room, like in a monastic retreat. Wooden blinds were drawn down, aqua drapes pulled nearly shut. There were two small sofas with what looked like a terracotta Indian design on them, and a blue rug lay on the floor.

At the far end of the room, beside the window, sat a small stereo—its dials illuminated by a lime-green LCD—and large Bose speakers. In the background, Deborah recognized Johnny Cash's melancholy *The Man Comes Around* album playing low. She had bought it herself downtown on the day it came out and the song sparked fond memories of Brett's parents.

Jenny Forbes motioned for Deborah to take a seat. 'Something to drink or eat?'

'No, thanks, I'm good.' Deborah sat down on one of the sofas. She smelled spicy home cooking and looked across at the other woman. 'Hope I'm not disturbing you.'

'I don't do visitors.' Jenny sat down. 'Thomas, my husband, has the children down at Mallory for the sunset. They love it.' She seemed edgy although she tried to appear laid-back.

'It's a great place.'

Jenny dropped her gaze.

'You've never spoken to the press, have you, Jenny?'

'No.'

'I guess I spooked you, turning up out of the blue.'

'A bit. Brought it all back—reporters on my doorstep in South Beach, creeping about my yard, peering through my windows, night and day. It was like I was under siege.' Deborah had read that Jenny's identity had inadvertently been revealed by the trial judge, thus alerting the media.

'That why you moved down here?'

'Yeah, I just wanted to try and forget my old life. Everything.' Jenny ran a hand through her hair as if she was nervous. 'So, you wanna know about this officer who kept in touch, right?'

Deborah smiled and nodded.

Was Jenny on Prozac to help her cope? Deborah had interviewed San Francisco rape victims for the Berkeley college newspaper, and many of them had been reliant on drugs, at least temporarily. She thought Jenny Forbes showed the same low-level signs of anxiety, despite years having elapsed since the attack. Hardly surprising. Being drugged in a busy bar and then dragged out by O'Neill as if she was drunk was every woman's worst nightmare.

'Does he still keep in touch?'

'To this day.'

Deborah nodded, glad that she'd finally connected. 'You mind me asking why?'

'Thought the trial was deliberately botched.'

'Look, Jenny, we don't have a whole lotta time, as you can imagine. Basically, I need to speak to this detective.'

Jenny winced as if that might be difficult.

'When's the next time you'll see him?'

'Around a fortnight, but I can't make promises. He comes down here once a month to see how I'm getting on.'

'What exactly is the detective's take on Joe O'Neill's trial?'

'Thinks it's something to do with the senator, plain and simple.'

'Senator O'Neill?'

Jenny nodded. 'Said he had some influential friends, people who knew how to play the system.' Goldberg had alluded to the same thing. 'Said it was impossible to prove.'

Deborah's heart thumped.

Had the senator or his associates got to the judge or jury? Maybe to both? The story might not have caught fire, but the embers were certainly aglow.

'Jenny, those are serious allegations. Why didn't this detective do something about it? I mean, if it was me I'd kick up a storm.'

Jenny shrugged. 'He tried, but he was warned off. Got death threats at his home from some guy saying they'd kill him, his wife, their four children, and the goddamned dog.'

Deborah's stomach knotted.

If this was true, it confirmed that there'd been a conspiracy to mess up the trial of the senator's son. Was all this done just to let him off the hook? Was that what it boiled down to? Was that what her boss and Mr Craig had alluded to when they'd told her to be careful?

'Jenny, are you sure about that?'

'Positive. He was the lead investigator. He knew that bastard did it. I knew who did it, but he had to back off when he saw how things were going. From what he said, Joe O'Neill was put on trial just to appease rank-and-file officers . . . but things were going wrong all over the place.'

'Going wrong? Like what?'

'Like in the DA's office important witness statements went missing, but it was all hushed up. A sample of DNA from Joe O'Neill mysteriously disappeared. The detective also got strange calls in the middle of the night, telling him not to push it. People were also following him. He came close to having a nervous breakdown. Eventually, they transferred him to another case.'

Deborah remembered the red Chevy the previous night, which had tailed her until Fort Lauderdale. Was this related? Was she just being paranoid? No matter. The story, if true, would be political dynamite.

Deborah shook her head and sighed. 'I don't understand. So this officer couldn't do anything about it? Why didn't he go higher up?'

'Reckoned that was where the problem lay.'

'Any proof of that?'

'No.' Jenny picked at the cuticles on her right hand. 'At grass roots, he said every police officer wanted the O'Neill boy to go down for a long, long time. The best evidence was messed up at the police labs with the DNA debacle. Weird things going on.'

'This detective, you say he's a regular down here?'

'Yeah, does some marlin fishin', and enjoys a few drinks, stays the night, and goes back to Miami. Like I said, he likes to know how I'm doing. He's coming round mid-October, but I'll need to speak with him first. If he agrees, I'll give him your number.'

'That could be too late,' Deborah said. 'I need to speak to him now—or at least in the next couple of days. Time's running out.'

'I can't contact him. He says the calls can be traced. He comes down here or phones me from a friend's cell phone. He's paranoid, as you can imagine.'

Goldberg would want something more concrete than Deborah waiting for this detective for a chat, but it seemed pointless to press Jenny Forbes harder.

Deborah pulled out her card from inside her jacket and handed it over. 'That's got my cell phone and office numbers. If he wants, he can speak in confidence.'

Jenny glanced at the card, then at Deborah, her eyes heavy. 'This detective, by coincidence, was present when my grandfather confessed. He knew how fucked-up the Joe O'Neill case was.'

It was pointless getting quotes from Jenny Forbes. Who would believe her? She had a vested interest and no proof about any cover-up. But this detective's evidence would carry weight. Still, time was not on Deborah's side.

'How is he?' Jenny asked suddenly.

'Who?'

'My grandfather. Did he ask about me?'

'I don't think he wanted to talk about you. He's very protective of your privacy.'

'Yeah.'

'How often do you make it up to Raiford to see him?'

Jenny bowed her head. 'I don't.'

'I'm sorry—I don't follow.'

There was a long silence. When Jenny did speak, her voice was low. 'I've not visited him for more than five years. That come as a shock to you?'

It crashed through Deborah's head like a sledgehammer.

'Thomas visits once a month. I don't even know what Grandfather looks like now. I've never written. Doesn't sound too good, does it?'

'I guess it must be difficult for you, Jenny.'

'I couldn't take seeing an old man like that, treated like an animal. Every time I saw him, he looked paler and paler. I couldn't take it any longer.'

Jenny's eyes filled up with tears. Deborah went over and put an arm around her and pulled her close. She felt her tense up.

How was it possible to imagine the depths of despair and isolation that she'd experienced? Of course, it wasn't just a matter of pulling yourself together. Time did not necessarily heal.

Jenny's body shook. 'I can't face the journey. The look on his face when I see him. Can't bear to look at him behind glass. His face.' She broke down and sobbed like a little girl, head in hands. 'I've let him down most terribly.'

Deborah squeezed her shoulder. 'He's smart enough to know what you're going through. He'll understand.'

'You think so?'

'I know so.'

Jenny dabbed her eyes with the back of her hand. 'It's not because I don't love him, but it's the only way I can cope. I've cut myself off from everything just to deal with life.' She shook her head and sighed. 'Y'know, I've never once told him I was glad he killed Joe O'Neill.'

'I'm sure his lawyers still have something up their sleeve to get a stay.'

'I doubt it. He's all out of stays.'

Deborah thought it was a good time to make tracks. 'You've been very helpful, Jenny. And I hope you manage to find the strength to get through the next few weeks. And maybe that detective can throw your grandfather a lifeline.'

Jenny nodded, but looked unconvinced. She stood up. 'Oh, before you go, there's something I'd like to show you. Remember I said I'd been trying to highlight my grandfather's case for years?'

Deborah nodded.

'Well, I went round every major paper in Florida showing them something I thought would make a good story for them. You know, show another side to my grandfather.'

'I see.' This was news to her. 'Did you try the *Miami Herald*?'

'I spoke to a guy called Harry Donovan.'

'Ah. He's the executive editor now. What was it

you had for them?'

'Stay right there.'

Jenny left the room. A couple of minutes later, she returned with a dusty green box. 'I took custody of my mother's estate. Included in it were my grandad's papers, all about his involvement in the war. I think it shows the real man, not the "Butcher of South Beach" as some of the press dubbed him.'

'In what way?'

'Letters home to his mother, pictures of him in uniform.'

Deborah felt her pulse quicken. 'Do you mind if I take a look?'

'There's one thing I want you to see before anything else.' Jenny put the box on the floor and lifted the lid. She pulled out a yellowing piece of paper and handed it to Deborah. A red wax seal was at the bottom right-hand corner. It was heavily frayed at the edges. 'Take a look at that.'

Deborah scanned the typewritten words on the nicotine-hued paper in silence. Her throat tightened.

Buried among Craig's war papers was a dramatic insight into his past . . . A past that had been kept hidden for more than sixty years.

6

Sam Goldberg stared out of the huge windows in his office, hands thrust deep into his pockets. Dark gray clouds hung over the skyscrapers of downtown Miami. It never ceased to amaze him how much the city had changed since his parents had moved from Philadelphia in the early 1960s when he'd been a young boy, setting up home in affluent, sedate Coral Gables. They had expected it to be a world of white picket fences, blue skies, and cocktails at art-deco hotels on South Beach.

Slowly, the cityscape began changing before their eyes, faster than they or anyone else realized. All of a sudden it seemed to become rough around the edges—graffiti, boarded-up shops, homeless people begging in the street. His parents saw the massive immigration from Cuba and Haiti as contributing to social tensions. That was only partly correct. What was indisputable was that the city had become a staging post to major US cities for international drug traffickers from South America.

Drug turf wars, murders and power struggles started, as the Colombians moved in big time. Social unrest and disaffection with Miami's crumbling infrastructure followed. The city was no longer a sunny retirement home for snowbirds like his parents. He remembered the darkest moment in the city's history: the riots of 1980, which started after an all-white jury in Tampa acquitted four Miami police officers of fatally beating black insurance executive Arthur McDuffie. The fallout claimed eighteen lives and caused one hundred million dollars' worth of damage. Sam, a twenty-three-year-old political science student at the University of Miami at the time, watched appalled from his backyard as the smoke rose above Liberty City and Overtown.

Goldberg remembered watching the TV footage as the orgy of violence and mayhem gathered pace, spreading from block to block downtown. In the weeks and months that followed, the money which had poured into the city, earmarked for Overtown's regeneration, didn't find its way there. To this day, the inner-city areas remained dreadfully poor.

Elsewhere, Miami underwent a rapid regeneration, as if Overtown had never existed. South Beach was transformed. Now, for visitors and those with a good job, Miami was a cosmopolitan city: chic restaurants, bars, nightclubs, a magnet for the beautiful people. Residential towers were coming out of the ground all over downtown.

Goldberg wondered if one day Miami would regret not learning the hard lessons of the past and ignoring sections of the poorest in society, their voices unheard above the noise of the huge cranes and other building work that was creating condos and lofts for affluent incomers.

He sat down behind his desk, thinking how much the city was evolving before reflecting that his wife wasn't there any longer to share it with him. He gazed at the picture of her. Sometimes he didn't want to look forward too far. He knew he wasn't over her. And the sadness lingered, occasionally threatening to swamp him with grief. He'd lost count of the number of times he'd covered up his black moods with bourbon and beer. He so badly wanted to move on, but her ghost always seemed to be following his every move. Her presence was everywhere. Her perfume still lingered in his home.

The picture had been taken on their last vacation. Two blissful weeks sailing around the

Greek islands, despite his wife's cancer being at an advanced stage.

What Sam remembered most was her bravery. Her once voluptuous figure had withered away before his eyes. The opiates pumped into her body by a doctor he had hired for the trip made the pain bearable, but she refused to accept that death was inevitable. Even at the end, she wouldn't give in.

He remembered the expression on her face one evening. She was sitting on deck, eyes closed as the sun set. Mozart played in the background and she held a glass of Cabernet Sauvignon—pure serenity. It was possible that she might even have smiled.

His phone rang, snapping him out of his reverie.

'Goldberg.' He expected it to be Deborah Jones giving him an update on her trip to Key West.

But it was Harry Donovan, executive editor of the paper, calling from a newspaper publishers' conference in New York. 'Sam, you got a couple of minutes?'

'Sure. What's on your mind?'

'I'm hearing that one of our most inexperienced reporters has just been sent to Raiford. Is that true?'

'You mean Deborah Jones?'

'Yes, of course.' Donovan paused for a moment as if waiting for an answer. He didn't get one. 'I'm surprised you sent someone so green.'

'I thought it sounded like a good story.'

'At her age, Deborah Jones is on a steep learning curve. She's ill-equipped to deal with such a job.'

Goldberg groaned inwardly. It was just typical of Donovan to query his decisions, thinking he knew better since he used to do the job. Truth was that the guy was more at home with flip charts and profit-and-loss printouts than with news. 'Harry, what do you mean, "ill-equipped"? She's a very competent journalist who's got a keen eye for a story. What's so wrong with that?'

'With all due respect, Sam, I don't think you've thought this through. This paper's got to think more political, understand that this might rub Senator O'Neill up the wrong way.'

'I don't give a damn about Senator O'Neill. I decide, as managing editor, what stories go in, and what stays out. You deal with the business, the politics, right? The link man with the owners.'

'That's technically correct, but I'm telling you, as a friend, that this was not a good decision.'

Goldberg felt his blood pressure rise a notch. 'Meaning?'

'I don't want to say it, Sam.'

'Say what?'

'People are talking in the newsroom. They say you've taken a shine to her.'

'And they'd be correct. She reminds me of me at that age. Hungry, committed and—'

'Stunningly beautiful.'

Goldberg felt his cheeks flush. But Donovan had hit a raw nerve. Something about Deborah's beauty and intelligence had definitely attracted him. He was also intrigued that she was interested in the case of William Craig. It made him smile to think that as a crime reporter he'd tried to get an interview with Craig but had failed. The fact that she'd done it said a lot about her. 'I'm not going to dignify that with an answer.'

'Sam, what you feel for her is your business, but I don't see how she could've been given that assignment.'

'Because she's good. Look, Deborah Jones is a journalist, first and foremost. And I like to see reporters carving out stories instead of rewriting AP copy.'

'She's not ready.'

'I'll be the judge of that.'

A silence opened up between them and Goldberg turned to face the granite skies above the city.

Sam heard Donovan sigh. 'Let's hope she proves me wrong. And the next time, I'd appreciate a little forewarning.' He hung up.

Donovan always seemed to want the last word. The guy had a way of pissing off even the most mild-mannered people. Sam's late wife had once poured a glass of wine over Donovan for being an 'idiot par excellence'. Goldberg had laughed so hard that he'd spat his beer inadvertently all over Donovan's wife, Jackie.

He became lost in his thoughts, wanting to disappear to a bar for a few drinks and some peace and quiet. But he knew there was more chance of Governor Wilkinson announcing the regeneration of Overtown and Liberty City.

There was a knock at his door, and he snapped out of his daydreaming. It was stick-thin Kathleen Klein, the politics reporter, whom he'd been avoiding for months, ever since she'd come on too strong at a bar, late one night after work. She was two years older than Sam—forty-seven—and a good-looking woman. But Goldberg had made it clear that he wasn't interested. However, it hadn't stopped the invitations to parties, clubs and functions, not to mention the incessant flirting. And, despite the awkward edge it had given to their working relationship, Klein was an excellent operator. She was an astute commentator on Republican politics, and had stellar contacts.

'You got a minute, Sam?' She smiled.

An ice-cold beer seemed like a good idea. 'Can't it wait?'

Klein shook her head, mouth turned down. 'I don't think so. We've got a problem.'

'What kind of problem?'

'There's something you need to know . . . about your new best friend, Deborah Jones.'

7

The following afternoon, after a marathon journey up from Key West—and after phoning ahead to make an appointment to speak to Craig—Deborah arrived at Raiford, mentally and physically drained, only to find that Warden Erhert had pulled the plug on any interview.

In his office he explained, while slurping a mug of coffee as Deborah sat quietly fuming, that the Florida State Prison was in 'emergency mode' after the leader of Neta, the Puerto Rican prison gang, had been fatally stabbed, prompting threats of reprisals from friends of the dead man. In addition, he said, the Florida Department of Corrections was concerned that any article by Deborah Jones might make a celebrity out of William Craig, not to mention the fact that the article could be offensive to the victim's family.

Deborah didn't buy it. She didn't want to seem paranoid, but it sounded like the senator's people had called in some serious favors. And she wasn't going to be put off. Not at this stage.

She called Sam on his cell phone and explained the development. He asked to speak to the warden directly. Still, Warden Erhert smirked and smiled and patted his ample belly, refusing to budge. The discussion with Sam continued for nearly an hour, but nothing changed.

Erhert sat and eyeballed Deborah, trying to make her feel uncomfortable. 'Guess you've been wasting your time, Miss Jones. Real shame, that.'

Deborah considered her options. She could take it on the chin and head back to the newsroom with her tail between her legs. Or she could fight back.

Erhert leered, as if taunting her. Perhaps he was just waiting to have an excuse to deny her access.

Her heart beat hard and she felt her mouth go dry.

She got up and leaned forward on Erhert's desk, spreading her palms on its imitation wooden surface, fixing her gaze only a few inches from his oily face. 'Okay, Warden Erhert,' she said, 'if that's the way you're going to play it, fine. Let's cut the crap. I've listened to your racist put-downs and flimsy excuses for canceling my interview, but I will not be intimidated. Now, I've driven all the way up here from south Florida and I am *not* leaving this jail until I speak to William Craig. Is that clear?'

The veins at the side of Erhert's neck bulged. 'Are you threatening me?'

'No. I'm simply telling you I will not sit back and accept flimsy excuses for not being allowed to see William Craig. Have the senator or his friends put pressure on you? Is that what this is about?'

'You're out of line, young lady. I could pick up

that phone to the governor right now and he'd personally order you to be picked up and thrown out of my jail for suggesting such things.'

'You think you know about pulling strings? Let me tell you, my father is on the executive of the National Association for the Advancement of Colored People. Now, how do you think that'll play with the black people of Florida, if they find out that you've denied an accredited member of the press the right to interview a man on death row because of the color of my skin? You do remember the dimpled-chad fiasco a couple of years ago, Warden, in the 2000 elections? You think there was an outcry over that? Trust me, you ain't seen nothing yet.'

For the first time Deborah saw real fear in Erhert's eyes. She was calling his bluff. But he didn't know it.

She pressed home her point. 'You want to see thousands of people protesting outside your prison because you don't afford the same opportunities to black journalists as you do to whites? You wanna go there? Is that what you want?'

Erhert focused on his phone, as if contemplating contacting the governor. Then he wavered, as though he'd realized that calling the governor wasn't such a good idea. Deborah couldn't believe it—she had him.

The loud ticking of the clock on the wall accentuated the long silence. When Erhert spoke, he could barely suppress his rage. 'You got one hour with him. Maximum. A minute longer, and I'll drag you out myself, y'understand me?'

Deborah took a deep breath. 'That's much appreciated, sir. I'm glad we came to that understanding.' Erhert gave a sickly smile.

* * *

Half an hour later, after more pat-downs and fingerprinting, Deborah was escorted to the same booth as before.

She sat down and drummed her fingers against her notepad as Craig was brought in. She smiled at him through the murky plastic, not wanting him to see that she was nearly hyperventilating with anger and anticipation.

Craig waited for the guards to leave him alone. Once they were out of earshot, he picked up his phone, double-handed like the last time.

Finally, Deborah pressed the yellowing paper with the red wax seal against the plastic. She thought her heart was going to burst. 'Why didn't you tell me about this?'

'Where did you get that?'

'Jenny. You want to answer my question?' Deborah withdrew the piece of paper. Craig's eyes were fierce.

'You'd no right bothering her, you hear me?'

'I'd no other way of tracing the police officer you told me about.'

'I never said track her down, did I?'

Deborah could see how much his family meant to him. She wished her parents had showed the same undying love, but it wasn't their way. She had longed for her mother to put her arm around her and display some affection, but it never happened. Her mother's tough upbringing in the cotton fields of Tunica County, Mississippi, had left their mark. Love to her was having food on the table. Close family bonds weren't encouraged for the simple reason that life was so hard. Her brothers, sisters and parents all worked the cotton. Sunup to sunset. Back-breaking, soul-destroying labor. She'd come a long way, but still, displaying affection was a sign of weakness. *'That wouldn't help you in no fields,'* she'd say.

'I didn't mean to offend you,' Deborah said. 'I promise.'

Craig nodded as though he had been appeased.

Deborah held up the yellowing paper again. 'What does this mean?'

'Can't you let me be?'

'Why didn't this come up in court?'

'It's worthless.'

'It's a citation.'

Craig closed his eyes and sighed.

'A citation for bravery. Didn't you think this was relevant at your trial?'

'It's too late for all that.'

'It's never too late.'

'Maybe. Maybe not.' His breathing sounded labored through the phone.

Deborah smiled and tried to engage with him again. 'I couldn't believe it when I read it. It transforms everything. We have a story. You want me to read it out?'

Craig just stared at her.

'Well, I'm gonna anyway.' Deborah held the citation in front of her. 'It says that despite being injured you fought off more than thirty paratroopers in a place called Máleme in Crete which you were trying to regain. You were part of a small group of reinforcements from the Argyll and Sutherland Highlanders sent by the British Army to fight alongside the Australians and New Zealanders.'

'Please stop.'

'It says you were bleeding from a shoulder wound, but you stormed enemy positions. It also says you rescued an officer from New Zealand's Second Division, Colonel James Beacon, who lay injured, and carried him to safety, on your back, after an ambush on German soldiers. Mr Craig, people need to know this. This is a citation to be proud of.'

'Nonsense.'

'It's a citation for a Victoria Cross, Mr Craig. You're a Second World War hero.'

Craig leaned forward, almost touching the Plexiglas. His eyes were cold; his face flushed purple as if it was ready to explode. 'I'm no hero, Miss Jones. I've seen real heroes. You want to know what they look like? You ever seen a young man screaming for his wife, just before he died? Have you?'

Deborah shook her head.

'I'm thankful. I knew many men like that. They were real heroes, all alone, thousands of miles from their homes.' Craig closed his eyes. 'Christ, I was just doing what I did. I was lucky, if you can call it that.'

'You were given a Victoria Cross.'

'Be precise, Miss Jones.' His tone was harsh, like her father's could be. 'A citation for a VC is what I was given. Nothing more, nothing less.'

'Let me get this straight. You got a citation for outstanding bravery, and nothing else? What about your medal?'

'There is no medal. I turned it down.'

'Why?'
'I had my reasons.'
Craig's obstinacy reminded Deborah again of her father. If she suggested he should stay inside as it was too hot, he'd go and sit in the Mississippi sun for hours. Infuriating. 'Look, I'm trying to help you. Don't keep me in the dark.'
He went quiet for several awkward moments, weighing up what he wanted to say. 'Hundreds, maybe thousands of us—many injured—were left behind on Crete. The officers, all upper-class Englishmen, made sure they got the hell off the island, back to Alexandria in Egypt.'
'I'd no idea.'
'Well, now you do. They boarded the ships before injured men . . . it was my understanding that no officer should ever leave an injured man to fend for himself, but that was what happened.'
'You were just left to your own devices?'
Craig nodded. 'Every day we'd look out at the sea hoping to spot British boats coming for us. They never did. We survived up there for years. Should've starved, by rights.'
Deborah scribbled down his comments with a rising sense of excitement. 'So, how *did* you survive?'
'Bully-beef army rations, handouts from the Cretans. They were the real heroes. Bravest people I ever met. Men, women and children. All the guys I fought with would say the same thing.'
'So you refused the medal because you were abandoned on Crete?'
Deborah noticed a tremor in Craig's left hand.
'You're holding out on me again, aren't you? Please give me the full story.'

'I saw things I don't want to think about, okay?'

'Mr Craig, please look at me.'

His piercing blue eyes had never looked sadder.

'I want to know,' Deborah said.

'I didn't even tell my wife, damn it.'

Deborah nodded and waited for him to continue. She'd read from court transcripts that he'd married his childhood sweetheart, Mary, in Belhaven Parish Church, Dunbar, in 1946, after being discharged from the army. They'd had three children, whom he had now outlived. Tragically, his wife had died in a car accident in June 1972.

'We had no secrets. But I didn't tell her what I saw.'

'Why?'

'Because I felt ashamed.'

'Mr Craig, I want to write your story. I want to tell them what you did during the war.'

'What use is it now? My life's over.'

Deborah banged on the plastic. 'No, it damn well isn't!'

'I've had enough of this.' Craig got up to leave.

'Please sit down, Mr Craig.'

He paused for a few moments, about to hang up. His eyes seethed with anger. Then he sat down slowly and readjusted his double grip on the phone.

'Thanks. Did you know that your granddaughter tried to persuade newspaper editors in Florida to let people know about this? About your heroism? No one was interested.'

'So what's so different now?'

'*I'm* interested. I care what happens to you. This guy that kept in touch with Jenny, I'm planning on speaking to him. If Joe O'Neill's trial was a sham, it would put you in a strong position to be moved off the row. So, you wanna try and help me help you?'

'How?'

'Mr Craig, if you were the governor, would you send a war hero to his death around election time? So, tell me, what were you so ashamed of?'

Craig grimaced. 'We watched a massacre, okay? Cretans mown down in cold blood. People who had baked us bread. Machine-gunned. It was payback for an attack we'd launched on the Germans. We couldn't reach the village in time.'

Craig gritted his teeth, tears welling in his eyes. 'It goes through my head every day. Why didn't we intervene? Why didn't we stand up and take some of them out?'

'Would you have saved the village?'

Craig shook his head. 'No. And after all that, they wanted to give me a medal. Would *you* have accepted one?'

8

Deborah was running on adrenalin but something was gnawing away at her as she checked into a Best Western motel on the outskirts of Starke. She unpacked her laptop and spread out her notes—including Craig's VC citation and the war papers that she'd borrowed from Jenny. She stared at the citation and realized what was bothering her.

She understood the reach of Senator O'Neill, making sure that newspaper editors in Florida ignored the story about Craig's outstanding bravery during the war. But what she couldn't get her head around was why the British papers hadn't unearthed the citation in their military records.

Over the next hour, Deborah made numerous calls to various press officers at the Ministry of Defence in London. Eventually she was told that records belonging to Private William Craig and thousands of other men and women had been destroyed in a fire at a War Office repository in Dartford Street, Southwark, London, in December 1952.

It explained why the British press knew nothing of Craig's war record. But it gave her a problem. She needed confirmation of the Victoria Cross citation before she could consider speaking to Sam. She knew Sam had a reputation for ensuring that facts were checked, double-checked and then checked again.

An hour later, after talking to military experts in London and Edinburgh, Deborah was given the number of a Professor Ernest MacKenzie, an expert on Scottish military regiments. She called him at his office at Edinburgh University. He kept her waiting for ten minutes, while he looked through his files. Eventually he came back on the line.

He had a copy of a letter from the Secretary of State for War, David Margesson, sent to the King, letting him know the names of four men who were to be given Victoria Crosses. Top of the list was Private William Craig, First Battalion of the Argyll and Sutherland Highlanders, Service Number 2982064. He scanned the copy of the letter and sent it to her.

Deborah had her verification. Now it was time to

work—and she started to type.

As she pounded the keys, she remembered what Larry Coen, the crime reporter, had told her in her first week at the paper—let the story be told in quotes and facts, but keep it simple. Let the reader make up his or her own mind.

Just before ten p.m. her eyes scanned the luminous blue screen for misspellings and bad punctuation. Then she sat back, hit the 'send' key and e-mailed the story to Sam Goldberg. Then she rang his cell phone and told him everything.

Sam didn't seem bowled over. 'Why wasn't this raised in court?'

Deborah rubbed her eyes. 'Craig told his lawyer and Jenny not to mention it at his trial. Not surprisingly, they begged him to change his mind. Jenny Forbes also told me that she'd tried to highlight the issue with newspapers across Florida after her grandfather's trial, including the *Herald*, but no one was interested.'

'I see.' Sam's voice sounded flat.

'Are you all right?'

'Yes—why wouldn't I be?'

'Sounds like something's wrong.'

Deathly silence.

'You still there?' Had she disturbed him at a bad time? Annoyed him in some way?

'Deborah, I know what happened to you.' The words echoed round her head as though she was trapped in a mausoleum.

'Know what?'

'You weren't totally truthful when I asked about your motivation for interviewing Craig.'

She paused for a few moments before speaking in a faltering voice. 'Perhaps not . . .'

'Why didn't you tell me you'd been raped?' She felt herself beginning to shake. 'You could've approached me in confidence.'

Deborah thought she was going to faint. 'How did you come across this information?'

'Remember I told you about the senator's influence?'

'Yeah.'

'Well, he has many friends in the police, national security, everywhere. It wouldn't have been too difficult to find out. Just like it wouldn't have been difficult to browbeat editors in Florida at the time to keep silent about Craig's side of the story.'

Deborah felt ice run through her veins as her mind flashed back to San Francisco.

* * *

It started with an argument in a crowded off-campus student bar, Logan's, on a Friday night. Deborah and Brett began quarreling in full view of many of their friends. Deborah wanted her father to officiate at their wedding. Brett wanted a close friend of his father, a Southern Baptist preacher in Florida. He wouldn't back down. And she stormed out into the cool San Francisco night air, crying and distraught, thinking her wedding plans were in tatters.

A little while later, she remembered a car pulling up, and two of Brett's buddies asking if she was all right. She knew they smoked dope, but they were friendly enough. She told them what had happened and that she was fine. They convinced her to have a couple of nightcaps.

Before she knew it, she was in a biker bar in downtown San Francisco, pouring her heart out as the drinks kept on coming. But she noticed she was the only woman and the only black person. Loud, crazy Metallica songs blared from the jukebox as she downed tequila shots, trying to numb the pain, as Brett's friends listened attentively.

Suddenly, she felt her world tip upside down. The next thing she knew, she was lying on the floor, staring up at a sea of unshaven white faces.

She tried to yell out for them to back off, but she couldn't. She was frozen.

Then, laughing, Brett's friends lifted her up. She tried to scream again but nothing. And the darkness descended.

The next thing she remembered, she was naked. Sore. Lying on a bed spreadeagled, ankles and wrists tied tight with leather belts. TV on. Disgusting pornography. Why was she watching it? Two young white men taking turns at a young black woman. They looked familiar. Very familiar. She looked drugged. Half asleep. Why were Brett's friends laughing? She watched aghast as they committed sex acts. Too vile to mention.

Please make this stop!

Motel. One bed. Her lying on it. She looked again at the video. The young woman's eyes were rolling back in her head like she was crazed.

No. Not possible. Was she going mad? It was her. Brett's friends were raping her. Deborah began screaming until the darkness came again.

* * *

Deborah felt the tears on her face, phone pressed to her ear, silence on the other end of the line.

'Are you still there, Deborah?' Sam asked

eventually.

Her relationship with Brett didn't disintegrate immediately. Bizarrely, she managed to sail through her exams, high on Prozac and Valium to numb the pain. They moved from Berkeley to a new apartment in Orlando soon after graduation, but things had changed. Brett didn't communicate with her anymore, having a full workload as a rookie lawyer. If she wanted to discuss how he felt, he just shrugged his broad shoulders. He wasn't the sort of guy who opened up his heart. Instead he worked long hours, sometimes not coming home.

Eventually, unable to come to terms with what had happened, riddled with guilt about not being able to protect her, he didn't come home at all. All he left was a note, saying he was sorry, but he couldn't cope.

Deborah was left alone in a strange city, struggling to make ends meet, starting out her new job in local journalism, drinking too much, doped up to the eyeballs, feeling suicidal. She had a mental breakdown and fell into a black depression.

Deborah wiped away the tears, trying to regain her composure. 'Who knows what happened to me?'

Goldberg sighed. 'I do and a senior journalist who was given the information.'

Please, no—not her.

'Kathleen Klein?'

Silence.

A million thoughts whirled around her head. 'Are you angry with me for withholding that from you?'

'It's understandable why you wouldn't want to share it.' Sam Goldberg paused for a few moments as if he was picking his words carefully. 'I don't want to find out from the senator's spin doctor, who just so happened to drop it into polite conversation with one of your colleagues.'

Definitely Klein. Oh God, how could she face the world? Everyone would know. They'd be laughing at her. E-mails would be sent about it.

Goldberg said, 'I'm sorry I had to let you know like this.'

Deborah looked out across the motel parking lot and wiped her eyes. 'If it's all right with you, I'd like to offer my resignation. I wasn't straight with you.'

'Not a chance.'

'Why?'

'Look, I feel bad raising this whole thing. It's deeply personal, I appreciate that. But it's impinged on your reasons for doing this story.'

'There's something else. I need you to know everything.'

'Deborah, I don't need to know anymore.'

'I want you to.' Deborah dabbed her eyes. 'My case didn't go to trial.'

'I'm sorry—what do you mean . . . ?'

'I settled out of court. I've been racked by guilt about it for the last two years. In effect, I took the money and ran.'

'Why?'

'My father wanted me to settle. He was ashamed. I was ashamed. He said he couldn't face his congregation. And I agreed to accept a substantial settlement from the boys that enabled me to buy my apartment overlooking the beach. You see what I'm getting at?'

'Deborah, I'm sorry I—'

'Look, I don't want any more secrets. You're

probably wondering what sort of person accepts money in return for silence, so the boys who raped her can go free?'

'Not at all. You did what you thought was best for you. And that's fine by me. So, let's draw a line under this, okay?'

'But it's not okay. It can never be okay. I have to live with this.'

'We're going to draw a line under this.' Sam's voice grew harder. 'Do you hear me?'

Deborah tried to get a handle on the situation. 'They're trying to get to me, aren't they? Trying to humiliate me, undermine me, aren't they?'

'It's dirty tricks, Florida-style. They're letting you know that they know about you. Erhert must have tipped off the senator's people about your visit. And they raked through your past in order to discredit you.'

Deborah watched a happy family in a battered Buick pull into the motel parking lot and wondered why she'd allowed her personal emotions to intrude on her professional life.

'Deborah, your single-mindedness on this story—it wouldn't be to do with a sneaking admiration for Craig?'

'Perhaps.'

Deborah's mind drifted as she tried to think about the sequence of events following her rape. Mental scars, alienation from her family, and a burning desire to find out everything about William Craig once she'd come across his case in the library at Berkeley.

Her father's reaction to her rape had been the most unforgivable. His reputation with his congregation and as a figurehead within the

NAACP seemed more important than his daughter. He'd turned his back on her. He blamed her for being so stupid, and going to the bar with the boys. He even blamed her for 'leading them on'. His very words. Unbelievably, he believed in forgiveness for the boys, but not for her. Reconciliation. But only for them. As a leading light in the civil-rights movement in the 1960s, 'non-violence' and 'love the enemy' were his watchwords.

Craig did what the Bible said—*an eye for an eye*. Why didn't her father want revenge? But she knew it wasn't his way. He was a gentleman. A peaceful man. A man of the cloth.

'I don't want to jeopardize this story,' she said. 'I want Mr Craig's heroism to come out, untainted by my motive. Maybe it'll be better if someone else takes it over.'

'No. This is your story, and it's a great story. I'm proud of you.'

Deborah felt the tears cool her cheeks. 'Are you gonna run it?'

'You bet. Senator O'Neill will not be happy, that's for sure. But our readers'll like it. We've got to do a whole lotta checks tomorrow. And then some more, before it goes in the paper. When it does, we're gonna be asking the governor to take Craig off death row.'

9

Forty-eight hours later, Senator Jack O'Neill sat poker-faced in the back of his limo in the capital holding a copy of the *Miami Herald*. The story of Craig's heroism was splashed all over the front page. They were headed north along First Street, in Washington's snarling rush hour. He handed the paper to Hal Lomax and gazed out of the tinted windows as they passed Capitol South Metro Station.

The story was like a bombshell.

It had erupted out of nothing and he wondered what impact it would have on his poll ratings. Might even send them into free fall. But worst of all was Lomax's failed ploy to leak details of Deborah Jones's rape to discredit her motives. O'Neill was ashamed of such action.

He stared straight ahead as he spoke to his director of media relations. 'Hal, why didn't you tell me you had something of that nature on Deborah Jones . . . ?'

'You wanted me to try and kill the story. That's what I tried to do.'

'I am not interested in descending into the gutter.'

'Jack, we have to fight them hard on this. We can't just wish this sort of shit away.'

O'Neill glanced at his aide and shook his head. Hal Lomax was a studious-looking man with horn-rimmed glasses, brow constantly furrowed. He was in his early fifties and had been with O'Neill from the start. 'Let's forget all this bullshit media-manipulation nonsense, okay? And no more digging into her past.'

O'Neill leaned over and turned down the volume of the limo's TV. Experts were talking on NBC about the 'Axis of Evil' and the possibility of a pre-emptive strike against Iraq. He shook his head.

He knew it wasn't just a possibility, but that a timetable had already been set by the military, and all the diplomatic talk to take it through the UN was just a ruse. In fact, plans for America to oust Saddam had been in place even before 9/11.

He knew of secret meetings in California, Washington and the Middle East where the talk was of a *coup d'état* in Iraq. Big Oil was pulling the strings, although some neo-cons were wanting to go the whole hog and destroy OPEC by flooding the world market with Iraqi oil.

Bottom line? If the American people knew what was being done in their name they wouldn't even believe it; it sounded too crazy.

Lomax tapped the newspaper. 'Jack, read the headline. *Death Row Scot is War Hero*. We need to address this problem, not bury our head in the sand.'

O'Neill lit up a cigarette, preoccupied with the TV. 'Any other bright ideas?'

Lomax coughed on the smoke. He pressed a button and the electric window on his side came down, letting in the welcome autumn air. 'I suggest we talk this through, but for Chrissakes let's not hide away.'

O'Neill was silent, thinking of how his wife would react to the story. She'd been on medication for depression and agoraphobia for years, haunted by her son's death. He'd battled on, consumed by work as he always had been, but the pain was sometimes too much to bear. Some nights, usually late, when Rose was in bed and the housekeeper Maria was away, the emptiness of their lives overwhelmed him. He knew there'd be no more children, no more fun. Now all he had was his wife, but she preferred the company of fine brandies and Jesus.

'Jack, God only knows how you feel about all this coming at you again, but let's be clear: the first priority is the election. And that's why this story on Craig, and anything else, needs to be closed down. We must also think about the donors, Jack.'

'How do you think they'll react to this story?'

'Depends how you respond. The corporate boys couldn't give a rat's ass if Craig gets the needle, but the blacks, the Jewish snowbirds, blue-collar whites and the low-income groups are a different kettle of fish.'

'So what do they think?'

Lomax shrugged. 'We'll arrange some focus groups. Leave it with me.'

O'Neill dragged heavily on his cigarette as the DC traffic became gridlocked outside the Corinthian splendor of the US Supreme Court.

Did the story originate with Craig? Did he write to the *Herald* and tell them his version of events? Maybe if O'Neill hadn't been so preoccupied with Pentagon briefings about Al Qaeda operatives, trips to Afghanistan and Washington, not to mention NASA officials who lobbied him for bigger budgets, he could have seen it coming. Maybe he could have done something about it.

O'Neill turned to face Lomax. 'What's our line, then? The press pack'll want to know if I think the execution should still go ahead.'

'We have no line.' Lomax held up a finger as if to stop further questions. 'So far. Look, you're due to meet Pentagon workers later today to see how the 9/11 damage has been repaired. You'd do well to act like the patriot. Just say, if anyone asks, that you're leaving it all up to the American justice system and God.'

O'Neill felt himself becoming increasingly irritated, boxed in by the story and the pressure of his job, not to mention concern about his wife. The thought of his beloved Rose having to relive the ordeal, seeing Joe's pictures in the paper again, alarmed him. He wanted to protect her from such things. And the story wouldn't stop here.

The car drew to a halt behind a long row of cars. Lomax made eye contact with the chauffeur in the mirror and opened his palms. 'What's the delay? The senator's got a meeting with Condi Rice at nine sharp. That name mean anything to you?'

The black chauffeur muttered, 'Nothing I can do, man,' into the intercom. Lomax shook his head and jumped out.

'I'll meet you in the office,' he said, and slammed the door.

O'Neill watched him walk the last five hundred yards. Then he picked up the *Herald* Lomax had left behind. He scanned Craig's proud features, the picture of him in military uniform, the citation on the inside pages, the letter from the British Secretary of State for War. This was the man, war hero or not, who had killed his son.

He wanted Craig to be held to account, but he didn't know if he had the stomach for the fight. The stomach to get him executed. Especially now.

He pulled out his laptop, logged on and checked his e-mail. The CIA wanted him to review his security arrangements for the fourth time in the wake of 9/11.

Maybe if they'd done their job in the first place, 9/11 would never have happened.

O'Neill logged off and checked the voicemail on his cell phone.

Damn. Everyone wanted to know what he thought of Craig being a war hero. He remembered what Lomax had said.

His cell phone went off and he picked up, expecting to hear Condoleezza's nasal drawl. The voice was from Brooklyn. 'It's Richmond.'

'You read the *Herald*?'

'I'm sorry, Jack. Listen, I've been doing some digging on this Deborah Jones, and—'

'Forget it. I've already had to tell off Hal for the same thing.'

'Whether you like it or not, you can't sit on your ass until this gets out of control. You need to get a grip of the situation.'

O'Neill didn't want to listen to the old man anymore. It was true that he was closer to Richmond than anyone, even Lomax. But the thought of prying into someone's personal life always left him cold. It wasn't the America he believed in.

'I've made a couple of calls already. She was born and bred in Jackson, Mississippi. Middle-class black background. Parents still live there.' Richmond paused for a moment. 'Did you know what happened to her in San Francisco?'

'Yes.'

Richmond ignored him. 'You'll like this, though. Turns out her father was a big shot in the civil-rights marches. Close friend of Dr King. Leading light in the NAACP.'

O'Neill felt a knot of tension in his back. He doubted whether all this trawling through a person's life would be helpful. It might even complicate matters if Deborah Jones's father got the blacks on Craig's side. He noticed the chauffeur glance in his mirror. He smiled back at O'Neill but looked away immediately as though he knew that he shouldn't eyeball his boss.

O'Neill said, 'Have you finished?'

'She's got an upscale condo in Miami Beach. Which raises the question, how can she afford that on a reporter's salary?'

'How many times do I have to tell you? I'm not interested.'

'She settled out of court with the two boys who raped her. A million bucks ended up in her account at a bank in Orlando eighteen months ago. One of the boy's fathers is a Beverly Hills plastic surgeon, and he paid up. So now we know why she was so keen to interview Craig. But it also leaves her vulnerable.'

'Richmond, do me a favor, and leave all that muckraking to some sleazy private investigators. That's not the way I do business.'

'Jack, you need to know everything about her. She has initiated this story, and we need to discredit her. You need to know what she eats for breakfast, about her boyfriends, lovers, her habits, what drugs she takes. Do you know she's a jibagoo?'

O'Neill ignored the racist jibe. The traffic was moving again and the concrete monstrosity that was the Hart Senate Office Building came into view. Armed guards swarmed all over the place. Another damned security alert. 'What's that got to do with anything?'

'It's got to do with your survival. This girl has somehow opened up the story, after all this time.

Do you think she'll be content with that?'

'I've no idea.'

'You can bet your ass she won't.'

O'Neill shook another cigarette out of the packet and lit up.

'I think this reporter could give us problems.'

O'Neill dragged hard on his cigarette and smoke filled the car again. 'Look, I've got my hands full with the election coming up. Gimme a break, okay?'

'Jack, we're keeping an eye on the situation. I just thought you should know.' Richmond's tone was ominous.

O'Neill hung up, wishing the whole mess would just go away.

10

Early in the evening—on the day the story made headlines across America—Deborah gazed out of the window beside her desk as a burnt-orange sunset enveloped downtown Miami. She was drained by the excitement of her first real scoop. She imagined William Craig, stuck in his stifling cell. All she could hope for was that her article would give the authorities something to think about. Perhaps they might even move him off death row.

Her mother had called from Jackson just after six to congratulate her. She said that she and Deborah's father were 'real proud' of their daughter. Deborah wanted to talk to her father, but her mother said he was busy, which meant he didn't want to speak to her.

Her phone rang and she heard a familiar drawl. 'Hi, Deborah. It's Brett.'

His voice reminded her of the first time she'd met him. He'd been captain of the college football team, she a reporter for the student newspaper. He was tough, tall and funny. He was also very shy. And she'd liked that. 'What do you want?'

'I read your story,' he said. 'Just wanted to say congratulations. Helluva good job.'

'Thank you.'

'So, how do you like the big city?'

'Suits me fine.'

Brett cleared his throat. 'I moved to a little place on the Gulf Coast. Beautiful part of the world.'

'How very nice.'

'Look, I don't want to fight.' He paused. 'Guess you're wondering why I've waited so long to contact you?'

'Not really.'

'Deborah, I just wanted to say I'm real sorry. I'm an asshole, okay?'

'Amen to that.'

'I couldn't handle it. I wanted to forget it happened.'

Deborah's throat tightened. 'You left me alone. I needed you. Any idea how that feels?'

'I can imagine.'

'No, you can't.'

A silence opened up between them as Deborah remembered the day she had returned from work at the *Orlando Sentinel* to see the note from Brett attached by a Mickey Mouse magnet on their fridge. How could he? Did the beautiful walks among the redwoods on the coast not mean anything? The great concerts? The glasses of wine, watching the sunset over the Golden Gate Bridge? The plans for their future. Children.

'Deborah, you wanna know why I left?'

She stayed quiet.

'Look, it's difficult to explain, but these were my so-called friends. I felt responsible. But . . . but, more than anything, I couldn't bear to think of anyone, let alone people I trusted as friends, doing such things to you. Bottom line? I couldn't live with myself because I failed to protect you. But I never stopped loving you.'

'I've moved on, Brett.'

'So have I. Look, I'm working out of a few places on the Gulf Coast.'

'Doing what?'

Brett paused for a few moments. 'I joined the FBI about a year ago. I found I wasn't interested in just sitting in an office all day, working as a lawyer. I wanted to do something useful.'

'Is joining the Feds supposed to be cathartic or something?'

'Gimme a break, Deborah. Look, I know I let you down. I let myself down. Perhaps you're right, maybe it is cathartic.'

'Can't really imagine you carrying a firearm.'

'Neither could I, until I went to Quantico.'

Deborah leaned back in her seat and wondered if he could be a potential source. She knew it was mercenary. But she was thinking of her job and her future. She tried to sound interested in his new career. 'Quantico?'

'The big time. I enrolled as a trainee special agent, and did the standard eighteen-week course—firearms training, physical fitness, defensive strategies, that kind of thing, not to mention law. Guess what? I aced it all. Top of my class. Now I'm a Special Agent of the FBI.'

Deborah couldn't resist probing. 'You wanna tell me what you're working on now?'

'Come on, Deborah, that's not fair.'

Deborah glanced up at the clock, which now showed 7:15 p.m. She was due for soccer practice in South Miami in under an hour. 'Brett, you mind telling me what you want?'

'I'd like to meet up again.'

Deborah drew in a sharp breath. This was what she had feared. Feared and prayed for. 'I'm real busy.'

Brett went quiet for a few moments. Then he spoke in a gentle voice. 'I knew you'd do it. I'm real proud of you. Mom and Dad called me to say they'd read your story as well.'

He didn't have to tell her what nice people they were. Deborah's throat tightened. 'Thank you.'

'Deborah, I'm not gonna push this, but I sure as hell'd like to give us another chance. Guess that's all I wanted to say.'

She so wanted him to hold her. Just to say he loved her and say it like he meant it. She imagined his muscular arms and his soft lips.

Damn.

He'd gone and done it to her again. It was as if he expected she'd be at her most vulnerable. Truth was, she wasn't. The past forty-eight hours had been a nightmare now that the fact of her rape was no longer a deeply private thing. The knowledge had plunged her back into those terrible memories. She wasn't sleeping. Even the enthusiastic feedback throughout the day about her story from her colleagues and friends didn't lift her spirits.

Why wasn't she more angry with Brett? By rights, she should tell him to go to hell. Deborah had suffered the agonies of intensive therapy sessions and bleak loneliness as she'd struggled to cope, without his support. Her girlfriends in Orlando had told her that she was better off without him, but that wasn't true. They were just trying to make her feel better. You'll find another man, they'd said. She wasn't interested in another. She'd had one. He'd left.

But the sound of his voice had revived all the sadness within her. The memories.

She remembered the look of anguish when Brett saw her in the hospital in San Francisco after her rape. The hurt in his eyes made her cry. She never wanted to see hurt like that again. And that's what she could never understand. How could he leave her, a few months later, in Orlando? How could the handsome young man she loved turn away from her, leaving a note for her to read after work? He knew how she was struggling to cope with the nightmares, pills and flashbacks.

'Brett, I gotta go.'

'I understand. Can I phone you again?' There was a tension in his voice.

'I don't know, I'm kind of mixed up and swamped with work and phone calls . . .' She was silent for a few seconds, wishing he'd say something to keep her on the line. Instead, she hung up.

Deborah buried her head in her hands and felt the ache of all the desperate months she'd endured rise to the surface. The emotion started deep down in her stomach. It made its way up through her chest, and then her throat, until she sobbed like a little girl, alone at her desk.

11

Thirty minutes later, after a short, tearful drive across the city, Deborah had swapped mental turmoil for physical pain. Her heart pounded and sweat poured down her face as she and thirteen other girls weaved in and out of traffic cones under the floodlights of the soccer field at Palmer Park. Everyone's expressions were etched with pain as they gasped for breath, but skipping training was not an option.

On the sidelines, wearing a red Adidas tracksuit and matching sneakers, was Deborah's best friend in the city, Faith King. She was a small black woman who coached them. 'Let's pick it up, girls,' she bawled, hands on hips. 'You've got to love the pain, y'hear?'

Deborah had joined the Overtown Women's Soccer Team—a motley collection of former hookers, junkies and other hard-luck stories—about four months ago after she had written an uplifting article on the team. Faith invited her to fill the vacant center-forward role until someone suitable turned up, but no one had. And so was born Deborah's friendship with the girls who'd grown up in Miami's crime-ridden Overtown, some of them in the notorious housing projects, now demolished, around NW 3rd Avenue.

Deborah sucked in the air hard as she underwent

another weaving sprint among the cones, but felt good that Faith was so near at hand. In the past, she'd confided in her about work, her family back in Jackson whom she missed and, most of all, about the recurring nightmares. She even told Faith that she kept the bedroom lights on, scared of going to sleep.

On the surface they had nothing in common, but Faith became a great shoulder to cry on, as did Deborah for her. Faith let her into a horrible secret she kept from most people. She'd been raped as well. Not at some fancy college, but in her grandmother's bathroom by her uncle. That link brought them even closer together. Like sisters.

Deborah saw that through the team and soccer, Faith—like a lot of the girls—could work out her simmering anger and sense of hopelessness. More importantly, it was also an environment in which she didn't feel threatened by men.

Faith's husband had deserted her. To feed and clothe her five children, the easy thing to do would have been to start turning tricks—like many of the women around her—in the sleazy Miami Beach hotels. But she wouldn't sink that low.

Faith wanted her children to respect her and be proud that their mother worked for a living. So she endured double shifts waiting tables at two different restaurants, one for breakfast/lunch and the other for dinner, and juggled the two jobs for years. It wasn't easy, but at least she slept well at night knowing her kids were growing up with the same values her own mother had instilled in her. Work hard, respect yourself, respect others, and never, ever turn your back on the needy.

Deborah, despite coming from a more affluent

and stable background—private school, loving parents, the works—tapped into the dignity and determination of the team, especially Faith, who was now a full-time community soccer coach. The rest of the girls had cleaned up their acts, ridding themselves of drugs and the prostitution rings that had ensnared them for so many wasted years. That was one of the team's hard and fast rules—no drugs, no vice, just soccer and Bud Ice.

Some of the players had gotten educations, some had started small businesses, one had even entered Miami politics, but they all found the camaraderie and spirit of their soccer team an inspiration.

Initially, there were some reservations from a couple of the girls about Deborah's suitability. One said that she didn't meet the criteria for the team—namely, being from Overtown—while another thought she was 'slumming it' to look cool.

Faith, being so respected, won them over and Deborah stayed. Since then, she'd become the star player and turned up religiously every Tuesday night for training and every Saturday morning for the game. She even babysat Faith's kids when Faith needed a few hours to herself.

After the sweat-drenched training session, Faith shook Deborah's hand, patting her on the back. 'Good work, girl,' she said. 'Surprised you managed to drag your bony ass down to see us tonight, especially after the big licks that story of yours got.'

'Gimme a break, Faith,' Deborah said, turning to give her a playful kick up the backside. 'And less of the bony.'

Faith laughed, but she seemed to sense that Deborah was more preoccupied than usual.

Half an hour later, the girls knocked back the beers as they watched English soccer on the big screen.

Deborah sat beside Faith in a quiet corner. The rest of the team crowded round Big Marcia who was cheering on her favorite team, Liverpool. Deborah pretended to watch the match, but her thoughts were elsewhere. Her story on Craig, Brett's call, the rape being water-cooler fodder.

Faith, as if sensing how she felt, turned to her. 'You gonna tell me what's on your mind?'

Deborah sipped her drink and smiled. 'What do you mean?'

'I don't know, you seem kinda edgy tonight. Thought you'd be on top of the world after that article of yours about that old white guy on death row.'

'I am.'

'So?'

Deborah sighed and bit her lower lip. 'I'm just a bit tired, that's all.'

Faith wasn't stupid. She leaned closer and Deborah smelled a new perfume. 'Hello? Deborah, it's Faith you're talking to. If you can't confide in me, who can you confide in?'

Deborah stared into her drink, not wishing to go into details.

'Don't keep it in. It's not good for you. Just let old Faith know what's the problem.'

'My boss knows about me being raped.'

Faith closed her eyes for a moment. 'I'm sorry, honey. How did that happen?'

'He just mentioned it out of the blue a couple of days ago. I'd rather have cut off my arms than have him know. I feel like I've been violated all over again.'

'You have. So how did he find out?'

'Senator O'Neill's media adviser dropped it into a conversation with one of my colleagues, during a lunch. She reported back to my boss.'

'Shit. How did O'Neill find out?'

Deborah took a sip of her drink. 'Who knows? He's a very powerful guy. Many connections. Probably pissed that I found out something positive about the guy who killed his son. Maybe he feels threatened, and wants to undermine me or my confidence.'

'And has it?'

'What do you think? Faith, I never thought people would stoop so low.'

A great roar erupted from Marcia and the rest of the girls as Liverpool scored.

Faith leaned closer. 'Listen to me. You're a great reporter and a great person. Don't let those bastards get you down.'

Deborah looked at Faith. 'It's brought everything back. Not only that, I'm imagining that people are following me again.'

'Girl, you need to get some counseling, you hear me?'

'I thought I'd got over it all. Damn. Miami was supposed to be the new start for me. *Now* look at me.'

Faith touched her hand, which held a glass of Diet Coke. 'How many times have I told you? You've got to open up. I'm here for you. Any time you want to speak about that or anything, you've got my number. Night or day, honey. You understand?'

'I don't know what I'd do without you.'

'I've been through all that stuff. And you can make it. You've just got to like yourself a little bit more. Lighten up.'

'That's what everyone at works says. They think I work too hard and don't have fun. But I don't want to go out partying with them. I don't feel ready.'

'I know, honey. One step at a time.'

Deborah looked up for a moment to sneak a glance at the soccer game. 'There's something else.'

'You're not pregnant, are you?'

Deborah smiled and lightly slapped the back of Faith's hand. 'Behave.'

'So what is it?'

'Brett phoned.'

'Hell is he wanting?'

'He wanted to get back together.'

'You kidding, after what he did to you? You should've told him to get lost.'

'Look, I'm feeling kinda fragile over this whole thing. He was being as nice as—'

'I'm sure he was, the rat.'

Deborah shook her head, wishing Faith would cut her some slack. 'I'm mixed up,' she said. 'I want us to get back together again, but I feel so let down by what he did. I know he felt bad because he couldn't protect me. He's a good guy, honestly.'

'There's no such thing.'

Deborah shot her a sharp look. 'What about William Craig? You feel the same about him?'

'You know I don't mean that.'

'I want him off death row.' Deborah finished her drink and glanced at her watch. 'I gotta go.'

'Look, I didn't mean to upset you.'

'It's not that, but I'm due at the office early

tomorrow.'

'Sure, honey, I understand. Don't wanna hang around for the sports quiz they're running after the game?'

'Maybe next week.' Deborah kissed Faith on the cheek. 'Thanks for listening.'

'Don't mention it. See you Saturday.'

Deborah said her goodbyes to the rest of the team and walked out into the still night air. As she got into her convertible, her cell phone rang. She reached into her bag for the phone and wondered if it was Sam Goldberg calling from one of his favorite haunts—the Tobacco Road Bar—to congratulate her again.

But the voice on the other end was an educated-sounding Englishwoman. 'I've just read your story on the Internet about William Craig with great interest, Miss Jones.'

Must've been diverted from the office phone to her cell. Deborah switched off her engine. 'Can you call back in the morning, please?'

'I'm sorry, but this is urgent. I think I have a story for you. I'd like to meet you in person to discuss it.'

Deborah closed her eyes and wondered if it was another Ricky Martin nut. 'Where're you speaking from?'

'The Mandarin Oriental. Do you know it?'

'Excuse me?'

The woman sighed like she was losing patience. 'I'm not used to being asked to repeat myself, Miss Jones. I'll say it again, do you know the Mandarin Oriental?'

'Yes. It's not far from where I am just now.'

'And you're the Deborah Jones who wrote this story?'

‘Yes—’

‘Don’t be late. Meet me at the Martini bar in the Oriental lobby at ten sharp.’

‘Ma’am, I don’t know anything about you.’

‘For now, all you have to know is that I’ll be wearing a white T-shirt and jeans,’ the woman said. ‘You’ll recognize me, I promise. Before I forget, bring something to record our conversation.’

* * *

It was only a short ride from the bar, across downtown towards the lights shimmering from the concrete and glass towers where the Mandarin was located. Deborah crossed the causeway and headed for Brickell Key, also known as Claughton Island, a man-made triangular island south of the mouth of the Miami River.

She pulled up outside the hotel, just before ten. She felt sweat on her back as she handed her keys to a valet. A concierge held open the glass door.

Deborah was wearing a black linen suit, carried a stylish briefcase, and felt good after the evening’s training session. The air-conditioning cooled her skin as she walked past the marble front desk into the soaring lobby.

Harp music mingled with the odd tinkling of Martini glasses in the M-Bar. Floor-to-ceiling windows allowed great views over the bay and of the countless lights of the Miami skyline. It was as if the people lived in a hermetically sealed universe, far from the pulsating beat and Latin influence of the city. Even further from Overtown.

Deborah’s gaze was drawn to a woman in her late thirties sitting alone by the windows.

Was she the one? She looked vaguely familiar.

The woman stared out over the bay and sipped a cocktail as if she hadn't a care in the world. All around, in the candlelight, couples chatted and flirted.

Everyone apart from the woman seemed to be paired off. Deborah walked over, briefcase in hand. The woman looked frail and her tight white T-shirt revealed pert breasts. Her faded Levis looked a couple of sizes too big on her frame.

'Hi.' The woman held out a bony hand and smiled. 'You'll be Deborah Jones?'

Deborah nodded and shook hands.

The woman's eyes were lifeless as she ran a hand through her messy auburn locks. 'You look surprised.'

Deborah sat down, briefcase on her lap. Close up, the woman looked more fragile and beautiful than she did on the big screen. She had eyes like faded emeralds. Her high cheekbones emphasized her red lips. Her arms were toned.

Rachel Turner was one of Hollywood's hottest and most volatile properties. She'd starred in most of the top-grossing films in the last decade. Bust-ups on film sets were her thing, if you believed the *Enquirer*.

'Can I get you a drink?' she said. 'You look like you need one.' Rachel Turner's accent was cut-glass, just like her film roles. She held up a black linen menu. 'They've got two hundred and fifty kinds of Martini. I'm working my way through them. Take your pick.'

'Just a Diet Coke, thanks.'

Turner ordered the drinks.

'So, you'll be thinking,' she said, 'what did I do to

deserve this unexpected pleasure?'

Deborah nodded and sipped her Diet Coke.

'If you can take out your tape recorder and pens and paper, I can let you in on my little secret.'

Deborah rummaged in her briefcase and brought out her mini recorder, paper and pens for shorthand. What could Rachel Turner tell her that related to her story? 'Okay,' she said, and switched on the tape recorder. 'Ready when you are.'

'Your article about William Craig was moving. Must've been, because I cried.' Rachel Turner glanced at the tape recorder. 'I rarely cry. Do enough of that in front of the cameras.' She took another long sip at her cocktail. 'I read the article on my computer at home this morning.'

'Where exactly is home?'

'Upper East Side of Manhattan, but I still like to keep up to date with what's happening down here.'

'Why's that?'

'I lived here briefly in the early 1990s. Before I go any further, I need to fill you in on my previous life for this to make any sense.'

Deborah looked up from her notes. 'What do you mean?'

Rachel Turner licked her lips and glanced out over Biscayne's sparkling water. 'I want to tell you what I did before I was famous. I'm originally from New Cross in South London. That mean anything to you?'

Deborah shook her head.

'Didn't think it would. For your information, it's a shithole. Gary Oldman's from there, so it can't be all bad, but this is not the accent I was brought up with. My mother, God bless her, worked in a bar. Scrimped and scraped to send me to elocution lessons hoping they'd pay off one day. Thought a working-class accent wouldn't get me far.'

'Didn't do Michael Caine any harm.'

Rachel Turner smiled and took another drink. 'I went to live in New York in the mid-1980s. Some hellhole on the Lower East Side. I thought with my new posh accent I'd get spotted immediately. I'd seen Joan Collins do it in *Dynasty* and thought, why not me? And wouldn't you know it, I got lucky. Got my big break and never looked back. There are literally hundreds of wannabe actresses in New York. Every one drop-dead gorgeous and would kill for my luck. And I mean kill. Think about it. How could a piece of white trash like me go to the top of the queue on the other side of the Atlantic?'

'I don't mean to be rude,' Deborah said, 'but what's this got to do with William Craig or my story?'

'I'm coming to that.' Rachel Turner finished her drink and her eyes got heavier. 'I enrolled at the Actors' Studio in New York. Things weren't easy. Waitressing at night in midtown to make the rent. I was star-struck. I was also dumb. Didn't realize that most people wanting to get into the movies head to LA.'

Deborah nodded.

'Where I worked, the clientele had cash to burn. Remember, by now this is the late 1980s. Conspicuous consumption. They tipped well. Wall Street guys thinking they were Charlie Sheen. One night a guy came in. He was the only customer. Good-looking. Young. I was supposed to lock up with the manager who was in the back counting the takings. This guy asked if I wanted a drink. I refused, said I didn't date customers, that kind of line. Said I needed my beauty sleep.'

Rachel Turner's lower lip quivered and tears streamed down her fine features, smudging her mascara. 'I'm sorry,' she said. 'You mind if we carry on this conversation in private?'

*   *   *

Rachel Turner's suite was on the twentieth floor and was, of course, the hotel's finest—'The Oriental Suite'. The private balcony spanned the full length of the huge room and boasted the best views of downtown, the waters of Biscayne below.

Deborah stepped out into the sticky air and looked across the city, inky darkness overhead.

Wonder where Brett is? She hoped it wouldn't be dangerous, but knowing him, he'd opt for a tough assignment instead of easy street. Always did like a challenge.

The smell of the Everglades drifted in on the breeze, grassy and damp.

Rachel Turner joined her, carrying a glass of champagne and a Diet Coke. Her hair blew across her face and she laughed. 'Sure you don't want champagne?'

'I don't drink.' Deborah didn't mention that she had given up liquor because she never wanted to feel out of control again.

'Smart girl.'

Deborah turned and looked through the floor-to-ceiling glass back into the suite. It was lit by huge lamps, which cast a golden glow around the room. 'Real nice place you've got, Rachel.' Wonder what her colleagues in the newsroom would make of this. Come to think of it, what would Faith and the

Overtown girls make of it?

They stepped back inside, and Rachel gave Deborah a tour of her suite.

The luxurious bathroom featured an oversized shower, a free-standing tub, a floor-to-ceiling window and Bulgari bathroom fittings. A huge bedroom was separated from the bathroom by a rice-paper sliding door. There were plasma-screen TVs in every room. The suite also had a state-of-the-art media room with theater-style seating.

'A girl could get used to this,' Deborah said, sitting down on a cream sofa.

'You wanna continue our conversation?' Rachel asked.

'Sure.'

Deborah started up her recorder and took out her pens and notepad, while Rachel picked up the champagne bottle and poured herself another glass.

'Something happened to me in New York which has dogged me for years.' Rachel slid the bottle back into the ice bucket on the marble table.

'I'm listening.'

Turner seemed reluctant to go on. 'As I said earlier, there was only myself, the manager and this young guy. The guy was persistent. "Want to come back to my place and party?" That kind of thing. Well, I joined him for a nightcap. Second mistake.'

Deborah said nothing.

'He spiked my drink.' Rachel ran her hand through her silky hair and locked onto Deborah's gaze. 'Woke up bleeding in some alley near Times Square. The bastard raped me.'

Deborah's mind was suddenly filled with men's voices, drunken laughter, screams and a blinding white light which shone on her as she was tied to the bed. *Animals*.

'I spent two days in hospital.'

Deborah sat dumbstruck.

'Your story about Mr Craig being a war hero struck a chord with me.' She switched on one of the huge TVs with a remote control and flicked distractedly to an old black and white movie Deborah had never seen. Bogart was in it. Rachel's eyes filled with tears. She then went quiet for nearly a minute. 'It was after reading it that I realized I'd been a complete fool.'

'How do you mean?'

'I decided not to press charges against the guy who did it.'

The words seemed to skid across Deborah's brain in slow motion.

'A company, a powerhouse LA talent firm contacted me out of the blue. They signed me, but only when it was too late did I realize their one proviso was that I kept quiet. From then on, my career took off. Tried to forget all about it. That is, until this morning. Your story brought it all back.'

Rachel Turner took a deep breath. 'The guy that raped me was the same one Mr Craig killed,' she said.

Deborah sat transfixed.

'Less than six months after I was attacked, Joe O'Neill did the same to Mr Craig's granddaughter. If I'd taken the case to trial, it would never have happened. Do you understand?'

Deborah nodded.

'I felt physically sick when I read about how that

poor man is going to be executed. And all for killing that beast. Should have been given a decoration.'

Deborah felt the same about Mr Craig. His concern for justice for his grandchild and women like her was more important to him than his own liberty.

Deborah's mind flashed forward. It was a fantastic story, but could it ever be told? 'This may ruin you, Rachel.'

'I'm way past caring. What that old man did was right. It's crazy that he's on death row. My story proves he killed a double rapist. You think about that.'

Deborah wondered if she should call Goldberg about the revelations. Probably best to. By now, Rachel Turner had closed her eyes and was humming a show tune to herself as if oblivi-ous to her surroundings. 'My own boss has his doubts about the veracity of the trials of Craig and O'Neill.'

Rachel opened her sleepy eyes. 'Your boss is correct. You think that with all my money I can't afford the best private investigators?'

'So who's responsible?'

'Who do you think?'

'I don't know—the senator?'

'He's got the money, the motive, and the manpower.'

'Manpower?'

'A guy called Paulie Fachetti is his link. He's top guy in the Miami Mob. Was once the underboss of the Gambinos in Los Angeles. Would wine and dine me at all these top restaurants in Beverly Hills, twice a year, just to remind me of my obligation to keep quiet.' This was the first time she'd heard of Mob links. It seemed far-fetched. Maybe Rachel had had one too many drinks?

'When did you first meet him?'

'Couple of days after I got out of hospital. Made it clear who he was and what he could do for me. He's a small, weedy little shit.' Rachel shivered and finished her champagne. 'You think the *Miami Herald*'s got the balls to put that on the front page?'

*   *   *

Deborah tracked Goldberg down to a nearby jazz-and-blues bar, one block west of Brickell Avenue. She had to shout loud as a B.B. King song blared in the background. 'Stay right there, I'm on my way,' he said.

Goldberg arrived less than fifteen minutes later. The actress told him the story again and he listened in silence. Rachel Turner cracked open another bottle of champagne and poured a couple of flutes.

'Ms Turner, I'll be frank,' Goldberg said. He sipped his drink. 'This story worries me.'

'Why?'

'Have you thought through the consequences? Both career-wise and the possibility of putting yourself in danger?'

'Look, it's time the world knew,' Rachel said. 'I'm financially secure for life.' She looked at Goldberg through dreamy eyes. 'All I ask is that you print the story. It's yours as an exclusive.'

Goldberg frowned and the lines on his forehead bunched tight. 'We'll have to do some checking.'

'Will you promise?'

Goldberg put his glass down and Deborah noticed that he wore a wedding band. 'We'll run the story past our executive editor tomorrow morning. Maybe we'll go with it the day after. Can't promise any more than that.'

'Make sure it happens.' Rachel Turner was really slurring her words now. 'Let's not let Mr Craig down again.'

The elevator door opened and Deborah and her boss stepped out into the lobby, to the familiar sounds of harp music, gentle laughter, and the tinkling of cocktail glasses from the M-Bar.

Neither paid any attention to the two thickset men in well-tailored suits waiting to go up.

* * *

Just after two a.m. Deborah lay on her sofa, as CNN carried details of a Palestinian bombing in the West Bank. She felt herself drift away into a deep sleep. Before long, the nightmares were there.

Two men laughing. Hands round her throat. More laughing. Screaming. Red-smeared vision. A face she knew. Please stop, someone was shouting. Was it her? He reeked of bourbon.

The excited voice of a CNN reporter woke Deborah and she sat bolt upright. Her heart raced and she was drenched in sweat.

'I'll say again,' the young reporter said, 'Rachel Turner is dead. She was found just before one this morning.'

Deborah felt her blood run cold.

'No one knows how she died. Police say she's

fallen to her death in a tragic accident.'

12

Just after dawn, a small team of bleary-eyed journalists—including Deborah Jones—assembled in the newsroom of the *Miami Herald*. It was like a scene from one of Rachel Turner's blockbuster films. No one thought her death was an accident. The general consensus—knowing what the actress had said to Deborah and Sam only hours before—was that she had been iced in a contract killing. Off-the-record comments from the FBI's Organized Crime Section in Washington DC confirmed that the senator and Fachetti were tight.

Thankfully, Deborah had a tape and excellent shorthand notes to prove that the interview had taken place. Both items were locked in a safe in Sam Goldberg's office.

Sam Goldberg wanted to know one thing: Was Rachel Turner pushed or did she jump? 'World-famous actresses don't just fall to their death from hotel rooms after having a drink or a pill too many,' he said. 'If they did, our papers would be packed with nothing else.'

A few wry grins.

'Now, I'm not ruling out that it was a tragic accident or suicide, but I think we all agree this stinks. So I don't want any detail, no matter how small or insignificant, to be ignored. Try not to piss off too many people. Everyone and their dog will want a piece of this, but they're not having it. This is our story. Don't mention to anyone that

Deborah was the last person to interview her. That's strictly confidential. Any questions?'

Larry Coen, the crime reporter, said, 'Did the night editor come up with anything?'

'A few bland quotes from the duty manager and the police, but nothing from hotel employees or guests. It didn't amount to much.' His gaze roamed from journalist to journalist, and lingered on Deborah. 'Any more questions?'

There weren't any.

Deborah, along with two other younger reporters, was assigned to speak to chambermaids, cleaners, tourists or anyone who'd stayed at the hotel. Two senior journalists stayed in the newsroom and phoned valued sources. Three more streetwise reporters met up in bars with police informants.

Deborah could see early on that something wasn't right. She spent just an hour badgering night-shift employees leaving their work, but they all said the same thing. 'Please speak to the management.'

Fifteen employees, some chefs, some bellhops, some security, uttered the same words. Someone had laid down the law.

According to Shaw Walters, a crime reporter around Deborah's age, it was rare if not impossible for all the employees to give the same response, unless national security was at risk. Some would always speak off the record, but not this time. Even hotel guests, tourists and the like, didn't seem keen to talk. They weren't as on-message as the staff, but still, it was disconcerting.

Deborah was about to head back to the newsroom when she had an idea. What about

Brett? He was in the FBI after all. And she figured he owed her.

It took six rings before his cell phone was picked up.

'Brett Pottinger,' he said. Butterflies fluttered in her stomach.

'Brett, sorry to bother you. It's Deborah.' She took off her sunglasses as another network TV van pulled up.

'Hey, how ya doin'? I knew you'd call. Said to my father you would.'

'Look, Brett, I'm sure you're busy, but I need a favor.'

'Just name it.'

'I'm working on a story in Miami.'

'Rachel Turner?'

Deborah paused and tried to think of what she'd say. 'Look, I need to get an inside track on this.'

Brett groaned. 'That's against regulations, as you know.'

'No one's saying a thing down here. I spoke to her only last night. Has the name Fachetti cropped up in the police investigation so far?'

'We're not strictly involved.'

'You will be.'

Brett paused for a couple of beats.

'Well, is Fachetti in the frame, or anyone who works for him?'

'I'd love to help Deborah, but I—'

'You'd be doing me a big, big favor. And you owe me one, don't you think?'

'I can't talk just now, but I might be able to help. Not on the phone, though. I'll be in touch.'

And he hung up.

Early in the afternoon, when Deborah returned

to the office, Goldberg filled her in on developments. Apparently, two stringers in New York had independently verified that Rachel Turner had been raped many years ago in Manhattan. They'd faxed over medical reports from her past—after getting copies from the same 'amenable' hospital administrator. Goldberg was confident of running with her story tomorrow or the day after. But first they had to give a statement to the Miami police. They seemed satisfied, but the day wasn't over.

*   *   *

Shortly after five p.m., Deborah and Goldberg were summoned to the office of the executive editor, Harry Donovan. He sat behind his polished desk and stared morosely at his laptop. He wore a dark blue pinstriped suit, white shirt, and pink tie. His sand-colored hair looked like a wig.

Deborah and Goldberg took a seat.

Donovan cleared his throat and leaned back in his black leather seat. 'So, Deborah, what the hell happened last night?' She felt uncomfortable, aware that he knew all about the past that she had been desperate to conceal.

'What happened was, I interviewed Rachel Turner, first in the bar, then in her suite. I called Mr Goldberg for guidance because her allegations were so extraordinary. He came up and heard the allegations himself. Several hours later, I learn she's dead.'

Donovan picked up a pencil and chewed the end. 'So the two of you were the last people to see her alive?' He shook his head. 'How did she seem to you, Sam?'

'Slightly tipsy, but genial. Cogent.'

'Slightly drunk?'

Goldberg shrugged. 'She knew exactly what she was saying.'

'Did she talk about taking her own life?'

'No. She wanted the story on Joe O'Neill to get out.'

Donovan arched his eyebrows. 'And this was all recorded, right?'

'You wanna hear it?'

'I've seen the transcripts. Although I haven't read the whole thing.' Donovan leaned forward, elbows on the desk. He steepled his fingers. 'I had a rather interesting call this morning. Some Miami chief of police I've never heard of wanting some help from us.'

'We've given statements to the police already.'

'That's what I thought, but seems like they want a whole lot more.'

Goldberg shrugged.

'Sam, they want access to last night's tapes.'

Goldberg flushed crimson. 'I hope you told him to go to hell. Haven't they heard of the First Amendment?'

'Sam, I understand perfectly well that journalists don't hand over tapes, notepads or whatever. I know that. But think about it. Rachel fucking Turner is lying on a mortuary slab and nobody knows why.'

'I don't give a damn who it is,' Goldberg said. 'We don't give up sources or confidential material.'

'You have no sources. Turner is dead.' Donovan sighed. 'We should consider it. It could provide clues for the police investigation.'

'Over my dead body.' Goldberg was having difficulty controlling his anger. 'Harry, we go back a long way, but I don't ever recall you taking such a line. And just so you know, I'd refuse to obey a federal grand-jury subpoena if it ordered me to hand over the tapes.'

Donovan banged the table with his fist and made Deborah jump. 'In the circumstances, I understand where the police are coming from.'

'Have you lost your mind, Harry? Who phoned you? Look, I'll speak to them and take the heat. Gimme a name.'

'Dennis Morrison.' He shrugged. 'That mean anything to you?'

'He's top dog down the beach. What the hell's downtown got to do with him?'

'Never mind, but he wants those tapes bad.' Donovan paused for a few moments. 'Sam, we're not talking about ethics. We're talking about people's lives. Deborah's tapes could hold the key.'

Donovan had been in the job for just a year. He was, according to some on *Metro*, a 'steady, dependable' type of journalist. He had got the job despite the protestations of staff unimpressed by his tenure as managing editor. Goldberg had been the newsroom choice when he was passed over, five years earlier, apparently because of his relatively young age.

Donovan didn't have much of a track record sniffing out stories. Not like Goldberg. Sam knew what a story was. And he wasn't afraid to put a few noses out of joint. He liked to make the analogy, according to a senior journalist Deborah respected, of a dog who peed against a lamp-post. He said that was how journalists should treat politicians. Not with respect, but with contempt.

'Look, I agree the tapes are important.' Goldberg was trying to be conciliatory. 'But they're ours and we're not giving them to the police. Who the hell would want to be interviewed by us in the future?'

Donovan looked at Deborah, long and hard. 'What else did Rachel Turner say?'

'It's all there in the transcripts, sir. She was raped by Joe O'Neill. That's why she contacted me after reading my story.'

'Where's the corroboration?'

'If I can just interrupt for a minute.' Goldberg handed over the two faxes. 'Two stringers in New York, independent of each other, faxed Larry Coen copies of medical reports which back up her story.'

Donovan speed-read the information. 'This doesn't mean shit. It could've been anyone who attacked her.'

'You think Rachel Turner made this up?' Deborah said.

'I don't know.' Donovan undid the top button of his shirt and looked at Goldberg. 'What's the latest on our investigation into Turner's death?'

'Not much. But an Australian tourist in the suite below—he was attending a computer convention—said he'd heard a struggle just after midnight. Some screams.'

'Did he report it?'

'Thought it was high jinks.'

Donovan pinched the bridge of his nose. 'Fox News just reported that police sources are talking about suicide. If she'd been drinking, that's possible.'

Goldberg said, 'No way. I don't buy that.'
'We can't rule it out.'
'I disagree, Harry,' Goldberg said. 'And not only that, we've got to decide how to run with the story for tomorrow.'
'It'll just have to be a straightforward "mystery surrounds the death of actress" line.'
'Harry, that's stating the obvious. The police have buttoned down this story good. No leaks. Nothing. We, though, have got a fresh line. We're sitting on a classic story.'
Donovan shrugged. 'What do you propose?'
'Let's do the right thing, Harry. Let's publish and be damned. We've got the tapes, we've had confirmation from the stringers and I think we should splash on Deborah's story about the rape tomorrow.'
'O'Neill's lawyers will rip us apart.' Donovan looked at Deborah and smiled bleakly. 'This story of yours on this death-row Scot is turning into a bit of a headache for us, Miss Jones.'
'I'm sure that Rachel Turner would've swapped a headache for her fate, don't you?' Deborah replied.
'Miss Jones, you're only just in the door at the *Herald*. I'd strongly advise you to be less headstrong. What would you say if I told you I wanted you to pass the tape on to the police?'
'The same as Mr Goldberg, with respect, sir.' Out of the corner of her eye, Deborah saw saw Goldberg grin like a proud father.
'That might not be such a great career move.'
Deborah smiled, but inside she seethed. 'This is not about my career, Mr Donovan. It's about principles. It's about truth.'

'Okay, Miss Jones, if that's your last word on it, so be it. Sam, seems like you've left me with no choice. Since the tapes aren't being handed over, which I think is a perfectly reasonable request under the circumstances, the rape story is on the back burner. I'm pulling rank on you. And that's my last word.'

Goldberg looked dumbstruck. 'Are you serious?'

'Deadly. The story's spiked until you come up with something more substantial.'

13

That night, in a town nestled in the foothills of the Blue Ridge Mountains—seventy miles west of Washington—a limo pulled up outside an exclusive restaurant and country retreat. Senator O'Neill stepped out and was greeted by hotel staff as if he were an old friend.

'Would you like to relax in the lounge before being seated for dinner?'

O'Neill nodded and was escorted into a two-story sitting room. A huge portrait of the French bon vivant and writer Brillat-Savarin hung over a marble fireplace. The senator sat in his usual leather chair and faced away from the window.

For the next ten minutes O'Neill sipped a champagne cocktail and munched on nuts from a silver dish.

He had had little sleep after Richmond woke him to tell him about Rachel Turner. He'd taken the call in shocked silence as Rose slept, unaware, but he could see this was way out of control. It had to end.

His diary was full. He was up at five for a six o'clock breakfast with his advisers, before flying to Washington. He listened to dire warnings from hawks in the administration giving reasons why Iraq had to be invaded following the routing of the Taliban in Afghanistan. And all the time he heard reports on CNN and Fox about the bizarre death of Rachel Turner. To cap it all, his driver got snared in heavy traffic on the Beltway.

A waiter asked, 'Sir, are you ready for dinner?'

O'Neill looked up and nodded. He was ushered to a table at the rear of the dining room.

The lighting seemed dimmer than usual, plum in color. The atmosphere was French and convivial. He saw that four other tables were occupied by out-of-towners in suits, accompanied mostly by attractive young women.

O'Neill couldn't abide infidelity. Reminded him of stories about his father leering at barmaids, or impregnating an eighteen-year-old schoolgirl, back in Brooklyn.

His mother had been a quiet Italian lady, keen that her son should concentrate on his studies. Should've left that Irish bum before she was too tired to run off. He remembered saying that, but she had just laughed. She went to church and told the priest her woes and applied a little make-up to cover the bruising from her husband's drunken beatings. The church made her feel better, at least for a few hours.

O'Neill spotted the table, tucked away in an alcove. He sat down opposite a frail old man who wore dark glasses. He looked like he'd lost a lot of weight, the cream linen suit hanging off him.

John Richmond looked ill.

Neither spoke as glasses of the restaurant's finest Chablis were poured.

When the headwaiter retreated a safe distance, O'Neill spoke. 'What're you trying to do to me? It's all over the media.'

'Know something? I don't give a damn. Anyhow, it was an accident.'

'That was no accident. Talk about attracting unwanted attention.'

'Don't tell me how to do my job. We dealt with a problem, okay?' Richmond jabbed a finger in his direction. 'You deal with the politics, we'll deal with the shit.'

Silence prevailed as a tray of nibbles was brought to their table. Richmond took a bite-sized biscuit with ham.

O'Neill ignored the food. 'The police aren't stupid,' he said. 'And they sure as hell won't buy the notion that Turner fell to her death accidentally.'

'You'd be surprised.'

'Things have got out of hand. I want nothing to do with you anymore, y'hear?'

Richmond wiped the crumbs from his cracked lips with the back of his bony hand. 'Jack, we go way back . . . You can't forget who we are or where we came from. Christ, I visited your home on the day you were born. On the day you were born. And I'll never forget your sweet mother, who I loved like a sister, saying it was the happiest day of her life. She was so proud of you.'

'What are you saying?'

'I'm saying that you and me can never, ever be separated. I love you like a son, always have. Look,

Jack, you're upset, but you'll come round and see I'm right.'

O'Neill sipped some wine. He thought back to his early days as a child in Brooklyn, remembering meeting Uncle Paulie, as he was then known. Uncle Paulie would give him candy, ruffle his hair, and take him for walks in Central Park along the Upper East Side where he had an apartment. On these walks they were always accompanied by fearsome-looking men. O'Neill was a bright kid, and kind Uncle Paulie had paid his fees at Harvard. A few years later, once he'd become established as a hotshot lawyer, his uncle pulled a few strings to get him nominated on the Democrat ticket in Florida. All he knew about the man who would one day call himself John Richmond was that he was just a neighborhood 'import-and-export guy' who wanted to help a 'local' Brooklyn boy better himself.

O'Neill didn't ask any questions when obscene amounts of money poured into his campaigns. Perhaps he was naive. Perhaps he just didn't want to know. But when, in the late 1970s, he did find out where it all came from—criminal connections and Teamster pension dollars—it was too late. *Way* too late to extricate himself from Richmond's clutches.

'You didn't have to do this.'

'Oh, but we did.'

'Why?'

'Why? Turner spoke to someone before we could get to her.'

O'Neill felt sick to the pit of his stomach. 'How do you know that?'

Richmond picked at some arugula glazed with

olive oil. 'We are persuasive people. But it's not so much a question of what she said as who she said it to.'

'Deborah Jones? Anyone else present?'

'Sam Goldberg.'

O'Neill groaned inwardly.

'Something else you need to know, Jack. The conversation was taped.'

'Can you get hold of it?'

'Maybe.'

'Christ, they could publish the interview tomorrow.'

Richmond's mouth curved into a snake-like smile. 'I don't think so.'

'Why didn't you stop her before she reached Miami?'

'I wish the fuck we had. The tip-off from Rachel's personal assistant, Becky, came too late. By the time we were on her case, she had already checked into the hotel under a false name.'

O'Neill shook his head.

'What did you want us to do? Whack her there and then in front of everyone?'

'I don't have time for this. Goddamn it, I'm in the middle of a campaign—or hadn't you noticed?'

Richmond leaned back in his seat. 'There is one bit of good news.'

'What?'

'Jones has got part of the story about Joe, but not all of it.'

'Is that supposed to make me feel better?'

Richmond smiled, exposing some small, stumpy yellow teeth. With all his money, O'Neill knew it'd be easy for him to get his teeth done, but apparently he had a phobia about dentists. 'Look,

Jack, I could get rid of her for you. You want that?'

O'Neill stayed quiet.

'Know something? She got lucky.'

O'Neill took another small sip of the wine. 'She got lucky *twice*. So the *Miami Herald* will know the story?'

'Up to a point. But not the full picture.'

'I want out.'

'You know how it works, Jack,' Richmond said. 'No one ever leaves without our consent. It don't happen that way. We're like a family.'

O'Neill closed his eyes.

'It'll blow over. There'll be a feeding frenzy for the next few days, and that'll be that, you'll see.'

The two men went quiet as their main courses arrived. O'Neill had chosen filet of rare tuna, which he duly picked at. Richmond had a salad. They finished the bottle of Chablis and Richmond ordered another.

Richmond was normally obsessive about his security, especially in public. He was convinced the Feds were after him. He often left his home, in the same gated community outside Naples where O'Neill lived, in a procession of identical limos. And they all took different routes. It was paranoid to the point of madness, but it seemed to work. Richmond had been allowed to do as he liked for decades, undisturbed. His wealth was immaterial; once you got past the first billion, who counted?

Over coffee, Richmond broke the silence. 'Jack, I know how you must be feeling, but trust me on this. There was no other way. You know we wouldn't do anything to hurt you. Christ, you're part of us. Who's supported you from the very beginning?'

'Okay, what's done is done. But I don't want any more nasty surprises.'

Richmond, as if reading his mind, said, 'You want us to keep an eye on Jones?'

O'Neill knew at that precise moment that he should've walked out and had nothing more to do with Richmond or his organization. But he didn't. All he could think of was Joe's killer, walking free. 'Discreet, you hear?' O'Neill knew then that he'd crossed an invisible line. 'Do not lay a finger on her. Keep me informed this time.'

'Understood.'

O'Neill sipped a Glayva liqueur. The honey-smooth texture of the sweet whiskey felt good. But he still felt as though he was drowning in quicksand, unable to get free, no matter how hard he kicked or screamed.

Richmond took off his sunglasses and smiled at him, eyes black. He patted the back of O'Neill's hand. 'You know, you worry too much.'

14

The days following Rachel Turner's death were like a blur for Deborah. Sixteen hours straight was the norm. The *Herald*'s investigation was now bigger than the Versace killing down on South Beach. No breaks were forthcoming for the first forty-eight hours as the team worked like crazy, but then Deborah made a breakthrough.

A hand-delivered package from an anonymous source, addressed to 'Deborah Jones: Private and Confidential', arrived in her in-tray. It contained

FBI reports on Senator Jack O'Neill and a mobster named John Richmond, also known as Paulie Fachetti. Deborah wondered if Brett was involved. It seemed strange that such information, presumably coming from top-secret FBI files, was leaked at all. If it was Brett, why didn't he say? Then again, why would he incriminate himself? It had to be him. For that, she was truly grateful, knowing he risked being thrown out of the Feds if it was uncovered.

Deborah devoured the material in a matter of hours, taking copious notes. The senator was from the same Brooklyn neighborhood as Paulie Fachetti, alias Richmond. O'Neill's family was poor, but he'd been the brightest in his class. His mother was Italian, his father Irish. He studied law at Harvard and got elected to the Senate in his early thirties. He escaped the Vietnam draft after a letter from a priest said that he did volunteer work with problem kids in Brooklyn. The draft board bought it.

Unfortunately, the files didn't contain any photographs of the men together. Even so, a picture of their relationship started to emerge.

According to the files, O'Neill, as a rising politician in Florida in the 1970s, was 'only too willing' to use his political clout to ensure that controversial projects including upscale condos, shopping malls, waterfront hotels and golf courses in sensitive locations were given the go-ahead. He cited jobs and prosperity. The unions loved the new Democratic senator. He dismissed environmentalist opposition as 'anti-progress'. In return, serious money poured into his campaigns to ensure that he was re-elected, time and time again. Pension money from labor unions found its way to the most extravagant developments across the state.

With Richmond—who changed his name from Fachetti in August 1988—bank accounts were opened on a regular basis. New companies—bars, liquor stores and restaurants—started up in low-rent areas and attracted government assistance, but as soon as one company opened, another shut down, leaving a trail of bad debts. No creditor ever complained. FBI case offic-ers also believed that Richmond was working in conjunction with the Colombians to use Miami as the staging post to flood the country with cocaine. The money made was channeled back into construction and property across Florida.

The Feds had been investigating Richmond since the early 1980s. Field officers had been assigned. Some had gone missing. Nothing was mentioned in the press for fear of sparking outrage among the American public. They tried to get him under RICO laws on four separate occasions, but nothing stuck. Richmond had the finest lawyers in America and always got off on technicalities. The Feds said in file notes that they believed some Supreme Court judges were in his pocket. It was a mess, but no one seemed able to do anything about it.

* * *

A week after Rachel Turner's death Deborah was in the office, watching live TV coverage of the actress's funeral in LA. A procession of limousines dropped off A-list movie celebrities including Tom Cruise, Julia Roberts, Robert Redford, Jane Fonda and Anthony Hopkins.

A horse-drawn funeral cortège made its measured way to Rachel Turner's final resting place amid the manicured lawns and alabaster statues of Forest Lawn Memorial Park. It overlooked the studios of Universal, Disney and Warner Brothers.

Deborah looked out over the MacArthur Causeway—linking Miami with the beaches—which was strangely quiet, sealed off for the filming of *Bad Boys 2*. The blood-red skies made the city look like the surface of Mars.

Suddenly her phone rang. It was Craig in his new death-watch cell, thirty feet from the execution chamber. He was obviously making use of his social-calls privilege with less than three weeks to go.

'You watching the TV?' he asked brusquely.

'Yeah, real sad.'

'That should be a warning to you.'

'What do you mean?'

'You're in danger. You should back off from this story.'

'Mr Craig, I appreciate your concern, but—'

'But nothing. Listen to me, Deborah, your investigation is leading only one way and that's to deep trouble.'

'I'm not backing off.'

'It's not going to stop here.' Craig's voice softened. 'Deborah, I don't want you getting hurt.'

Deborah looked up and saw Frankie Callaghan hold up his phone to indicate that a call awaited her. 'Mr Craig, I gotta go. We'll talk soon. A lot of good people are thinking about you and praying for you. We're gonna do our utmost to get this story out.'

Craig hung up.

And the call from Callaghan was transferred. A man's voice came on. It sounded Deep South gruff.

'A young lady in Key West asked me to call you,' he said.

'Look, sir,' Deborah said, not wishing to say his name on the line, 'no disrespect, but I don't know who you are. Can you give me a clue?'

'Jenny Forbes. Happy?'

'Thank you.' Deborah had checked through the newspaper's archives and had found that the lead investigator was Detective Richard Manhart.

'Listen, I've got something you may be interested in.'

Deborah picked up a pen.

'You still tryin' to piece together this story, ain't you?'

'Yeah, that's right. How do you know?'

'Still see my ex who works with you. You might know her. She's a professional ball-breaker.'

'Who?' Deborah looked over at Kathleen Klein. She too was on the phone, running a hand through her blonde highlights. 'Does she use Senator O'Neill as a regular contact, by any chance?'

He gave an eerie laugh. 'You got it.'

'Why haven't you called until now?' Deborah asked.

'You want my help or not? I ain't got time for no bullshit.'

'I'm listening.'

'You've got to promise that you won't divulge this conversation to anyone, y'hear?'

That was a given for any journalist. Deborah prized her contacts and kept their names and phone numbers in her Palm, which she kept locked in her top drawer.

'Of course.'

'Name Jimmy Brown mean anything to you?'

'No—should it?'

'Lives in a trailer park outside Naples.'

'Sorry—what relevance does this have to my story? Anyway, how do I know you are who you say you are?'

'Shut up and listen. Jimmy used to be the senator's chauffeur. If you play your cards right, he could get things moving again.'

'How?'

'Rachel Turner's not the only one with a little secret. Jimmy's got one as well.' His voice went quiet, as if he was covering the mouthpiece of his phone. 'We're talking about a cover-up. Only . . . only the Miami Beach police and the senator would rather you didn't get to hear about it.'

15

Sam Goldberg leaned forward, elbows on his desk, and took a long, hard look at Deborah. She was dog-tired—shadows under her dark eyes.

The whispers from Capitol Hill were that O'Neill was 'bombproof'. It followed an investigation by the *Washington Post* into the links between military contractors, the procurement people within the Pentagon, and the politicians with the muscle to get a slice of the action. Despite revealing kickbacks involving defense contractors and senior politicians, Senator O'Neill came out of it smelling of roses.

Requests by the *Miami Herald* to interview Governor Wilkinson at length about William Craig's case were denied. Goldberg wondered if he was wary of getting sucked into the mire, following the sudden death of Rachel Turner. He knew the governor was a clean-cut modern politician who talked enthusiastically about e-commerce and the 'Information Superhighway'. He wanted technology to revolutionize lives. But in many ways, like most politicians, he was old hat. He seemed to have perfected the art of saying everything, yet saying nothing. And, all the time, he loved soft-focus *People* magazine-style features—dreamy photos of him and his pearly family posing as a unit in the front row of church, or cooing over his latest child, or talking about the importance of God in the world, or his college-sweetheart wife showing the reader round the governor's Tallahassee mansion.

'So, tomorrow you're going to see what this is all about?' Goldberg smelled that great perfume of Deborah's again.

'I'm planning on heading across to Naples tonight, stay in a motel, and get out to the trailer park in the morning.'

'A motel. Is that such a good idea?'

'I don't follow.'

'Look, you're going to be in the backyard of the senator. I don't mean to get you alarmed, but I'd be a lot more comfortable if you stayed at the Ritz-Carlton on Vanderbilt.'

Deborah smiled. 'Isn't that going to knock a big hole in my expenses?'

Goldberg remembered being stung for three

thousand dollars after a three-night stay with his wife in a deluxe room. The bill had included breakfasts, meals and booze, but still, he had rechecked the extras to make sure they were counting correctly. 'It was a favorite of ours. Check in there and I'll be a lot happier.' He didn't say out loud that the thought of her staying in some cheap Naples motel, with dodgy locks and lax security, didn't fill him with confidence, especially after what had happened to Rachel Turner.

'Thanks for that.' Deborah knew exactly what he meant.

'I've not had a chance to speak to you in person since our conversation about what happened to you.'

Deborah gazed at the floor.

'I'd like to say that I'm very sorry.'

Tears welled in her eyes and Goldberg wondered if he should've kept his thoughts to himself.

'I had no right to say that you should have declared that to me beforehand.'

Deborah curled some hair behind her ear. 'I'd rather not speak about it.'

'Listen to me,' Goldberg continued. 'Don't beat yourself up over Rachel Turner's death. You weren't to blame.'

'I feel bad.'

'I feel bad, too. That's natural. But what we need to do is focus on where we're going with this.'

Deborah nodded.

'Be careful,' Goldberg said.

'I can look after myself.'

'And keep in touch.'

Deborah left his office and shut the door.

Goldberg had been in journalism too long to

ignore the warning signs of a reporter who was obsessed with a story. It had its advantages. He'd done the same thing, a decade earlier. One time, a black guy called Leroy McKenzie was going to be fried in 'Old Sparky' at Raiford for setting fire to a house in which his ex-girlfriend's daughter had died. Goldberg had found out that the little girl who was killed had several weeks earlier tried to set fire to a hedge outside her home in Jacksonville. But despite Sam's efforts, and despite doubts remaining about the man's guilt, he was fried anyway.

Goldberg had become so obsessed with the case that it was all he talked about. He bored friends in bars, his wife and his sister in Wyoming whom he'd phone nightly. They were all sympathetic, but they thought he should let it go.

Goldberg knew they were right, and gradually he moved on. In a way he'd compartmentalized the state execution. If not, he'd still have Leroy McKenzie's crazy red eyes staring back at him through the glass, burned into his psyche.

And that was what was worrying him about Deborah Jones's fixation with William Craig. She was getting deeper into a story as dark and inhospitable as the Florida swamps.

He turned to look at the picture of his wife and closed his eyes. He couldn't be bothered with the hassle anymore. The long days and the longer nights. All he wanted to do was go home and fall asleep in his quiet house, not having to worry about the responsibilities that went with his six-figure salary. The bullshit from Harry Donovan. The grind of getting enough good stories to fill the paper each night.

All he wanted to do was turn the lights off, listen to his wife's treasured Beatles albums until dawn, and get lost in whiskey and sweet memories.

But Goldberg knew that he'd be back tomorrow, sitting behind his desk, talking about stories that mattered, holding the elected representatives of the people to account, hoping beyond hope that some of the readers cared enough as well.

16

The following morning, Deborah pulled up at Pitch 582 at the Sunshine Hitching Post, outside Naples, after an overnight stay at the Ritz-Carlton on Vanderbilt.

Jimmy Brown's rust-encrusted trailer was the one located furthest from the entrance. Deborah knocked twice and waited for a reply. Loud country music filled the glue-like air. A few snowbirds lounged in plastic chairs outside their homes. Dogs barked several lots away and a couple shouted at each other about who should take out the trash. She smelled old garbage and disinfectant from a nearby bathhouse.

Deborah knocked again and wondered if Jimmy Brown was out working.

Still no answer.

She knocked three more times. She was starting to get cold feet. What had she got herself into? She didn't know this man Jimmy Brown, if indeed he even existed. It was insane to travel across to Naples at the behest of a detective who used to be in charge of the Craig investigation. She was taking it on trust that it really *was* Manhart. For all she knew the whole thing could be a set-up.

Maybe she should phone Brett. He would know what to do. Probably tell her to haul her ass out of there. But she didn't have time to make a call.

The handle turned, and the door opened.

Standing before her was a tall black man with sad eyes. He looked to be around her father's age. Spots of white shaving cream were still on his face. His huge torso was bare and his belly hung over his scruffy jeans. He held a towel in his right hand.

'I'm looking for a Mr Jimmy Brown.'

His unfathomable eyes—like oily water—scrutinized her face. 'Who wants to know?'

Deborah smiled. 'I do, sir.' He kept on staring as if he was not used to visitors. 'Name's Deborah Jones.' She flashed her credentials.

The man wiped away the last of the foam with his towel. 'I don't speak to no press, sister. Nuthin' personal, y'understand?'

'Just a few questions for you.'

'I don't need no hassle. I just do what I do.' But he hadn't slammed the door in her face.

'You used to work for Senator O'Neill.'

'Ain't got nuthin' to say about him.'

'Sir, we're carrying out an investigation into the senator. A man is due to die for killing the senator's son. You might've heard about him.'

'The old white guy, yeah?'

'That's the one.'

'Read in the paper that he'd fought in the war. Some kinda hero. You wrote that story?'

Deborah nodded. 'I've got a couple of questions I'd like to run past you.' She shrugged and smiled. 'Maybe you can help, maybe not.'

The old man looked at her long and hard. 'I'd like to help, but I gotta think about my family.'

'Sorry—what do you mean?'

'Look, it all happened a long time ago. Trying to get on with my life—I'm sorry.' He began to close the door.

'Mr Brown, I appreciate your reluctance to speak, but you could be of real help to our investigation.'

'You mind getting off my property? Anyhow, what the hell do I care about your goddamn investigation? Go on, get.'

'I need your help, Mr Brown. It's really important. A man's life is at stake.'

Brown was silent.

'Can't you at least think about it?'

'And what's old Jimmy gonna get, apart from some bad memories?'

'I promise I'll report anything you say with utmost discretion, if you're reluctant to go on the record. Mr Brown, we think Senator O'Neill's covering up his son's crimes.'

'How do I know you won't twist my words?'

'I'll record what we say.'

Brown glanced left and right at the adjacent trailers, like he was worried his neighbors might overhear him. 'Guess you better come in.'

Deborah squeezed past Brown's huge frame into the trailer. It smelled of furniture polish and fresh coffee. The air-conditioning unit growled low in the background.

Beside the window was a white Formica table surrounded by black leather seating. At the front left was a shower room, shielded by a dandelion-patterned plastic curtain. At the front right, a bunk with neatly folded blankets at the end, and a pile of ironed clothes. Between the front and back was a storage area. A dark blue uniform hung from a door, the word 'security' in yellow lettering on a lapel. Below it was a pair of newly shined black leather shoes.

Although the space was tight, everything was clean and tidy. Deborah could see this man took pride in where he lived. This was a man who liked order.

'Take the weight off,' Brown said. 'I'll put a shirt on.'

She sat down. 'Hope I'm not disturbing you.'

'Naw, I work nights. I'm off for the next three days. Gonna do some fishing.'

Brown pulled across a striped partition curtain near the front of the trailer. 'Just make yourself comfortable, miss,' he said from behind the screen.

Deborah didn't want to admit it, but being in a strange man's trailer made her feel nervous. The air conditioning continued to splutter in the background. No dishes had been left on the metal draining unit beside the sink and no old clothes nor any rubbish had been dumped on the floor. Back issues of *Time* magazine were stacked in a tidy pile on a small coffee table outside the bathroom.

Arranged proudly on the windowsill were silver-framed photos of young black people around her age. They looked like his children, maybe even his grandchildren. Beside the picture was a color photo of a younger Brown, laughing with some army buddies in a jungle clearing.

Vietnam vet.

Brown came back in wearing an aqua Dolphins

T-shirt and fresh jeans. He sat down opposite the table from her. 'You wanna soda, water, coffee, something to drink?'

'Large glass of water would be fine, thank you.'

He fixed them two large glasses of mineral water with ice.

'I should like you to tell me about Senator O'Neill, your former employer.'

Brown leaned back on the cushioning. His face was leathery as if toughened by years of salty winds and Gulf Coast heat. 'I don't know . . . it all happened a long, long time ago.'

Deborah switched on her tape recorder and thought of Rachel Turner.

Was she signing Jimmy Brown's death warrant?

'Okay, I'll start with a few basics. Tell me, Mr Brown, when did you start working for Senator O'Neill?'

'Fall 1972. I was his chauffeur. Paid real well.'

'So you drove him to functions?'

Brown glanced at the recorder as if suspicious of new technology. 'Yeah, y'know, Democrat conventions, meetings with advisers, party donors, fundraising people, even the president.'

'Describe your relationship with him in the early days.'

'He was a nice guy.' He sipped some water. 'Asked after my family. Felt kinda privileged to work for the senator after leaving the army. Y'know, the status. I come from nuthin'. And my family was real proud of me, y'know what I'm saying?'

'Sure. When did you leave his service?'

Brown scratched his short gray hair. 'Let's see now, I guess it must've been 1990. March 1990.'

'That's a precise recall.'

Brown paused for a few moments. 'It was the day I was fired.'

Deborah felt the butterflies in her stomach.

'Said I was drunk on duty.'

'Were you?'

'Like hell. I ain't drank or smoked since Nam. Don't believe in it. Seen what it can do to a man.'

'So he got rid of you as his chauffeur for something you didn't do?'

'Correct.'

'That doesn't make any sense.'

'It was bullshit.'

'Why would he make up this accusation if it wasn't true? Surely he must've had a good reason.'

Brown took a deep breath and let out an elongated sigh. 'I overheard Joe O'Neill speaking to his father in the back of the limo one night. He broke down crying. He admitted to his father that he was in trouble again. He said police had accused him of raping a girl in a park in South Beach.'

'You overheard this?'

'Guess they forgot to switch off the intercom.'

Deborah sat transfixed.

'Joe said he was sorry for causing all this trouble.'

'And you heard all this?'

'The senator said he'd deal with it. Swear to God, that's what he said. Told Joe to forget about it. Said he had friends who'd help him. I couldn't believe what I was hearing.'

Deborah felt as though time had stopped. Her heart was beating hard and she took a drink of water. 'Sorry, Mr Brown, can you repeat that so there's no misunderstanding?'

Brown stared at the mini-recorder. 'The senator said he'd deal with it. Said he had friends, told his son not to worry about it. Said it was all in hand, or something.'

'You absolutely positive?'

Brown shot her a mean look. 'Course I'm sure.'

'Why didn't you go to the police with this information?'

'I did. Gave a statement to the Miami Beach police, because that's where it happened.' He disappeared behind the curtain and reappeared a few moments later with four pink pieces of paper, Miami Beach PD notepaper. He handed it to Deborah. 'This is the copy of my statement. Take a look for yourself. It's dated, 'n' all.'

Deborah's eyes scanned the pieces of paper. The writing on them described the confession that Brown had heard in the back of the car. She looked at the date at the bottom, beside Brown's scrawled signature. 'Six months before Joe's trial, May fifteenth, eighty-nine.'

'That's right. Told them everything like I just told you.' Brown pointed at the paper. 'There. It's all down in black and white.'

Deborah couldn't believe her eyes. The statement clearly referred to the 'rape of Jenny Forbes'. 'So why weren't you called to give evidence in court?'

'Who knows? Assumed the police would pass on the information to the DA. Never heard nothing again.'

'What do you think happened?'

Brown shrugged. 'What do you think?'

'And you were sacked after the trial?'

Brown cleared his throat. 'Fired in March 1990,

about four months after Joe was acquitted. Don't know if they found out about my statement, but there ain't no other explanation I can find.'

'What did you do then?'

'Couldn't get another job as a chauffeur, that's for sure. No reference. Ruined my life, the son of a bitch. Wife left me, took the kids. Said I couldn't provide for them. Had to sell my nice house in Riviera Beach. Didn't work for a coupla years.'

'And then?'

'Got a bullshit security job working nights.' He finished his iced water. 'So, now you know, sister. The senator ain't no regular guy.'

'Why haven't you come forward since then?'

'What's the point? No one's listening to black folks like me. You educated, sister, so you can try, but remember this here is Florida. O'Neill's not the kind of guy you wanna mess with.'

'Are you under protection from the police, or the Feds?'

'Never been offered any protection. Guess that tells you all you have to know. I reckon that, because my statement was buried somewhere, the senator and the people who protect *him* are happy. They've probably forgotten all about old Jimmy.'

Deborah's mind was racing. 'If I get this in the paper, the senator will know that you've spoken to me. You could be in danger.'

'Don't matter to me. In a week, I'm heading out west to stay with my brother in California. I'll take my chances. Had my fill of Florida.' Jimmy Brown dropped his gaze and shook his head. 'Had my fill.'

*　　*　　*

Deborah got back to her hotel room and wrote up the story in a couple of hours. She e-mailed it to Sam Goldberg and wondered how he'd respond. She didn't have to wait long. Fifteen minutes later, he called back.

'He could've nailed the senator's son with his confession,' he said.

'You think we can run with this?'

'Oh yeah, tomorrow for *this* baby. Donovan can't ignore this. You got a copy of Brown's police statement?'

'Right in front of me.'

'Scan it and send it. Assuming we can stand this story up, our line is simple. "The Intercom Confession", we'll call it. Was information withheld in the trial of Joe O'Neill? We might not be able to get out the Rachel Turner story just now, but this is going to make a real stir. Wonder what the DA's office will say?'

Deborah felt mixed emotions.

'I think this'll give credence to our calls for Craig to be moved off "the row",' Goldberg added.

Deborah walked onto her balcony and gazed out at the turquoise waters of the Gulf. A young man beside the pool laughed and he suddenly reminded her of Brett.

'Just be careful. Oh, and stay another night on us. I think you've earned it.' That was strange. *First, he tells me to check into the Ritz, puts me up at the paper's expense. And now he's letting me stay another night. Is there something he's not telling me?*

'I appreciate that.'

Goldberg hung up and Deborah put down her phone. Almost immediately, she was annoyed at herself for doubting Sam Goldberg's loyalty.

She looked back down beside the pool. The young man with the laugh like Brett's was arm in arm with a beautiful blonde girl. They walked out to the beach and she wondered if she would ever find a man she could love. If she did, would he disown her when he found out what had happened to her? Would he leave, like Brett? Her feelings for Brett were still unresolved. She made a mental note to schedule an appointment with her therapist.

Deborah watched the couple as they paddled in the water and laughed like they'd be together forever. Why couldn't she have that in her life?

Her cell phone rang. A man's voice spoke.

'Deborah Jones?' he asked.

'Speaking. Who's this?'

'John Richmond's waiting for you downstairs in the private dining room. He's looking forward to meeting you.'

17

The mahogany-paneled dining room seemed like an elegant gentlemen's club from a bygone era. Chandeliers, white tablecloths and fine silver laid out as if awaiting diners at an anniversary dinner. An old man wearing sunglasses was eating alone at the far end of the room.

That had to be him.

He sat beside floor-to-ceiling French windows that were framed by silk draperies. At the next table a group of four burly men sat in silence, their stares crawling all over Deborah like insects.

The old man was picking at a salad. His hair was gray and wispy, his complexion weathered, Mediterranean. His cheeks were pinched, though, as if he was ill. He wore a white shirt, chinos and white sneakers. He didn't look up as she walked over to his table.

'How ya doin', Miss Jones?' he asked, in a streetwise New York accent.

Deborah stared down, hands on hips, her legs feeling like jelly. 'What do you want?'

Richmond cocked his head in the direction of his men. 'Check if she's wired.'

Before Deborah knew what had happened, a pair of huge hands frisked the inside of her legs, the lapels of her jacket and her waist. 'Get the hell off me!' She pulled away, shuddering. The man just grinned back at her, dead-eyed.

'Gotta check,' Richmond said. 'Can never be too careful. Take a load off, kid.'

'Is that how you greet everyone you meet?'

Richmond shrugged his bony shoulders and adjusted his dark-brown-tinted sunglasses.

Against her better judgment, Deborah sat down, arms folded on the starched tablecloth. The expensive aftershave that wafted off Richmond made her feel vaguely queasy.

'Believe you been snoopin' around,' he said, chewing slowly.

'Excuse me?'

'You heard.' Richmond put down his knife and fork, and then took off his shades. His rheumy eyes looked stagnant. 'The senator,' he said. 'You been asking a lot of questions. It's annoyed him.'

'I'm a journalist. It's my job to ask awkward questions.' Deborah's shaky voice betrayed her bravado.

'If you annoy him, honey, you annoy me—y'understand?'

Deborah wondered if he knew about her trip to see Jimmy Brown.

He pointed a bony finger at her. 'We know more about you than you'll ever know.'

'You threatening me? Want me to contact the police?'

Richmond smiled as the men at the next table snickered. He opened the palm of his right hand as if to say, 'What can we do with this girl?' Lowering his voice to a steely whisper, he said, 'We're far more powerful than the Naples police, believe me. You go to them with accusations that an old man—enjoying his retirement years in Florida—is threatening a pretty little black girl while he enjoys a meal at the Ritz. Who's gonna believe that? And I've got witnesses. Go back to Miami and forget about the senator. Never bother him again, y'understand? And forget your heroics on Craig. He's dead meat. Whatever you do or dredge up's gonna make no fucking difference. Trust me.'

Deborah stood up to leave. Richmond grabbed her by the wrist.

'Don't fuck with us. We know everything about you. We know that you were raped, and who raped you. You wanna know how much Steven Cartwright earns as a broker in Dallas?'

Deborah felt her insides go cold. Her mind flashed a picture of his longish hair, leering smile and horn-rimmed glasses.

'Then there's Ben Hamilton. Turns out he didn't like Texas too much. Last year he headed back to his family mansion in Beverly Hills. But according to my sources he's just landed a job as a pediatrician in Miami. Isn't that cozy? You wanna know where he lives? I can tell you if you want. If you left it with me, I could arrange for him to take you out for the night. I'm told by those who know about these things that he still has a voracious sexual appetite.'

Richmond smiled at her and she wanted to die.

Deborah pulled her wrist away. 'In case you didn't know, Mr Richmond, this is America. Some of us still believe in free speech. And no hoodlum friend of Senator O'Neill is going to dissuade my paper from unearthing the whole damn story.'

She turned on her heel and walked out, chin up. Just like Momma told her.

As Deborah passed him, one of Richmond's men sniffed her. Like a dog.

18

Back in her room, Deborah locked the door. Her heart was racing and her mind was in meltdown. She called Faith. She knew that her friend would be putting the kids from a local middle-school soccer team through their paces. When Faith answered, Deborah heard the excited shouts from children in the background.

'Can we speak for a second, Faith?' Her voice cracked with emotion as she paced the room.

'Of course, honey. What's going on?'

'I'm scared. I'm really scared, Faith. I don't know what I'm—'

'Hey, slow down, honey. Now, what's the

problem?'

'You're not going to believe this, but I've just been threatened by the Mob. I know it sounds nuts. But I'm in Naples, in my hotel room, and I'm terrified to leave in case something happens to me.'

'Hold on one second, honey.' Deborah heard Faith shout at one of the parents to take charge for five minutes. A few moments later, she was back on the phone. 'Okay—first of all, who threatened you?'

'It doesn't matter, but he's bad. And I'm scared.'

'Shit.'

'I feel like I'm losing my mind. I'm wondering if my boss, Sam Goldberg, could have set this up. It was his idea for me to stay at the Ritz, after all.'

'Now that's just plain silly.'

'I don't know who I can trust. It's like how I felt back in San Francisco after the—'

'Okay, honey, this is what you do. You pack your bags and get back to Miami, right now. And you tell your boss everything, okay?'

Deborah sobbed. 'I don't know if I can do this. He said that one of the boys that raped me is living in Miami.'

'If you're being threatened, maybe it's a good idea to back off.'

'I can't. I wanted this story.'

'Then you've got to find the strength to go on. You can do it. There's nothing you can't achieve, girl, you hear me? You're going to do it.'

'I'm not tough like you.'

'Think of your daddy, Deborah.'

'What's he got to do with this?'

'Remember you told me about him in Mississippi

during the civil-rights marches?'

'So?'

'He didn't back down, did he?'

'No.'

'They spat on him, but he kept on marching. Marching for the right to vote . . . Marching for the right to exist as an equal. To exist as a human being.'

Deborah felt ashamed of the fear she felt. 'I'm not him.'

'I'm not saying you are. But if you want to do this, seems like you've got to come out of your shell and show them what you're made of.'

'I'm not as brave as my daddy. I'm not brave at all.'

'You're tougher than you think.'

Suddenly Deborah felt less afraid. 'Okay. Thank you, Faith. You're a real friend. I'll call you when I get back home.'

*   *   *

Deborah checked out of the deluxe hotel immediately, and was soon heading back along Alligator Alley as an orange sun blazed above the Everglades.

How did Richmond know where she was staying? Was he still in there? Was he watching her now? It was like something out of a creepy late-night horror film . . . finding him sitting downstairs like he owned the place.

Deborah bit her lower lip and wondered if anyone had followed her. She glanced in her rearview mirror, but there was no sign of a red Chevy.

She switched on the car radio and the swaggering hip-hop of Mary J. Blige pounded out into the sultry air. And she felt better.

Ahead of her, Deborah saw a young girl lean out of her father's pick-up and wave a small stars-and-stripes flag. The reminders of 9/11 were never far away. Americans felt patriotic like never before, stoked up by the government and people like Senator O'Neill who demanded astronomical levels of military spending to defend the homeland. Whether it would stop another attack was a moot point.

She put her foot on the accelerator.

Deborah's cell phone rang. She turned down the pounding music and picked up the phone from the passenger seat, keeping one hand on the wheel.

Classical music played in the background and a man was laughing. Then he said, 'Slow down, bitch! We can't keep up. You hearin' me, nigger bitch?'

19

Two hours later, Deborah's car screeched into the underground garage below her Miami Beach condo. Her mind was still racing and her heart seemed to alternate its beats.

She cut the engine and wondered if someone really had followed her.

Could they be watching her now?

Deborah scanned the other vehicles dotted around the shadows of the concrete catacomb. Shiny BMWs, Jaguars, Escalades and Hummers in neat rows.

She sat still, locked in her car, watching and waiting. Where were the valet-parking guys when you needed them? Probably stuck in their booth at the Collins entrance. The strange thing was that the place was usually bustling with them, keen to pick up healthy tips from her well-heeled neighbors.

She hated these places. It reminded her of a bizarre and scary moment when a young addict—the only son of a woman who attended her father's church—mugged her father while he walked back to his car. She reckoned her fear of underground parking zones could all be traced back to that incident.

Deborah gripped the wheel, trying to pull herself together.

Don't let your imagination run wild. But her deepest fear was nearing the surface. A fear she'd only told her therapist. The fear that the two boys who raped her might one day track her down.

Deborah closed her eyes and tried to let her muscles relax, something she practiced in cognitive therapy classes. It took a few minutes but, as if by magic, the waves of anxiety seemed to subside.

But she remained in her car for the next ten minutes. Looking for any suspicious movements in the deep shadows. But there was nothing. Just concrete, chrome and steel.

'This is stupid, Deborah,' she said aloud and opened the door, wincing at the noise of the mechanical locking system.

The glass doors that led to the elevator were around fifty feet away. She started walking, the noise of her shoes echoing around the concrete walls.

Her gaze darted from side to side.

She glanced up. Closed-circuit television cameras strafed the area.

Thank goodness, at least the cameras would track her movements.

Deborah quickened her step. It seemed to take forever just to walk that short distance, but she made it and pushed open the doors. The elevator door was open.

Excellent. She wanted to get back to the safety of her apartment.

She punched in number 33. Nothing. She tried again. Still nothing. She stood and waited for the doors to close. *These things happen, just relax*. She stared at the button as if it had a mind of its own for what seemed an eternity. She punched it again. The doors remained open.

Goddamnit.

Deborah glanced up at an elevator camera. It'd never happened before.

Just then, voices . . . Voices that sounded like they came from the garage. Men's voices. The men were arguing. Her stomach knotted as the footsteps got closer. Voices louder.

Goddamn this elevator.

She punched the button again and closed her eyes. *Please don't let this happen*, she thought. *Please just shut*.

'Come on!' Deborah jabbed the button repeatedly. It seemed to have frozen. She looked up again at the camera and showed her palms.

She imagined a bored round-the-clock security guy sat at his monitor in the bowels of the huge tower, watching reruns of a ball game, eating doughnuts. And never checking his monitor.

Two men walked towards the doors. Both were white and wore good suits and sunglasses, black shoes polished to a deep shine. They weren't talking anymore.

'Goddamn it, close.' She punched in the number 33 with the knuckle of her index finger. The door shut.

Deborah felt like sinking to her knees as the elevator climbed quickly. She arrived at her floor and stepped out, rummaging through her bag for her front-door key. Her hands were shaking.

She gripped the key tight and slid it into the lock. The sound of the deadbolts unlocking first time was reassuring. She opened her door, secured it behind her in the blink of an eye and listened for the special locks to click back into place.

Safe at last.

Deborah was okay, high up above Collins. Immediately, she felt the apartment's air conditioning brush her hair and chill her hot skin. She didn't need a therapist to tell her that her home had become her sanctuary since she'd moved to Miami. She'd read too many stories about women being raped in their own homes to take security lightly. She figured it was better to be safe than sorry.

She turned on some Louis Armstrong. 'Basin Street Blues' blasted out in all its jazzy glory. She felt better.

Good old Satchmo. Her musical tastes were, by and large, more country-oriented. Willie Nelson a particular favorite, and Gram Parsons . . . But she did like her father's tastes as well. Traditional jazz, Paul Robeson, gospel. The occasional R&B, like

Mary J., was the exception.

She switched on her lamps and they cast a reassuring soft jade light around the room. Then she went into her bedroom to check her e-mail.

Nothing. Good. She needed some time to breathe.

Deborah shut the blinds and took off her clothes. Her muscles ached. An early night sounded like a good idea. She thought of calling Sam or Faith, just to let them know that she was back in Miami, safe and well, but she was too tired. She'd call them in the morning.

Then she remembered that her story about Jimmy Brown was going in the following day's paper.

Like all journalists, she couldn't wait to see the story in black and white, with her byline beside it.

She'd have to thank Manhart for that. With a bit of luck, he might have some more information relevant to the case. Anything that kept the story in the public eye, and concentrated people's minds on the imminent execution of William Craig, had to be worthwhile.

Richmond could threaten her all he wanted, but she wasn't going to back down.

Deborah caught her reflection in the full-length mirror beside her wardrobe. She turned sideways and glanced at her profile. Despite her figure, what she saw depressed her.

When would she be able to face having a boyfriend? Brett hadn't wanted her when he'd found out. Would anyone else? Probably not when they saw her body.

She twisted sideways so she could see the half-inch-wide vertical scars that ran the length of her back . . .

They'd never go away. Clawed into her skin by the sadistic rapist's nails as he took her from behind. Branded for life. What man could possibly find her attractive?

Her gaze dropped to her small brown belly. She patted her stomach and shook her head. Soccer wasn't enough—she needed to start doing sit-ups. Her slight physique had come under sustained attack from the combination of rich five-star hotel cooking and fast food eaten on the run as she drove up and down Florida.

In the huge bathroom, the music still played, part of the hi-fi electrics hooked up by the developer when the tower was built. Deborah ran her tub and splashed in eucalyptus bubble bath. She stayed with the trumpet playing of old Satchmo and let the music sweep over her.

The bathroom was steaming up. Just the way she liked it.

The music reminded her of a trip to New Orleans with Brett. Late-night drinks on Bourbon Street as they soaked up the vibes. It also reminded her of New Year's Eve in front of a roaring fire as Daddy entertained family and friends, the music and warm aura of love all around. Happier days.

Deborah tied back her hair and checked the temperature. She didn't know one woman on the planet who didn't enjoy soaking in a huge bath.

The sheer pleasure.

The bubbles were up to her chin and the warmth eased her tight lower-back muscles. It seemed an age since she'd had a spare evening without work or commitments. She knew that her fellow journalists thought she was a naive workaholic, but she couldn't change. As it stood, her work ethic was one of the few things she still had.

Deborah wondered if her attitude was anything to do with her schooling at the exclusive Woodland Hills Baptist Academy. Even then she had striven to be top of the class, thanks in part to her father.

'We've got to work harder, think quicker, and aim higher so white people don't do us down,' he would say. She learned all about the Selma civil-rights march with Dr King at the head of the rally. Her mother showed her terrible pictures of her father. Blood ran down his face—he'd been beaten by the billy clubs of the white police force for daring to challenge the Jim Crow laws. 'Don't you ever forget, child, y'hear?' How could she? Segregation, she was told, was the work of the devil, but her father stressed that white people were not the enemy. 'They are our brothers and sisters. Together we shall overcome.'

Sorry if I hurt you, Daddy. Please forgive me, Momma. Even after two years, the rape still made Deborah feel like the guilty party. The soiled girl. The soiled virgin.

Was it possible that her father's health suffered as a direct consequence of her rape? She remembered the shock of seeing him in his hospital bed with his twisted mouth. Her mother told her one night that he couldn't cope thinking that his beloved daughter had been drugged and raped. Two days after he was told, she said, he had the stroke. Maybe it was just coincidence, but Deborah didn't think so. Maybe that was one of the reasons she'd been so keen to settle out of court.

Waves of tiredness swept over her and she drifted away. All of a sudden, Deborah heard the 'You've got mail' voice from her computer.

Just leave it. It would still be there in the morning.

She waited for a couple of minutes and tried to empty her mind of the investigation. It didn't work.

Was it Sam Goldberg? *Could be urgent.*

Groaning at her own diligence, she stepped out of the bath. She realized she was her own worst enemy. She wrapped herself in a white terry robe and padded across the hardwood floors of her bedroom in her bare feet, leaving a trail of foam in her wake.

Deborah leaned over and scanned her in-box. The new e-mail message was from 'National desk'.

Strange.

Deborah never, as a rule, opened e-mails without knowing exactly where they came from. She assumed it was something Frankie Callaghan wanted to talk to her about. The subject was entitled 'Photo you might find interesting, Deborah.'

She maneuvered the mouse and clicked to 'open'. Her gaze locked on to the image and her brain struggled to process the signals.

It didn't seem possible.

She shook and started hyperventilating. *Relax, Deborah. Relax just like the therapists told you.*

Stumbling backwards, she knocked over her computer seat. She sat down hard on the floor and stared transfixed at the image on the screen. A photo of her naked and patting her stomach—taken only minutes before.

*   *   *

Deborah stood on her balcony, arms folded. Her cozy bathrobe had been abandoned for the emotional armor of jeans, sneakers and an oversized T-shirt. She gazed out into the darkness of the Atlantic. She'd been violated.

Through the half-open French doors lay her living room, a hive of activity, with the incessant buzz of uniformed Miami Beach police and cold-eyed detectives who talked loudly into their cell phones.

It was a relief to see Sam Goldberg push his way through the throng. She immediately felt guilty for thinking negative thoughts about him, back in Naples.

'I came as quick as I could.' He stepped onto the balcony, his tie askew. 'What the hell happened?'

'Someone got hold of my private e-mail address.'

One of the detectives shouted out, 'Found them!'

Deborah and Goldberg went back into her living room, where the younger of the two detectives waved some wires which hung from three square-shaped black plastic devices, each less than an inch long. He handed them to the man leading the investigation, Lieutenant Jonny Hernandez. The Latino cop turned to Deborah, his eyes fierce and brown. 'You know why someone would wanna bug and film the inside of your home?' It was like something out of Watergate.

Deborah felt her legs nearly give way. She glanced briefly at Goldberg. Anxiety clouded his eyes.

'This is a video transmitter and receiver, Miss Jones,' Hernandez said. 'It's an XLT-900.

Professional. Battery-operated, range up to one thousand feet, built-in antenna and real good resolution. Private investigators like these babies. Some people use them to watch their cruisers, y'know, outside their house.'

'Someone has broken into my house? And bugged me? Where did they put them?'

'Inside three specially designed smoke detectors.'

People were spying on her as she was naked? It was sick.

Deborah closed her eyes. 'This is too much. I feel so stupid for not noticing anything.'

'You weren't supposed to. Someone's beamed back a real-time picture to their computer, then they've e-mailed it back to you. These guys are pros, believe me.'

20

Next morning Sam Goldberg sat at a sidewalk table outside the News Café on Ocean Drive as the sun blazed down. He was nursing the hangover from hell. His pounding headache was compounded by thoughts of the latest development in Deborah's investigation. He'd called her first thing, asking her along for an informal chat about the sequence of events. What he hadn't told her was that late the previous night he'd spoken to Donovan and they'd agreed that she'd be pulled off the story for her own good.

She'd hate him for that. But it had to be done.

Goldberg brushed some croissant crumbs off his chinos and dark blue Ralph Lauren shirt. On the table in front of him was an untouched espresso to help wake him up when his stomach got over the croissants, a large glass of water with ice and a slice of lemon, and a copy of that day's *Herald.* The front page was dedicated to Deborah's story on the statement given to Miami Beach police by Jimmy Brown, alleging that he had heard Joe O'Neill telling his father that he had raped a girl. Even Donovan was blown away by the story.

Goldberg's head felt like someone was drilling inside it and his throat was like sandpaper. Why did he drink so much? Why couldn't he be like his father? Goldberg senior was a man who enjoyed one malt whisky and a bottle of Schlitz on a Saturday night, content to sit at home with Sam's mother and watch sitcoms.

Goldberg picked up the water and noticed how his hand shook. He needed to cut down. His doctor had warned him often enough. He took two large gulps of water which momentarily quenched his thirst. Shit, this was ridiculous. It wasn't that long ago, shortly after his wife died, when he'd had to go to the doctor's after starting to piss blood. Afterwards he altered his lifestyle briefly. But now the pull of the liquor was as great as ever.

He gazed across Ocean Drive, towards the beach. A few people were already enjoying the sun. A young couple were playing volleyball, watched over by a lifeguard lounging in the sand. Driving past only a few yards from him, a flashy car with a bass-heavy sound system pumped out Snoop, disturbing his thoughts on this Saturday morning.

What he wouldn't give to disappear for a few months. Maybe that was what he needed most. A long vacation to recharge his batteries. He was running on empty, using alcohol to smooth over the cracks.

Goldberg glanced up and saw Deborah approaching. She looked stunning with her athletic figure, yet her face was drawn. She wore a deep gray Nike tracksuit, battered old sneakers and a white headband. As she got closer, he smelled her scent, which reminded him of flowers in a summer meadow. He stood up and shook her soft hand. 'Sorry to bug you out of hours.' It was a lame joke.

She sat down and slung a huge sports bag onto an adjacent chair.

'Can I get you anything?' Goldberg said. 'Coffee, tea, beer?'

'A freshly squeezed orange juice would be good.' She smiled.

Goldberg caught the eye of a waiter and ordered the juice and another espresso for himself, despite not having started the first one. He looked at Deborah. 'How you feeling?'

'Freaked out.'

'That's to be expected. Get any sleep?'

'Not really. I kept thinking there were still bugs in my apartment. I looked in all the lampshades. I just gave up trying to sleep about four.'

Goldberg groaned. 'That's about when I got to bed.'

'Ah, hah. Anything special?'

'No. Just some drinks with old buddies from the paper. You wouldn't know them—retired a couple of years ago.'

'Old-timers?'

'Hey, less of that.' Goldberg felt a wave of exhaustion sweep over him as he remembered what he had to say. 'Look, we need to sort things out. I've got a responsibility for my journalists. And I've got a proposition for you.'

Deborah shrugged her shoulders.

'Now, don't take this the wrong way . . . Deborah, I'd like to take you off this project until things cool down.' She opened her mouth to speak but Goldberg held up a hand to silence her. 'Now, I know this isn't what you want to hear. But I've been talking to our lawyers and Harry Donovan, and they think the warning from Richmond, or whatever his name is, in addition to the bugging, is a very worrying development.'

'Sam, this isn't the time to back off. We're on to something.' Deborah lifted up the front page of that day's *Herald* so he could see her story. 'Jimmy Brown's risking his life to try and help William Craig. *Risking his life.* Are you seriously saying we should just let Craig die?'

Goldberg took off his sunglasses and placed them on the table. 'Listen to me—'

But Deborah didn't let him finish. 'Sam, I'm on this assignment, and I want to see it through. Either that or you give it to someone else. And that person will no doubt be threatened as well. I'm prepared to put my neck on the line over this.'

Goldberg was not in the mood for an argument. His gaze was drawn to a limbless veteran, maybe in his late fifties, begging in Lummus Park, which separated the white sand from the traffic of Ocean Drive. He'd seen the guy several times before sleeping off the effects of cheap wine under a bench.

Poor bastard.

'You're making this very difficult for me,' Goldberg said.

Deborah leaned forward, inadvertently brushing his arm. He felt his stomach knot. It felt good just to be touched by her. 'Trust me, I can do this.'

'I haven't got time for personal crusades,' Goldberg said. 'I'm a newspaper editor. We have to think story. Besides, we're in very dangerous territory.'

'Don't get cold feet on me, please. Look, how about reviewing the situation if things change—what do you think? Gimme a break, Sam.'

'You think Senator O'Neill is pulling the strings?'

'I know it. You said it yourself. He's the key.'

Goldberg sipped some more water.

'Let me continue working on this,' Deborah said, 'reporting directly to you.'

Goldberg shrugged. 'I must be nuts, but okay, I give in.' He'd clear it with Donovan that afternoon. Sure, Donovan would hit the roof, but Goldberg would take the flak and leave his journalist, no longer so green, to get on with her investigation.

Goldberg looked at Deborah's elegant, manicured hands, and he wanted to hold them. Hold them just to say he cared for her. Nothing more, nothing less. 'But I'll be keeping the situation under review on a daily basis. Is that understood?'

She leaned forward and pecked him on the cheek. His heart started pumping faster.

'What was that for?'

'For having faith in me.'

Maybe Harry was right. Maybe he wasn't thinking straight. But Goldberg was too exhausted to dig his heels in. If Deborah wanted this story so badly, so be it.

21

After a great game with the Overtown Women's Soccer Team, Deborah was enjoying a barbecue with Faith and the others in the shade of some huge oaks in a corner of Palmer Park.

Deborah had scored a hat trick, which put the team in the top three of their league. Beer, wine, and cheap champagne were flowing. Salsa music blared. The smell of burnt hot dogs, hamburgers and chicken wings filled the steamy air.

Faith sidled up to Deborah and nudged her in the side. 'What you on, girl? Last time you played like that was when you first joined.'

'Guess I owed you all a good game.'

'A good game, honey? You gave us more than that. You got everyone talking about us. Now they'll know the Overtown girls are no lazy street sluts . . . We're here because we love playing soccer.'

'Amen to that.'

Deborah looked around at the rest of the girls. Some danced, beer in hand, some fooled around, some lay back on the grass and chilled out.

The cell phone in Deborah's bag rang. Faith shook her head. 'Just ignore it, honey. It's Saturday.'

Deborah wished she could, but that wasn't the way she worked.

It was Frank from the newsroom. 'Hi, Deborah, got something for you.'

'Hi, how's it going?' She smiled as she watched Faith join some of the girls and dance beside the

CD player.

'Good. Sorry to bother you on your day off, but I've had a Mexican lady pestering me, wanting to speak to you.'

'Can't it wait till Monday?'

'That's what I said, but she said it was important. Mentioned today's story. Thought you'd be interested. You want her number?'

'Shoot.' Deborah scribbled the information down on the back of a napkin. She thanked Frank and called the number he'd given her.

She sat down cross-legged on the grass.

A woman's voice answered, a heavy Latino accent. 'Carla speaking.'

'Hi, Carla, it's Deborah Jones of the *Miami Herald*. You called my office.'

The woman gave a long sigh. 'My sister call me this morning, after reading story of Senator O'Neill's chauffeur. She has story to tell as well. I tell her to go to police, but she doesn't listen. I say go to lady who wrote the story in newspaper, but she doesn't listen. She is scared. She say they will kill her.'

'Sorry—*who* will kill her?'

'Friends of Senator O'Neill.'

Deborah felt her stomach knot. 'Can you say that again, please?'

'My sister's name is Maria Gonzalez. She works as a maid for Senator O'Neill in Naples.'

Deborah felt her heart skip a beat. 'Your sister works for the senator?'

'For many years. She cleans and cooks.'

'And you're saying someone threatened her. When?'

'First thing this morning. They visit her at her

house. Two men. She'd never see them before.'

'Why doesn't she go to the police?'

'Miss Jones, listen to me. My sister is a simple woman. She love her church and place her trust in God, not in the police.'

'I still don't understand.'

'I'd like that you to speak to her. Perhaps then you will understand.'

'Does she live in the senator's home?'

'No. She live in North Naples, that's all I know.'

'Hang on. You're saying you don't know your sister's address?'

'She doesn't have much to do with us anymore. She only go out to work or go to church.'

'Do you know the name of the church?'

'I know that, yes. St John the Evangelist Church on 111th Avenue. She say the priest is very nice.'

'Okay, that's something.' The music from the girls was getting louder. Deborah signaled with her free hand for Faith to turn it down.

'My sister and I speak on phone only one hour ago. She is scared she will be deported if she speak about what she know.'

'Deported? For what?'

'The senator is sponsoring her green card. She cannot say nothing against him.'

'I see.'

'So you will speak to my sister?'

'Very well,' said Deborah. 'If I can find her.'

22

Early the following morning, just after seven, Deborah sat in the shadows near the back of the St John the Evangelist Catholic Church in North Naples. The first Mass of the day.

She'd got up just after four, headed across to Carla Gonzalez's house in Little Havana—where she'd picked up a picture of Maria taken three years earlier at a family funeral—before making the two-hour journey to Naples. She arrived just after dawn had broken and had blanketed the pretty Gulf town in a tangerine glow.

Deborah glanced at the small color picture. Maria Gonzalez was a chubby woman, well turned out in a very conservative trouser suit. But her eyes conveyed a strange sadness.

Deborah looked around the congregation and felt like an impostor. It was strange to be back in the city, after her run-in with the man called John Richmond. Perhaps she should have told Sam Goldberg before she set off, but he would probably have tried to dissuade her.

Most of the hundred early-morning churchgoers were white, although not particularly affluent-looking. Deborah counted five Hispanics, seated close together near the front. Maybe one family.

Mass started and the thick smell of incense wafted through the church. The priest was a thin, whey-faced man who wore half-moon spectacles. He was draped in the traditional full-length black cassock and the white surplice with wide sleeves worn over it. Looking around and smiling, he welcomed everybody before asking God to forgive their sins.

In her father's Baptist church, after a brief welcome, a hymn was the order of the day. As a little girl, Deborah had taken great pride in sitting beside her mother as her father began his sermons. What a voice he'd had—strong, passionate, and full of life. By contrast this priest sounded like a dull scientist explaining the laws of physics to kids.

Father Tobias Bruskewitz read from the Bible, and Deborah noticed a young girl with pigtails near the front turn round as if she was bored. Deborah smiled across the pews at the girl, and she smiled back. *Oh, to be young and innocent.*

Deborah bowed her head as prayers started. After each prayer, the congregation responded with 'Lord, graciously hear.'

After a long twenty minutes the bread and wine were offered up as the body and blood of Jesus.

Deborah watched everyone carefully, but no one matched the description or photo of Maria Gonzalez.

For some reason, she'd expected to see the woman as soon as she entered the church. Deborah left after the blessing and stood outside in the hope that she might've missed her. A few minutes later, the worshippers walked past her, blinking into the fierce morning sunshine.

The priest shook a few hands and offered gentle pats on the back for some, whispered condolences to others.

Deborah hung around until only she was left. Deflated, she went back to her car, parked a block away.

What should she do now?

The next Mass was at nine, then at eleven, then at one and, finally, at six.

She felt silly having come all that way. She hadn't even asked Carla what time her sister usually took Mass. 'Deborah, you idiot,' she said, and banged her palm on the steering wheel.

She contemplated calling Carla but decided against it, as she didn't want her to think that Deborah was some airhead. Damn. She knew that if Maria talked it would open up the story again. But time was running out for William Craig. He needed someone to put their neck on the line, just like Rachel Turner and Jimmy Black had.

But look what happened to Rachel, Deborah thought. Perhaps it would be an idea to let someone know where she was and why. Someone she trusted.

She bit her lower lip, not sure what to do. It was too early to call Sam Goldberg, especially on a Sunday.

What about Faith? Who better? Deborah knew her friend took a nine o'clock Sunday-morning soccer session for girls, and would probably be getting ready. She called up her number from her cell phone and it was answered on the second ring.

In the background, children shouted and cried as a TV cartoon blared at full volume.

'Morning, Faith, sorry to bother you.'

'Hey, what's happening, honey?'

'A few moments of your time.'

Faith shouted for someone to shut the door, and the noise subsided. 'Sorry, honey, they're all acting up.'

'Faith, I'm back in Naples.'

'You're what?'

'I know, I know.'

'Thought I told you to get the hell out of there.'

'I know, but a lead's come up. Look, I want you to write down the following, in case something happens to me.'

'Honey, you're scaring me again.'

'Just do it, okay?' As a rule, Deborah never snapped at Faith, but her nerves weren't holding up too well. 'Write down that I'm going to be attending five Masses at St John the Evangelist Catholic Church in North Naples. The last one is at six.'

'You flipped your lid, honey?'

'Remember that call I took yesterday afternoon? Well, that was the sister of a woman who works for Senator O'Neill.'

'I hear you.'

'Anyway, just write down the name Maria Gonzalez.'

'What does she do?'

Deborah paused for a moment, slightly reluctant to tell her who it was. 'She's Senator O'Neill's maid.'

'I got you.'

'I believe she has been threatened by friends of Senator O'Neill.'

'Hold on, hold on.'

'You writing?'

'Yeah, yeah, okay, got it. So, what do I do now?'

'Keep that bit of paper close to you and don't tell a soul.'

'I don't like the sound of this.'

'It's just a precaution. If something happens to me, I want someone to know what I've been up to.'

'Come home, honey, it's not worth it.'

'I've got to see this through. I'm getting closer.'

'You're getting sucked into something you don't have the faintest idea about, honey.'

Deborah paused for a moment. 'Maybe I am.'

*　　*　　*

Over the next few hours, Deborah attended the nine o'clock, eleven o'clock and one o'clock Masses. Afterwards, feeling tired and extremely bored, she was tempted to head on back to Miami, just like Faith had advised.

More than four hours to wait until the last Mass of the day.

She decided to buy lunch—a chicken sandwich and Diet Coke—at a nearby deli. Afterwards, she walked off her lunch down the oak-lined streets around the church. Then she returned to her car and enjoyed some shut-eye as the sun beat down.

Just before six, Deborah was back in the church, ready to go through the same routine.

As the Mass started, she looked around her, desperate to see Maria Gonzalez. The congregation's gazes were all focused on the priest. He looked bored, now on his fifth round of Mass. There was no sign of Carla's sister. In fact, there was not a single Hispanic in the church.

Afterwards, Deborah once more watched the churchgoers leave and shake hands with the priest. A short while later, feeling depressed and even more tired, she was the only one left outside.

As the priest turned to walk back inside, Deborah decided to approach him. 'Excuse me, Father.'

He turned round to face her and smiled. His

teeth were stained yellow at the front.

'I'm looking for Maria Gonzalez.'

The priest dabbed his forehead with a hankie. 'You were sitting near the back, weren't you?'

'Yeah, that's right. I'm trying to find Maria. Her sister Carla's a friend of mine.'

'I'm sorry to disappoint you, miss, but I've not seen Ms Gonzalez in the church for months now.'

'Months?' According to Carla, her sister was a regular. Devout. 'Are you sure?'

'Quite sure.' Something about the man's staccato response made her wonder. There was an edge to his voice, as if he didn't like being asked unnecessary questions.

Deborah's eyes were drawn to the index finger of his right hand, which was stained nicotine brown. 'I've traveled quite a distance, and I really hoped to see Maria today. Is it possible that you can tell me where she lives?'

'I'm sorry, but we're not in the business of giving out the home addresses of those who worship with us. I'm sure you understand.'

Deborah's heart sank. 'I only want to speak to—'

'Maybe I didn't make myself clear. I hear confessions and preach the Christian gospel. Whether you need to speak to one of my flock is not really for me to get involved with. Now, if there's nothing else, I've to get ready for confession.'

Deborah nodded as she shook the priest's sweaty palm. 'I appreciate your time.'

He turned and walked slowly back inside the church, but something about Father Tobias Bruskewitz told Deborah that he wasn't telling the whole truth.

23

Deborah sat for a while in her parked car, until the street lights came on. Her stomach rumbled for food. Suddenly a thin, stooped figure strode quickly past her car, books clutched to his chest.

It was the priest.

Deborah's heart thumped and she wondered where he was going. Perhaps he'd finished confession and was going to visit friends. But his demeanor suggested someone who wasn't about to wind down. Quite the opposite.

He walked further down 111th Street, then took a sharp left.

Deborah waited a moment before she started up her car. She eased off slowly, careful not to rev the engine. At a safe distance, she took a left.

Father Bruskewitz was walking fast down 6th Street North. There was front-yard parking here, paint peeled from some houses in need of repair, and she passed a couple of wrecked phone booths. This was a world away from the Ritz-Carlton.

Further down 6th and then the priest turned on 99th Avenue North. Deborah squinted into the darkness. There was very little street lighting here.

She pulled up beside the curb and noticed a placard tied to a broken street light. It advertised a public meeting of the Naples Park Coalition for Community Involvement.

The priest had stopped. He opened a gate to the front yard of a prim house.

Deborah edged off, again slowly, and parked diagonally opposite the house, shaded by a huge oak, as she watched the priest knock on the screen door.

She slunk down low in her seat and peered out of the window. A few moments passed before the door opened. Smiling at the priest was a plump woman, perhaps in her fifties. It was Maria Gonzalez. She opened the door wide and Father Bruskewitz was ushered inside. Was he about to tell Maria about the young black woman—a supposed friend of her sister—who'd attended all five Masses?

Deborah glanced in her rearview mirror and was blinded as a police car turned the corner. She sank deep into her seat as the lights got stronger.

Please drive on.

The brakes squeaked as the police car came to a halt. Deborah's stomach knotted. She started thinking of the red Chevy and Richmond's threats. Were people following her?

She closed her eyes and prayed that the police wouldn't get out. As if on cue, she heard one of the doors slam shut. The sound of heavy footsteps approached. Immediately, the beam from a flashlight temporarily blinded her.

She squinted into the light.

A patrolman said, 'Get out of the car, ma'am.' He took a step back.

Deborah did as she was told. Florida was not the sort of place to enter into discussions with the cops.

'Can I see you driver's license, ma'am?' he said.

Deborah reached over into the glove compartment and handed it over. He scrutinized the details and the photos.

'Can I ask why you were sitting crouched in your

car, ma'am?

'I'm sorry, officer, but I was just taking a nap. I'm conducting an investigation for the *Miami Herald*.'

'ID?'

Deborah flashed her press card. At the same time, the patrolman's colleague, a woman, stepped out. She spoke into her radio. 'I want some plates given the once-over,' she said.

The patrol officer scanned the press card before he looked up at Deborah. 'Is this how you conduct your business, hiding like some peeping Tom?'

Deborah stole a glance at the house. No one was looking out of the front window, which was a relief. 'I wasn't hiding, sir. I was resting.'

'You really expect me to believe that?'

'It's true. I need to interview the lady in the house opposite. But she has visitors. So I decided to take forty winks. I've been working since early morning.'

The policeman arched his eyebrows as if he'd heard it all before. 'You been drinking, ma'am?'

'Absolutely not.'

He leaned closer and sniffed around her chin. 'Don't smell of liquor.'

'I can assure you, sir, I don't drink.'

The policewoman's radio crackled into life. 'Plates are clean. Vehicle belongs to Deborah Jones of Collins Avenue, Miami Beach. No violations outstanding.'

The policeman's expression didn't change. 'You mind if we check your car, miss?'

Deborah shrugged. 'Be my guest.'

The next ten minutes seemed like an hour as the policeman peered into the trunk, shone the flashlight into the passenger seat, driver's seat, and finally the ashtrays, perhaps for any signs of reefer. He probably assumed that because Deborah was young and black she'd done drugs. It was a lazy and outdated assumption, not to mention racist.

Eventually, after much muttering and groaning as he examined her convertible in minute detail, the patrolman left, along with his female colleague, having apologized for the intrusion.

Deborah had been lucky. A patrolman who hadn't liked the look of her might've easily taken her downtown on a number of trumped-up charges. Thankfully, this police officer was just being diligent.

Suddenly, the screen door across the road opened and Father Bruskewitz emerged. He shut the door quietly behind him . . .

Deborah crouched low again as the priest hurried down the narrow path. She watched him disappear into the distance and finally felt safe when he turned back onto 111th Avenue.

24

When the coast was clear, Deborah got out of her car, briefcase in hand, and walked up to the door. The muggy air was filled with hundreds of lightning bugs flickering in the dark.

She knocked twice, stood back and waited. Eventually, the door creaked open. Maria Gonzalez's face was rounder than in her picture, eyes heavy as if she'd been crying.

'Good evening, ma'am, sorry to bother you,' Deborah said. The woman looked frightened. 'My name is Deborah Jones of the *Miami Herald*, and I was asked by a member of your family if—'

'What are you doing here?' The woman's tone was sharp.

'That's what I was about to explain. I'd like to speak to you . . . You're Maria Gonzalez, the maid for Senator Jack O'Neill, right?'

She shook her head. 'I am sorry you waste your time, but I have nothing to say.'

The door was slammed in Deborah's face. She stood for a few moments, feeling foolish. She felt beads of sweat on her brow. She turned around and noticed the police car circling once more.

Damn.

Deborah knocked on the screen door again.

Maria Gonzalez opened the door again, this time wider, her face red with anger, a silver crucifix round her neck. 'I tell you already, I have nothing to say.'

'Please . . .'

'I call the police.'

Deborah pointed to the patrol car, which had slowed to a crawl. 'Go right ahead. I spoke to them ten minutes ago.'

Deborah fixed her gaze on Maria's black eyes. 'I'm here to talk about the threats. Made yesterday morning.'

Maria looked away. She held on to the screen door, her plump frame blocking the entrance. Her black hair was tied up in an old-fashioned bun.

'Can I please come in?'

'Who spoke to you?'

'A member of your family.'

'My sister, wasn't it? Carla. I might have known it would be her.'

The sadness in her eyes made Deborah look away for a split second.

'Ms Gonzalez, a few minutes of your time, that's all I ask.'

'I don't want to talk. Can't you understand that?'

'Look, if in five minutes you don't want the conversation to go any further, I'll leave and that'll be the end of it. Your sister cares very much about you. She is worried.'

'I am very scared. People could hurt me.'

'Then let me come in.'

A long silence ensued. Then she spoke in a quiet voice. 'Very well.'

Deborah followed Maria through a narrow hall that was festooned with wooden crosses and pictures of an Aryan Jesus into a small living room. The sky-blue sofas clashed with the lime-green wallpaper. A large metal crucifix was above the mantelpiece.

Deborah sat down and placed her briefcase on the floor beside her.

Maria took the sofa opposite.

'First of all,' Deborah said, 'I won't record anything or write anything down unless you want me too, okay?'

Maria Gonzalez eyed her briefcase. 'Sure.'

'Yesterday the *Miami Herald* carried the story of Jimmy Brown, the senator's chauffeur, who reported a conversation he overheard to the Miami Beach police, with Joe O'Neill saying he had raped a woman in a park in South Beach.'

'I read that.' Maria went over to the windows, pulled the drapes shut and switched on a large table lamp that rested on a huge TV.

'Your sister told me you'd been threatened. Who

by? What are you so afraid of?'

'You don't know what these people are like.'

'What people?'

'The senator, his family, his friends. They can do anything. Anything at all. They are untouchable.'

'I'm listening.'

Maria shook her head. 'I can't say any more.'

'Can't or won't?'

'They said they would kill me if I spoke about what I knew. They said Jimmy Brown was going to die. I am simple woman. I am scared. And I don't want trouble. I rely on the senator's money.'

'Ms Gonzalez, a man is about to be executed. The man who killed the senator's son for raping his granddaughter. What about justice?'

'What about justice? My family needs to survive. What happens if I speak out? I will lose job, will be deported to Mexico.'

'Who says?'

'Senator. My priest. He say it is better to be quiet and dignified.'

Deborah's blood ran cold. 'The priest said that? What does he want you to be quiet about?'

'He said I a good woman, but should not bring shame on good man like Senator O'Neill.'

'I'm sorry—you've lost me.'

'He says God wants me to be good. Good for my family and good for my employer.'

Deborah reached across and held her hand. 'Maria, look at me. What is it you know?'

'It is difficult to talk about.'

'Maria, your sister loves you very much.'

'I love her.'

'So why don't you visit? Why only call? What is it you're afraid of?'

Maria shook her head and scrunched up her face as the tears fell.

'You must speak to me.'

'Please, please, you are making it very difficult. My priest says—'

'Your priest?'

'He is friends with Senator O'Neill. Senator O'Neill gives money to Catholic charities. He is a generous man. I am just cleaning lady who runs around, picking up the mess in the house, carrying out trash. That's me.'

Deborah clutched Maria's hand. 'You know something, don't you? Something about the senator? Something about his son, maybe?'

Gonzalez's hand trembled slightly. 'What will my priest say?'

'He is most definitely not your friend.'

Maria dabbed at her eyes with a small pink hankie with her initials on it. 'I don't know where to begin.'

'Okay, let's take this nice and easy. If you wanna stop at any time, just say. This is an initial interview only, for the *Miami Herald*.'

Gonzalez blinked away the tears and blew her nose.

'Whenever you're ready, Maria.' Deborah switched on the recorder.

Maria took a deep breath as if she'd waited a long time to divulge her information. 'I work in house of Senator Jack O'Neill. I have kept secret for many years. I have been sending money home illegally.'

'Sorry?'

'I was given money by Senator O'Neill to keep quiet. One thousand dollars a month.'

'Maria, what was the money for?'

'To keep quiet about Joe O'Neill.'

'Maria, what do you know? What do you know about Joe O'Neill?'

Maria Gonzalez closed her eyes tightly as if in pain. 'He . . . he rape me, too.'

Deborah felt like she'd been thrown in a freezing cold bath.

'He rape me when senator and his wife were at function.'

Deborah said nothing for a few moments, trying to regain her composure, her mind working overtime. 'When exactly did this happen, Maria?'

Gonzalez touched the crucifix around her neck. 'March 1986. Joe O'Neill was around sixteen or seventeen.' *Nearly three years before Jenny Forbes,* Deborah thought.

'Tell me about it.'

Gonzalez looked at her nails. 'He spike my Coke with something and I wake up bleeding all over. He rape me with bottles as well. I think he drug me.' The maid averted her tear-stained gaze. 'It is horrible to tell you. I am so ashamed.'

Deborah leaned over and patted Maria Gonzalez on the knee. 'I think you've done a brave thing by telling me this. This happened at the family home?'

'Yes, in West Palm Beach where he stay at time.'

'Why didn't you report this?'

Maria's bottom lip quivered. 'Senator O'Neill threaten to have me deported.'

'This might sound like an obvious question, Ms Gonzalez, but why do you think the senator would want to cover up such things?'

'So he be American senator. No?'

'Tell me about the money you received.'

'He give me money in cash. I think about my mother and father and the things I could buy for them. Same with my children. My man blame me. Say I was dirty. And he go away.'

Brett didn't even take the time to pack. He just left Deborah wrestling with the demons inside her head. 'Ms Gonzalez,' she said. 'I need to know if you are willing to be identified in any article?'

Maria looked up, her gaze steady. 'Yes . . . that's what my sister want.'

'But what do *you* want?'

Maria closed her eyes and touched her crucifix again. Then she looked straight at Deborah. 'I cannot live with this any longer. I want to tell people what happen.'

'It can't be easy working in the house, after what happened.'

'I pray every day. I glad to be alive. I provide for my children.' She bowed her head. 'But now I want to help the man who kill that animal. I want to help him.'

*   *   *

Just before dawn, Deborah—after a sleepless night—was in Sam Goldberg's office. His feet were on his desk.

She had phoned Goldberg immediately after the interview ended, just after ten p.m. Initially, he was furious that she'd gone back to Naples. But when she told him the story his tone changed.

The sun rose and streamed through the blinds, suffusing the room with a yellow tint.

Goldberg punched a number into his phone.

'Harry, it's Sam here. Sorry to disturb you. Need to see you ASAP. We've got a major development in the O'Neill story.' A brief pause as he nodded, listening to Donovan. 'See you then.'

He hung up and looked at Deborah, determination in his eyes. 'I want you to go out there and write up this story. Harry says he'll be in by nine. This is your baby, but I want it written straight. Senator covers up son's rapes, okay? That's the angle. Use extensive quotes from Rachel Turner and what we've got off Maria Gonzalez. Also add in a couple of paragraphs from the chauffeur.' He was wired, his eyes like pinpricks. 'You must also link in the mysterious John Richmond and speak to our FBI contacts. They'll give you the inside beef on the Mob aspects. In addition, we should have clippings of Paulie Fachetti somewhere in our files. Make the quotes watertight. I don't want some smart-ass lawyer catching us out on a technicality. Send over your story to me personally. I'll let Harry see what we've got, and then we'll get it vetted and laid out. We're gonna get that son of a bitch O'Neill.'

'What about Mr Craig?'

'We're gonna be asking for him to be freed and moved off death row.'

25

In the dead of night, the lights were on in the tenth-floor boardroom of the Washington law firm of Stone, Finkelstein & Black in the impressive Willard Office Building, downtown on

Pennsylvania Avenue. Senator O'Neill sat in silence as the senior partner, Anthony Stone, speed-read an early edition of the *Miami Herald.*

O'Neill watched as Tony Stone—an old friend from college—adjusted his metal-rimmed glasses and took notes. He knew that the revelations spelled trouble. For as long as he could remember, he'd sailed close to the wind. Even in the Senate, the number of times he tried to railroad legislation amazed his colleagues, but that was just his way. Perhaps a more sophisticated approach was sometimes required. Stroke a few cheeks, massage a few egos. But that wasn't his style. Better to be blunt.

O'Neill sighed as Stone repositioned the huge green reading lamp in front of him and highlighted a crucial passage in yellow marker pen. Proof from Maria Gonzalez that one thousand dollars in cash had been paid into an account in Mexico every month.

Talk about dumb, Jack.

O'Neill was glad he had such an excellent lawyer. Stone headed up the feared litigation practice department. He had twenty-eight years' experience and had appeared before federal and state courts and administrative agencies. His reputation for aggressive courtroom tactics and hardball cross-examinations had resulted in billions of dollars in out-of-court settlements over the years. His specialties included antitrust, government contracts and international trade. But he was best known for white-collar criminal proceedings and congressional inquiries.

Was the FBI already on to him? The sound of a police siren outside startled him and he looked up.

Another shooting in the projects, no doubt. Parts of America's capital city were no-go areas after dark.

O'Neill's mind flashed back to the time when he and Stone had first met, in the late 1960s. It had been over a few beers at Charlie's Kitchen bar on Harvard Square. The start of an unlikely friendship. Stone, the Connecticut boy born with a silver spoon in his mouth, educated at the best of schools, with impeccable manners and singled out for Ivy League at an early age. O'Neill, by contrast, was a smart but foul-mouthed boy from the backstreets of Bensonhurst, but they hit it off right away. He remembered the drinking competitions in the frat house and their 'work hard, play hard' mindset.

O'Neill cleared his throat. 'Tony, gimme it straight. And no bull.'

'I think you're in deep shit, Jack.' Stone stretched back in his seat, hands behind his head. 'Okay, I need to know where I stand. Firstly, is what's in the paper true?'

O'Neill took a deep breath and looked around the oak-paneled boardroom. The oil paintings on the wall showed every president of the company since it had been founded in 1885. They all seemed to glower down as if they knew he had a guilty conscience.

'You really want me to answer that?' O'Neill said.

'Yes.'

He had to pick his words carefully. 'The story is not incorrect. That answer your question?'

Stone picked up a pen and nibbled the end. 'You bribed your maid to keep her quiet?'

The words didn't sound good and the senator felt his neck flush. He'd done all this out of misplaced devotion to his son. A son he couldn't have loved any more if he'd tried.

'And Richmond got Rachel Turner lined up with a Hollywood agent which kick-started her career, again to keep her quiet?'

Would Stone still want to be his friend after hearing all this? Would he be flying down for his election-night party? That would certainly not go down too well with his other clients—who included a couple of Hollywood directors who'd used Rachel Turner in their films.

O'Neill nodded.

'Fuck a duck, Jack, this is bad.' Stone leaned forward, elbows on the highly polished boardroom table, and clasped his hands together like a pious priest. 'Who knows the truth?'

'You, me and Richmond. And now, just about the whole world.'

Stone shook his head. 'Jack, before I talk about how we're gonna tackle this, I need to say something you might not like.'

'Fire away.'

'John Richmond is Mafia.' Stone took off his glasses. 'I know it, you know it, everybody knows it. I know he's helped you move into the big time, but believe me, you don't need friends like him. *I*'m a friend. He's not.'

'I've known Richmond since I was a boy. I didn't know what he was until it was too late. That's the goddamn truth.'

'Ditch him. Now.'

'I can't. We look after each other's interests.'

'Jack, you're involved in illegal activities. You

want me to list them? Just for starters, let's see, there's bribes and corruption of an elected public official which could result in grand-jury subpoenas, court proceedings, search warrants for your house and whatever else they care to throw at you.'

O'Neill looked at his watch—quarter to three in the morning. He sighed and picked up Stone's copy of the *Herald*. He scanned the story's headline for the umpteenth time since Lomax had faxed it through, just before eleven the previous night.

Florida Senator Covered Up Son's Sex Attacks

The byline was that of Deborah Jones. What did this woman have against him? Had this become personal for her?

O'Neill's mind drifted.

Wonder how Rose is taking it?

He'd phoned her just before midnight at their beachfront house in Southampton and had woken her up. He gave it to her straight. She didn't freak out. Just listened. She knew about the foibles of politicians, their tricks and their bullshit. She was friends with Hillary Clinton and knew about the darker side of political life, but all she said was, 'We'll discuss it at a more opportune moment.' O'Neill already had a small plane waiting to fly him to the Hamptons for the showdown. It crossed his mind to leave the country. Richmond had suggested that. He'd said that Belize would be a great place to disappear to. But O'Neill knew that if he disappeared it would make it far more likely that Craig would be moved off death row.

That couldn't happen. Never. He couldn't allow Craig to live, despite any reservations Rose had.

O'Neill shook out a Winston from a silver

cigarette case and lit up. He watched the smoke drift towards the huge windows. 'He was my son,' he said, 'and I'm going to defend him until I die. My son is my life. Like Josh is your life.'

Stone shook his head. 'Jack, listen to me. Joe's dead. You need to move on and forget about loyalty and family ties.'

'Not an option.'

'Are you prepared to lay down your career and liberty for Joe?'

'Absolutely.'

'Jack, we could sort this out. We could explain away the Gonzalez bribe, the driver or whatever they've thrown at you. But not your involvement with actresses who mysteriously fall to their death.'

'There's something you need to know,' O'Neill said. 'I met up with Richmond after it happened. I asked him to find out some stuff about Deborah Jones of the *Herald*.'

Stone winced. 'Okay, here's the choice. Either you deal with it my way or your way. My way, you stay a senator but Craig will be released. Your son's accusers are vindicated, in effect.'

'Tony, I want to sue those bastards at the *Herald*. Can I do that?'

Stone shrugged. 'Sure, you can sue them. But it'll cost you a fortune and you'll also foot their costs as well, if you lose. It's high-risk, but since you intend to defend Joe it's probably your only option. It can be done. It could buy you time.'

O'Neill nodded. 'I've got plenty of that, unlike Craig.'

'I see. You plan to string this out through the courts, tie down the paper in litigation so Craig gets executed before everything is done and dusted, right?'

O'Neill gave a thin smile. 'It's my only option.'

'You want us to sue the goddamned *Miami Herald*?' Stone shook his head. 'You'd be risking everything for one throw of the dice.'

'I'm a politician. That's what we do.'

* * *

An hour later, O'Neill was enjoying a stiff whiskey as his private jet took off from Reagan National, bound for the Hamptons, before flying on to Naples in the morning. He knew the press vultures would be waiting for him at the gates of the community when he returned home.

He wondered how the party would react. He remembered the Jesse Jackson affair when he didn't answer his home phone for a week. Lomax had insisted on it. Another time, during the Clinton scandal, he'd gone to Puerto Vallarta and had claimed it was a fact-finding mission. Everyone knew it was politics.

He felt relieved to have told Stone the story, but there was one thing he hadn't revealed. He figured that was a secret only Richmond could keep.

The phone on his seat rang and he picked up.

'Richmond here.' He sounded as if he'd been shouting. 'Looks like someone's gonna pay for what that bitch has done.'

'Listen,' O'Neill said, as the plane climbed into the dark sky, the lights of Washington below, the rippling water of the Potomac visible with the full moon, 'I'm handling this in my own way.'

'I'm sorry, Jack, but that won't do. *We*'re gonna deal with this.'

'I've spoken to my lawyer and we're gonna sue.'

Richmond snorted in derision. 'Know something? I'm sick of talking.'

26

Deborah strode into the office just after nine, and was cheered by her colleagues. She'd already read her sensational exclusive—which spanned pages one, two and three—down at the News Café on Ocean Drive, accompanied by the two Feds assigned to protect her. They had agreed to stay in reception vetting everyone who entered the building, as opposed to tracking her every move. It was all a bit scary and unsettling. But she was glad to have them in the building.

Frank Callaghan, Sam's closest friend at the paper, looked up as she passed. 'You've crossed the Rubicon, Deborah. You're in with the big boys now.'

'Thanks.'

She smiled as an old-timer on the National Desk held up the front page and shouted across, 'Way to go, Debs. Kick their asses, that's why I say. The senator won't know what's hit him.'

Then it was Larry Coen, the great crime reporter, who came up and shook her hand, smiling. He was, without a doubt, the man with more exclusives on Colombian drug gangs and corrupt Miami police officers and Miami-Dade County officials than anyone alive. He'd filed thousands of homicide stories. And in 1999 he'd won a Pulitzer for ten unrelated police-beat stories, out of the two hundred he had covered that year.

'I've been trying to pin something on that bastard for years,' he said, in his languid style. 'If you're looking for a job on the crime desk, just let me know.'

'Hey, Debs,' a female voice said. She turned round and Michelle Rodriguez, the features editor she still technically worked for, came to give her a big hug. 'I never in my wildest dreams thought you were cut out for the hard-edged stories. Shows what a poor judge of character I am. Unbelievable, honey. Everyone is raving about what you've done. I'm so proud of you.'

Deborah smiled, feeling slightly tearful with all the attention. 'What can I say? I got lucky.'

'Like hell. You worked your ass off, and you got your rewards.'

Deborah's head was spinning with all the compliments. And it continued.

Goldberg came out of his office and presented her with a magnum of champagne in front of everyone. She didn't have the heart to tell him that she didn't drink anymore.

No one could fail to notice that as everyone congratulated Deborah, Kathleen Klein remained serenely in her seat, phone pressed to her ear, studiously avoiding eye contact with Deborah. She didn't even glance up or give a little smile.

Goldberg came over to Deborah. 'Can I see you for a couple of minutes?' he said.

'Sure.'

She followed Goldberg into his office.

'Pull up a seat,' he said, and pointed to the chair opposite his desk. 'Proud as hell of you. But now for the comedown. Harry phoned me ten minutes ago. The senator's lawyers have been in touch. Apparently, Jack O'Neill is refuting the allegations.'

'I see.'

'That's not all. They're launching a multimillion-dollar lawsuit against us.'

'But we've proved—'

'I know what we've proved,' he said. Goldberg undid his red tie. 'Jack O'Neill is a dangerous man with dangerous friends. And he's mega rich. You don't need me to tell you that rich men love libel lawyers.'

'We in trouble?'

'To be frank, I'd have been surprised if the senator didn't set his lawyers on us. Whether he carries out his threat is another matter. Don't worry about it. You did great, but this is a time for caution. Ms Gonzalez has been taken into protective custody and is safe from Fachetti. Jimmy Brown's speaking to the Feds in LA. That leaves you.'

'I've got two Feds following my every move.'

'Where are they now?'

'Waiting in reception, checking everyone's IDs.'

'I'd be happier if you stayed away from your condo for now. Maybe even from Miami, just for a couple of days.' Goldberg cleared his throat. 'We need to move this story on. Fancy a six-hour trip back up to Raiford with your Feds and interview Mr Craig? Find out how he's feeling?'

That was what Deborah had planned anyway.

'Sure.'

'His hopes and dreams are important to understand. His story is now taking center stage.

But this turns everything on its head.'

'In what way?'

'Deborah, your safety is paramount. The Feds will be with you. But I want you to stay in a different motel or hotel every night. May seem crazy, but just do it, okay? And file your stories to my e-mail address from your laptop, okay? Any questions?'

Deborah leaned back in her seat and smiled. 'Yeah,' she said. 'When do I get a raise?'

Goldberg pointed to the door and tried hard to stifle his laughter.

* * *

It was a tedious six-hour journey up the Florida Turnpike with her two Feds for company. The heavily wired Pete, who chewed gum as fast as he talked, and Robert, laconic to the point of being mute, obviously didn't get on. They disagreed about everything. How many houses did Shaq own? Three? Five? They even argued about CNN's Paula Zahn's beautiful teeth. Pete thought they were perfectly natural, while Robert disagreed, saying they were all porcelain veneers.

Halfway up the turnpike they tried to put on a show of unity. It lasted for about half an hour during a painful silence. Before long, Pete was teasing Robert, asking him when had been the last time he'd fired his gun. Robert tried to make light of the comment, inferring he wasn't usually in the front line of operations. Eventually Robert went quiet, preferring not to goad his colleague into further comment.

The last two hours of the journey were relatively

good-natured. They sat back and enjoyed the scenery, asking Deborah about her work. They seemed genuinely interested, especially Robert, whose brother worked on a local paper in Memphis.

It was late afternoon by the time they arrived at Raiford.

Deborah went through the pat-downs and metal detectors like the last time. The stale smells of cheap perfume, body odors and bleach still hung heavy in the air. She took her seat and waited.

The heavy steel doors screeched open on the other side of the Plexiglas and made her flinch. Craig's cropped hair came into view. His orange prison-issue top was stained with sweat under the arms and down his front.

Craig sat down and picked up the phone, double-handed.

'Good to see you again, my dear.' He smiled and the lines around his eyes creased up.

'And you.' Deborah held up the front page of the *Miami Herald* and pressed it against the Plexiglas.

It took him about five minutes to read everything.

'You can put it down now,' he said. His face was white. 'Christ, I'm lost for words . . . The senator's involved in all this?'

'All down the line. After this, it'll be difficult for them to keep you on Death Watch.'

'Deborah, I don't want you to get your hopes up. I'm scheduled to die in twenty days. They're watching me every second until they strap me down.'

'Polls show only ten percent support your execution.'

'But it's the influential people who make up that ten percent.' Craig scrutinized her face. 'You look tired, my dear.'

Dog-tired would've been more accurate. Craig himself seemed to have aged since her last visit. His skin was grayer—as if the blood had stopped pumping properly.

He leaned forward and winced as the chains restricted his movement. 'Once this is all over, Deborah, I'd appreciate if you could do me a favor.'

'Of course.'

'Tell Jenny I love her. Tell her I understand why she couldn't come and see me these last few years.'

Deborah felt her throat tighten. 'Don't speak like that, Mr Craig. It's not over.'

'It might've been misguided, wrong or whatever, but I did it for her. If you're lucky enough to have a family one day, you'll know what I mean. You'll run through walls for them.' It was ironic, because that was probably how Senator O'Neill viewed his own position.

Deborah found herself thinking of Brett and what could have been. He had talked about it at Berkeley. They'd planned to get married as soon as they graduated and set up home together. She imagined taking their kids to the zoo, Disneyland or whatever else came to mind. It would've been great.

'If you were my daughter, I'd be damned proud of you.'

Why did she crave Craig's recognition so much? It was like when she was a little girl and wanted her father to compliment her on her piano playing. He never did, not coming up to the mark. If she got ninety-five percent in a piano exam, he wondered what happened to the other five percent. It was never enough, but she strived to please him.

This man did not seem embarrassed to wear his heart on his sleeve. That meant everything to Deborah.

*   *   *

As she was escorted out of Raiford, Deborah reflected how glad she was to have told Craig what type of young man he had killed. Not an innocent, but a serial sex attacker. It hadn't vindicated his actions, but it explained them. Craig saw what kind of man Joe O'Neill was when no one else did. That was to his eternal credit. And only he took action when no one else could or would.

Pete and Robert leaned against the cruiser beneath the archway, jackets slung over their shoulders. They straightened up and smiled back at Deborah as she approached.

It'd been a long day for everyone, but it had been the best in her short career.

Robert opened a rear door for her and she ducked down to get in. Just then her cell phone rang.

She rolled her eyes at the agents who nodded as if they understood what it was like to be at the beck and call of a demanding boss. But it was her mother.

'Deborah,' she said, letting out a long sigh. 'Got some news for you.'

'Momma, what's wrong?' She got back out of the cruiser and turned to face the chain-link fence. The razor wire glistened in the last remnants of the early-evening sun.

'It's your daddy, Deborah.'

'Daddy? What about him?'

'There's not an easy way to tell you this. Daddy's in the hospital. Two men threatened him.' Her mother's voice broke with the emotion. 'Deborah, your father collapsed, clutching his chest. He's fighting for his life.'

27

Early the following morning, after an exhausting ten-hour drive north through the night in pouring rain with the same two Feds, Deborah arrived at the Cardiac Observation Unit on the first floor of the Mississippi Baptist Medical Center in Jackson.

Her father's eyes were closed as he snored softly, hooked up to an intravenous drip that she knew administered thrombolytics to help destroy clots.

Sitting at his bedside and holding his hand was her mother. She looked up and gave a weak smile.

Deborah walked over, threw her arms around her and broke down in tears. It seemed so long since she'd done that. 'What happened, Momma?'

Her mother shook her head and wiped away her daughter's tears. 'We were leaving a church coffee morning when two white men jumped out of a car. The smaller of the two looked like a bodybuilder, although he was wearing a real fine suit. He grabbed your daddy by the throat. Said some terrible things, Deborah. Said they were gonna do bad things to you, y'understand? Said they'd hired some men to rape you.'

Deborah's stomach knotted. It had to be Richmond's men. Who else knew? Was it one of the goons sitting in the private dining room at the Ritz-Carlton who'd tried to frighten her father to death? It was smart. Threats don't leave any physical trace.

'Luckily I had some aspirin with me.'

Deborah remembered her mother had attended a first-aid course after her father had had the stroke.

'Doctors say it probably saved him. But he's not as strong as he used to be.' She turned to face him and leaned over to stroke his peaceful face. 'God bless him.'

Deborah was engulfed by waves of guilt. Was this Richmond's way of getting to her?

He'd warned her in no uncertain terms. But she'd ignored those warnings. All of a sudden, her father's sleepy eyes opened as if he'd heard her voice.

Deborah leaned across the bed so he could see her. 'I'm here, Daddy,' she said, gazing down at him through a film of tears.

Her mother pecked him on the forehead and smiled at her daughter. 'I think you need some time together, don't you?'

Deborah nodded and her mother left the room. Deborah looked into her father's eyes. 'I came as soon as I could, Daddy.'

It had been nearly a year since they'd last spoken. A Christmas dinner, stilted and strained.

His drugged eyes were heavy.

'I'm so sorry,' she said. 'If I knew that my work would result in this, I'd never have started.'

Her father didn't say a word. His steady

breathing and a low background hum from the medical equipment were the only noises.

'I know we haven't been close for a while. But I'm here to say I love you and I'm here for you.' She squeezed his hand like she had done when she was a little girl. It was their secret code. *I love you*, it meant.

His eyes misted over. When he spoke, his words were more slurred than she remembered. 'Your mother looks after me so well. Don't know what I'd do without her.'

Deborah wiped her eyes. 'Oh Daddy, I'm just glad to see you alive.'

'Best hospital in Mississippi. And it's run by Baptists.' There was a twinkle in his eyes now and a smile crossed his handsome unshaven features. It was the first time she'd ever seen him not closely shaven in her life. 'I have the Lord to thank as well.'

Deborah averted her gaze, no longer a believer.

'Look at me,' he said. 'Can you ever forgive me, Deborah?'

She thought her heart was going to burst. 'I've nothing to forgive you for, Daddy.'

'I'm a foolish old man. I turned my back on you when you needed me.' The tears spilled down his face and ran past his twisted mouth. 'My beautiful daughter. I don't know what to say, I'm so ashamed.'

'Hush now, Daddy—you're getting yourself all riled up. You need to rest.'

'Foolish pride, that's what it was. My pride and joy had been damaged, and I turned my back on you. All I was thinking about was how our friends and neighbors and my congregation would react, knowing that you'd been raped. About how the people at the NAACP would react. I knew it would all come out. It always does. And I was scared. Scared what they'd think of you, scared what they'd think of me. Stupid pride. What I wasn't thinking about was to support my beautiful daughter when she most needed it. When she most needed it. I'll have to live with that for the rest of my life. I'm a simple man who doesn't understand much about the secular world. Bars, nightclubs, young people.'

'Please, Daddy. You don't have to—'

'All I know is my church, my wife and my God. But I forgot the most important thing. My child. I forgot that you needed me to be there, and all I was thinking about was my position in society.'

'Daddy, you don't have to explain.'

'Oh, I do. You want me to tell you something else?'

Deborah nodded, her heart breaking.

'I thought it was God's way of punishing you for choosing a secular path far away from us.' Her father had wanted Deborah to attend Mississippi College in Clinton, the second-oldest Baptist college in the United States. 'But those are the thoughts of a fool. A pious fool whose pride was destroyed. I should've taken you up in my arms and hugged you, like I used to.'

Deborah squeezed his hand again. 'That's in the past, Daddy.'

'My heart was broken into a million pieces. But it's back together now that you're sitting here, beside me.' He stroked her hand. 'You never turned your back on me. And that tells me everything I have to know about you.'

Deborah wiped the tears from her father's eyes. 'I wish this had never happened to you. I feel this is my fault.'

'I don't blame you for what these men did. Listen to me. Do not be swayed by what has happened to me. Do your job. They are simply trying to intimidate you, by getting at me. But it'll take more than idle threats to send me to my Maker. I'm not ready just yet.'

Deborah wanted him to rest, not talk.

'Remember I told you many years ago when you said you wanted to be a journalist, about that quote by Edmund Burke.'

'Yes, Daddy.'

'Well, think about it now.'

All that is necessary for the triumph of evil is that good men do nothing.

'Anyone can be intimidated. But it takes a stronger man or woman to look evil in the face.'

'I'm scared, Daddy.'

Her father tried to sit up. 'Dig deep and find the strength that the Lord gave you. It's something we all have.' He laid his head back down on the starched white pillow and took hold of her hand. 'I read all your stories on the Internet. Even that one about Ricky Martin. That surprise you?'

Deborah was unable to look him in the eye. It had taken two long years for him to lift the burden of guilt she'd felt.

'Your story on William Craig brought a lump to my throat. And I understand your reasons for doing it.'

Deborah kissed the back of his hand.

'But what happened yesterday to me was only the start of it. If you are to proceed, be prepared to look into the face of evil.'

* * *

Later that evening, as Deborah sat alone at her father's bedside, mopping his brow with a cold cloth—after ordering her mother home to get some rest—a visitor arrived. It was Sam Goldberg.

'You didn't have to come all this way,' she said.

Goldberg pecked her on the cheek. 'Course I did.' He looked at her father. 'What's the latest?'

'Seems like he's over the worst, thank God.'

'Deborah, if I'd known the investigation would've resulted in this, I'd never have given the go-ahead.'

'No one could've foreseen anything like this.'

Goldberg paused for a few moments as if reluctant to say what was on his mind. 'That's why I'm taking you off the investigation. It's for your own safety.'

'I thought we'd already been through that?'

'Deborah, we're in uncharted territory. Fachetti or Richmond—or whatever his goddamn name is—isn't going to stop. He'll go after you. This was just a warning. The next time he'll kill you.'

'This is my investigation and I'm going to see it through.' She sounded tougher than she felt.

Goldberg shook his head. 'Look, I spoke to Harry Donovan about this before I left, and he agrees. We don't want anything else happening to you or your family.'

'I can't believe I'm hearing this.'

'Deborah, it's my duty as managing editor to protect my staff. I know this isn't easy for you to accept, but it's for the best.'

'If you honestly think I'm gonna just forget about

Mr Craig and everything I've uncovered, you better think again.'

'The hospital is ringed by Feds, Deborah. They've advised us on this.'

'What's it got to do with them? Are they running policy at the *Miami Herald*?' It was a bitter remark that didn't do her any favors.

'It's got everything to do with them. They think you're at grave risk. You can't go back to the office until this blows over. You'll have to do what they say. And yes, that means protection in a safe house.'

'Sam, try and look at it from my perspective.' Deborah felt her neck flush. She'd called him Sam. 'This case is not just about doing some fine investigative journalism and getting a pat on the back, nice though that is. This has got to be about saving Mr Craig. And myself. Otherwise, what's the point?'

Goldberg's expression softened. 'You're not going to be satisfied if I move you back to features when this is all over, are you?'

Deborah shook her head. 'I want to get back to the office and work on this story now.'

'It's too dangerous.'

'If I agree to be protected by the FBI, what's stopping me working the story using e-mail, cell phone and laptop?'

'I've asked Larry Coen to take over the investigation. The decision's been made.'

Deborah felt her mouth go dry. 'When was this decided?'

'Last night. Ongoing stories will be handed over to his crime reporters. He's happy to continue your investigation and I've assigned two extra people to help because we're running out of time. But Larry wanted me to stress to you that you can call him anytime for updates. I'm sorry, Deborah, but it had to be done.'

'I need to be part of it.'

Goldberg went quiet and began pacing the room, occasionally glancing at Deborah's father. She noticed how tired he looked and realized that the story and its ramifications were affecting him as well.

'Okay, work on the story,' he said eventually. 'If you must. But you will be in protective custody until this thing is over. That's the deal.'

Deborah knew that she didn't have a choice. 'Okay.'

Goldberg held her hand again and smiled. 'We're going to get through this. All of us. Trust me.'

28

The following morning, at the senator's sprawling Naples home, the mood among O'Neill's advisers—forty-eight hours after the revelations first surfaced—was edgy as they drank coffee, watching CNN coverage of the affair.

Outside the main entrance to the gated community, journalists, photographers and TV crews had laid siege to the man at the center of the storm. All the major papers—the *New York Times*, *Washington Post* and *LA Times*—had gone big on the story that morning and followed up the *Herald*'s allegations.

On TV, political pundits and commentators

speculated on the scale of the crisis that had engulfed O'Neill and said it threatened to derail both his election campaign and Craig's execution.

Away from the prying eyes of the press, O'Neill and his people were trying to find a way out of the quagmire.

O'Neill sat on a black leather sofa, papers on his lap. He wore a blue pinstriped suit, black shoes, white shirt and a blue tie. The plasma TV was on and the sun streamed in through the windows. He gazed across the bay as he fielded questions from his chief spin doctor, apoplectic at the turn of events.

Hal Lomax said, 'Jack, are you telling me that you *didn't* cover up Joe's rapes?'

CNN experts in the background filled a brief silence. Lomax held up that day's *Miami Herald*. 'They're calling for you to be put on trial. And if that isn't enough, they say Deborah Jones's father is in protective custody after death threats. What've you got to say about that?'

O'Neill shot Lomax an angry look. 'I've told you, it's a smear campaign.'

'Jack, these claims are fucking insane. It can't go on.'

O'Neill picked up a packet of Marlboro from a newspaper-strewn coffee table. He shook out a cigarette, lit up and looked around at the rest of his advisers. 'Politics is a dirty business, folks, as we all know.' He inhaled deeply and blew the smoke away from them. 'In Florida, it's dirtier than anywhere else. You know that.'

'Jack, this comes back down to one thing,' Lomax said. 'John Richmond. The guy's bad news, I've said that before. He's got you messed up in shit so deep you'll soon be choking on it.'

'Leave John out of this. He's a trusted friend . . .'

'Jack, wake up. It's time for a reality check. Richmond's rotten. Accusations of flaky land deals in the Everglades are one thing but this is way out of control. Christ, they're saying he heads up the Mob in Florida. And if that's not enough, they say he's one of the leading crime-syndicate figures in the States. Jack, you told me he was a businessman.'

'He is.'

'Look, I've had every journalist in the western world on my back since this story broke. They want a line and they're outside the gates. I tell you, they're gunning for you.'

O'Neill picked up his mug of cold coffee and gulped it down. 'You think they're gonna stop my career after all these years? You think those guys at the gate had to fight like I fought to get where they are? Not a chance.'

'Let's get this straight, Jack. You're saying there's nothing in these allegations? You seriously expect us to believe that?'

O'Neill glanced at Jodi Perkins, his legal adviser. Her face was impassive. This pleased him. Loyalty was important, after all. 'None at all. Look, Hal, I'm the one who should be angry, not you. They're dragging my name through the gutter. And I'm sure as hell gonna do something about it.'

'What . . . ?'

O'Neill dragged heavily on his cigarette. 'I'm suing.' He watched their faces for any sign of dissent as the smoke filled the air. 'We're goin' after Sam Goldberg, Deborah Jones and all those rats. I'm gonna bring them to their knees. They can't get away with this.'

Lomax seemed satisfied. 'We can deal with that.'

O'Neill felt his body relax. He gazed at the modernist pictures on his wall.

Damn awful. His wife had picked them at some fancy galleries in the Hamptons. She was probably in one right now. He could see her leafing through brochures as she tried to keep her mind off things. She was good at burying her head in the sand, but as long as her mind was elsewhere, that was all that mattered.

O'Neill turned to Jodi. 'You finished drawing up the statement?'

'We can issue it to the press later this morning.'

'Let's hear it.'

She cleared her throat and tucked some of her blonde hair behind an ear. ' "As a result of intense media scrutiny following an unfounded series of articles in the *Miami Herald* regarding myself, my dead son and my business associates, I feel it is necessary to clarify my position. With immediate effect, I am resigning my position on all Senate committees to devote time to clearing my name and that of my son. My family has been put under appalling pressure because of the bizarre allegations made in this newspaper. My lawyers are preparing the groundwork to commence proceedings against the *Miami Herald* forthwith." '

O'Neill crushed the end of his cigarette in an ashtray. He looked around the group approvingly. Glasser, his focus-group and numbers specialist, just nodded. O'Neill looked hard at Glasser, who sat with reams of computer printouts and graphs on his lap. 'What's the latest on our private polling?'

'Your numbers are heading south, big time, Jack. Telephone canvassers say, overwhelmingly, that Craig should be moved off death row.'

'Percentages, Bob.'

'Single figures.' Christ, it was meltdown. 'But it might be a blip.'

'Before I forget, Jack,' Lomax said, 'we've had a request from Oprah for Rose to appear on her show. You know, heartbroken mother of murdered son opens her heart. Admittedly, that was before the latest story.'

'I don't know if she'll feel up to that. Rose is kinda wary of the press, as you can imagine. She's upset by the allegations.' O'Neill turned to Jodi Perkins. 'You can understand how a mother and wife must feel, right?'

She nodded sympathetically.

'Can you ask her?' Lomax was persistent. 'I think it would go a long way to getting the family viewpoint across.'

O'Neill couldn't see Rose agreeing to that. She was a very private person. 'Leave it with me.'

'You know what I think we should do?' Perkins said.

The senator shrugged.

'Keep your head down, act dignified and both you and Rose stay off TV. Let justice take its course. After Craig's dead, who gives a shit?'

O'Neill lit up again. 'Indeed,' he said, and turned to face Lomax. 'We need a media strategy to counter these allegations. And quick. What do you say, Hal?'

His media man took a sip of his coffee. 'My advice is straightforward. I've listened to what you've said, Jack, and I apologize if I came across as a non-believer—'

'Perish the thought,' O'Neill said, sarcasm in his tone.

'Look, there's only one way to deal with such an onslaught and that's attack. It's the best form of defense. I must say that I disagree with you, Jodi. I say you should get out there, do the news shows, do the circuit, do the TV interviews, go coast-to-coast, national, cable, every goddamn thing.'

Jack O'Neill was incredulous.

'We're not gonna hide away. That's an option, but it'd be the wrong one. Come out fighting. Tell Larry King, Barbara Walters and all the rest the heartache you're facing. Say it's the ultra-liberal elements in the media who are against the death penalty. Lay it on thick.' Glasser and Perkins nodded. They saw the value of Lomax's media experience. 'Jack, you're gonna pitch yourself as the small man versus the unseen corporate behemoths. America will love it. Remember Clinton, when he and Hillary went on TV and faced down the doubters? Well, I want you to take the fuckers on by showing your human side.'

O'Neill reflected that whatever he was paying Lomax, it wasn't enough. The media man had learned a lot from the British tabloids. He'd worked at the *Sun* and the *Daily Mirror* in his younger days and knew the importance to the Democrats, just like to Labour in the UK, of the aspirational working-class vote.

Lomax added, 'You're gonna speak to your core constituency. Blacks and Hispanics, trade unionists in the defense industry, blue-collar whites, Jewish snowbirds, and generally press the flesh, in addition to TV. You're gonna appeal to the voters of Florida above the heads of the politically motivated liberal elites. And you're gonna say those words—*politically motivated liberal elites*—time and time again. People don't like elites. Hell, *I* don't like elites. America is for the common man. Egalitarian. See what I'm saying?'

O'Neill watched his cigarette smoke drift across the room and smiled.

29

The following night, just after ten p.m., while her father slept soundly in his intensive-care hospital bed in Jackson, Deborah kissed him on the forehead before being taken away by her FBI minders to a secret location. She cried all the way, not knowing if he was going to live or die. She ended up ensconced in a safe house—a log cabin—in rural Arkansas, where two new FBI officers were waiting. One of them was Brett.

Was this somebody's idea of a sick joke? Or had he requested the assignment?

For the first few days, Deborah locked herself in her room, blinds permanently drawn, and e-mailed Larry Coen for updates as Brett and his boss spoke in hushed whispers, afraid to annoy her. Furiously, she asked the FBI if Brett could be reassigned, but her request was turned down.

But on the fourth night she found herself alone with him. Deborah was waiting for the kettle to boil in the small kitchen when Brett came in, empty coffee mug in hand. She didn't say anything, and stood, arms folded, gaze averted. They both felt awkward. He apologized for his actions again, and said he was sorry that things had turned sour for her. They drank their coffee in silence before she retreated back to her room.

The monotony and her feelings of isolation intensified as time dragged on. But it wouldn't be dragging for William Craig.

At the end of the first week, Deborah, along with Brett and Simon Wilson—the special agent in charge—were watching Senator O'Neill being interviewed by Mike Wallace. Her father was still in intensive care, being monitored round the clock. The FBI had a three-man team protecting him at the Jackson hospital, and a two-man team to protect Deborah's mother back home in Farish Street.

Deborah stared at the large screen, knees tucked under her chin. She wore a gray Berkeley University sweatshirt, pants and pink sneakers. 'You believe that guy?' she said to Wilson. 'After our exposé and what happened to my father, and he's got the temerity to sit there and plead his innocence.'

'He's a politician, Deborah.'

She watched the second hand on the cabin's huge clock tick on, second after second. 'I've had my fill of sitting around,' she said to Wilson. 'When can I go back to work?'

'Cabin fever?'

'I want my old life back.'

Wilson nibbled on some pretzels. 'Not an option.'

Deborah noticed out of the corner of her eye that Brett was shifting awkwardly in his seat. 'I want to speak to Sam Goldberg about my story.'

'Not possible.'

'Am I a prisoner of the FBI?'

'You're in protective custody until this blows over. You don't need me to tell you how dangerous these people are. Those guys are just warming up, trust me.'

'Have the Jackson police not got an ID on the guys who did this to my father?'

'Your father and mother provided great descriptions . . .'

'But?'

'They don't match the IDs of those on our files or on police files in Florida. We think these guys were maybe brought in from out of town. And they're obviously pros.'

'I don't mean to be a pain in the ass,' Deborah said, 'but a man is gonna die in ten days.'

'Appreciate that, Miss Jones, but we're under orders from the top.'

Deborah shot Brett a scornful look. 'And what do *you* think, Agent Pottinger? Have you any views on the matter?'

Brett cleared his throat. 'Simon's right. We are only thinking of your safety.'

'But I can't just sit back and wait till Mr Craig dies.'

Wilson shrugged as if it wasn't his problem.

'You can't force me to stay here, can you?'

Wilson said nothing.

'You can't physically restrain me here, against my will, can you?'

Wilson gazed at the TV and munched more pretzels. 'Miss Jones, you don't wanna put yourself in harm's way.'

'Answer me. You can't keep me here, can you?'

Wilson turned to Brett. 'Tell her what we can do.'

Brett flushed a dark red. 'We *could* hold you against your will. Just need a material witness warrant.'

'Are you kidding me, Brett? What judge would grant the FBI that? You aren't going to get that warrant or any warrant, are you? I wasn't in Jackson when my father saw those guys. So how can I be a material witness?'

'If you leave, it may jeopardize the protection we're willing to offer you in the future. You think about that.'

Deborah looked at Wilson. 'You're the man in charge. Am I free to leave?'

Wilson fixed her with a long, hard stare. 'I wouldn't advise you to take that course of action.'

'Am I or am I not free to leave?'

'I'd have to check.'

'Can you call your superiors in Washington, right now?'

'Miss Jones, I'd rather you—'

'I appreciate your help, really. But I need to do this.'

Wilson got up. 'Gimme five minutes. But I'm not promising anything.' He went into his bedroom, shutting the door behind him.

There was a long and uncomfortable silence. Then Brett said, 'Whatever you think, and you're quite right to be angry with me, I want you to know that I'm here for you now.'

He didn't wait for her reply but retreated to the edge of the room and sat on the windowsill. At that moment, Deborah realized that there was too much water under the bridge for her to even contemplate trying to make a go of it with Brett again.

Wilson suddenly came back into the room, snapping Deborah out of her thoughts.

'I've spoken to my boss,' he said. 'There's nothing stopping you.' He paused for a moment. 'Only don't come running to us if those guys try and whack you.'

* * *

The following morning, Brett drove Deborah to Little Rock National Airport, off Interstate 440. It felt strange to be sitting in the same car with him, probably for the last time. He didn't say a word, his eyes focused on the road ahead.

She thought of the good times. Watching sunsets over the Golden Gate Bridge, sipping a glass of wine, enjoying a hot-fudge sundae at Ghirardelli's, checking out new bands that were in town. And then there'd been those unforgettable Sunday hikes among the thousand-year-old coastal redwoods of Muir Woods.

Brett pulled up outside Thrifty and Deborah returned to stone-cold reality. He asked her to reconsider her decision to leave FBI protective custody. She declined politely, but thanked him for his help. She shook his hand and he said, 'Best of luck.' At that moment, a part of her wanted to kiss him on the cheek, for old times' sake. But she didn't. She just smiled. He was an FBI man now and was creating a new life for himself. And so was she.

Brett took her bags out of the black SUV and put them in her rental car, a Mercedes convertible. As he slammed the trunk, she reflected that it really was over.

Deborah headed southeast under leaden skies, glancing in her rearview mirror to see Brett disappear from sight. It was the start of a fifteen-hour journey that cut through the Deep South, through Alabama, northern Florida and finally down I-75.

She stopped three times for coffee and snacks. The final hours of the journey she drove in sultry darkness. FM stations on the west coast of Florida pumped out Led Zeppelin, the Stones and the Who. The kind of music that Brett loved.

She saw a road sign for Naples and her stomach knotted. Two miles away.

A short while later, the sky inky-blue, humidity like glue, Deborah drew up by an imposing stone gatehouse flanked by an avenue of brightly lit palm trees. Two men, both sporting side arms and shades, watched her roll down the car windows.

30

'Here to see Mrs Rose O'Neill,' Deborah said.

The guard checked a clipboard. 'Name?'

'Deborah Jones.'

His eyes scanned a printed list. 'Sorry, you're not on the authorized list of visitors, ma'am.'

'I know. Short notice. Can you let her know that I'd like to see her on urgent business?'

'Wait there.' The guard turned his back on her, picked up a phone in the booth and waited for a few moments before he spoke. 'Sorry to trouble you, Mrs O'Neill, at this hour, but we have a young lady, a Miss Deborah Jones, saying she is here on urgent business.' He nodded and turned around to get a good look at Deborah. 'Yeah, she's alone.'

Deborah's heart pumped hard. If that wasn't enough, one of the armed men pulled a cell phone from his back pocket, his eyes trained on her.

This was either the dumbest thing she'd ever done or the most inspired. Truth was, she was clean out of ideas. It was a gamble, with the odds on success not too high. She'd checked the senator's media itinerary and he was too busy doing the rounds of the TV networks in New York.

'You're in luck,' said the security guard. 'She'll see you.'

She was? 'How do I get there?'

'Quarter-mile through here, and fourth left after The Avenue. Take a second left after that. And take it nice and slow, y'hear?'

'Thank you.' Deborah felt sweat run down her back. The barrier lifted up and she drove past the gatehouse and the armed guards. They just stared, one of them still on his cell phone.

Towering palm trees lined the meandering main road. The scale and opulence of the houses was staggering.

She kept to a steady fifteen miles per hour through the winding streets. The smell of mangroves and cut grass filled the heavy air and reminded her of summer picnics with her parents at Bienville.

She also got a whiff of azaleas, her father's favorite. Most of the virgin lawns out front were twice as big as basketball courts. Driveways full of BMWs and Lincolns and Porsches. The stillness was eerie, like a necropolis.

Only the night birds in the trees were making any noise.

On her left, Deborah spotted a small opening in the palms and turned down a gentle incline which led to a narrow road, and an oak-lined cul-de-sac. The house at the end was the biggest and most outlandish house she'd ever seen. It was Guggenheim in concept with sharp angles and futuristic design. It sprawled in all directions as if the architect had not worked to any precise plans.

Deborah pulled up behind a black BMW. She got out and admired the awesome scale of the coral-pink home.

Lights on inside. Cameras strafing the front.

She headed down the red-brick path and experienced a slight surge of fear.

What if the senator himself had returned? What about Richmond? She hadn't worked on a contingency plan if things went wrong. If Goldberg knew where she was now, he'd have a fit.

She pressed the buzzer and waited. She heard movement inside, footsteps clacking along what sounded like a wood-floored hall.

Then the door opened wide and standing before her was a thin woman with a watery smile. Rose O'Neill didn't say a word for a few moments. Then she stood aside and Deborah walked in.

In silence, she followed Rose O'Neill down a long corridor—modernist pictures on the wall—that led to a dining room.

Places set for twelve.

They continued down into a candle-festooned living room which overlooked the water. It was like a monastery. The air was cool, a welcome relief.

Signed Picasso prints and sketches on the wall.

Floor-to-ceiling windows overlooked the moonlit bay.

Deborah said, 'Wow, what a beautiful view.'

Rose gestured for her to take a seat. She seemed nervous and pulled at the cuffs of her mint-colored silk blouse. She was a plain-looking woman, shadows under her eyes.

Deborah sat down and looked around. With its indigo walls the O'Neill home reminded her of a Mediterranean villa. It was right on the bay and had its own personal jetty. In the distance, the flickering lights of other such houses could be seen through the palm trees and mangroves.

Rose picked up a full glass of brandy. 'Nice of you to turn up without prior notice so late in the evening.'

Deborah attempted a half-hearted smile. 'I can explain.'

'Can you now?'

'I've been in FBI protective custody since my father had a heart attack. Last night I decided I'd had enough protection and needed to speak to you direct.'

'You're on the run from the FBI? My, how brave.'

Deborah shifted in her seat. 'First, I'm glad you've given me the chance to meet you face to face.'

'Your picture in the paper doesn't do you justice.'

Deborah cleared her throat. 'You're probably wondering why I'm here.'

'It had crossed my mind.' Rose O'Neill leaned back in her seat. Her emerald eyes were watery and sad. She fixed Deborah with a long, unsettling stare. 'My husband wouldn't have allowed you to set foot on our property. Guess you're lucky he's on *Primetime* tonight.'

'Did you watch?'

'I don't think so.' Rose stared at Deborah as if trying to work out what made her tick. She checked her black suit and designer shoes. Then honed in on her hands. 'Not married, Miss Jones?'

'No.' Memories of Brett returned. His face. Kind eyes. 'Never found the time.'

'Let me tell you, Miss Jones, a mother can't brush aside the loss of a child.'

Deborah nodded and gave an empathic smile.

'By rights, I should have nothing to do with you. Your article about my husband was devastating. I . . . I felt dirty. Soiled. What you were saying portrayed my dead son as a sex monster and my husband as a conniving son of a bitch who covered it up. Those aren't the people I knew.'

'So why did you let me in?'

Rose gazed into her brandy. 'Guess I wanted to meet you. Your story's turned my world upside down.'

'Mrs O'Neill, I won't waste your time. I'm here to talk about William Craig.'

'Thought you might be.'

'What do you want to happen, Mrs O'Neill? Does another life have to be lost? More blood shed?'

'I'd rather we didn't execute Craig. But I can't go against my husband's wishes. This is off the record, right?'

'Completely. Look, Mrs O'Neill, you have the right to disagree with your husband in public. William Craig's gonna die otherwise.'

'He killed my son.'

'He didn't deny that.'

Rose closed her eyes for a moment. 'My marriage vows meant something to me. In sickness and in health. For richer or poorer. My husband's in some difficulty—'

'Your maid Maria Gonzalez said that your son raped her and your husband bought her off. What more evidence do you need? Do you know that she is in FBI protective custody now?'

'I didn't know that.' Rose glared at Deborah. Then she picked up a framed photo from a coffee table and handed it to her. It was a picture of Joe O'Neill. Handsome, healthy, white teeth and short hair. 'That was taken the day before William Craig killed him.' Her eyes misted over. 'If only we'd known what was going to happen.'

Joe O'Neill had the preppy good looks of the two boys who'd raped her.

'My husband doted on him. Still does. He'll never allow William Craig to be freed.'

Deborah handed back the photo. 'What about you?'

Rose finished her brandy and placed her glass and the framed photo on a table in front of her. 'If I spoke out it'd be the end of us. I feel as if I'd be deserting my family, my son's memory and my husband if I offered clemency.'

'Your son raped women, Mrs O'Neill. Pure and simple. You think that was right?'

'Might sound strange in this day and age, I know, but I still love my son and my husband, despite all they've done.'

Deborah kneeled down beside Rose and held her hands. She smelled of a flowery perfume, the sort that Deborah's own mother wore. 'I'm begging you to do the right thing. See it from William Craig's perspective. How would you feel if the young man who raped your granddaughter wasn't convicted?'

Rose closed her eyes.

'You were at the trial, weren't you?'

'Every goddamn day.'

'So you'll know better than anyone what a sham that was.'

Rose nodded and gazed at the floor.

'Look at me,' Deborah said, her voice edgy. 'Tell me what you see.'

'I don't understand.'

'What do you see?'

Rose shrugged. 'I don't know. A young, professional black woman?'

'But do you know I was raped just like Mr Craig's granddaughter . . .?'

'I'm sorry, I didn't know. How could I? But I see now why this case means so much to you.'

Rose turned around and peered into the darkness of the bay. A powerboat pulled up to the senator's jetty and two stocky men jumped off.

As they approached the house, Deborah felt all her senses switch on. 'Call the police!'

Rose did nothing.

'Do it now.'

'I've seen those men before,' Rose said.

'Call the police! They're Richmond's men.'

'The windows are locked. We're safe.'

Under the bright exterior security lights, Deborah got a better view of them. Each had a boxer's nose, a thick neck and raven-hued eyes. She felt herself begin to shake.

This was not a social visit. *Damn*. Why hadn't she

listened to Simon and Brett?

The men smiled through the glass as if they were dinner guests who'd arrived late. Dressed in chinos and sneakers and Hawaiian shirts, they looked like tourists. But the way they expertly snapped the locks off the French windows told another story.

Rose O'Neill gave a high-pitched scream. It was like one of her nightmares.

The smaller of the two men was grinning from ear to ear. He had no teeth. He took a small glass bottle out of one of his pockets, a white handkerchief from the other.

Deborah stood transfixed and watched as he poured some of the liquid into the hankie. Suddenly he lunged forward and pressed the sweet-smelling cotton over her nose.

31

After a sleepless night, Sam Goldberg stared out of his rain-streaked office window as a thunderstorm lashed Miami. It was important not to panic. But he had to face facts: Deborah was missing, almost certainly after being kidnapped by Richmond's men.

According to a statement that Rose O'Neill had given to police from her hospital bed where she was being treated for acute shock, two men had broken into her house and taken Deborah away.

Goldberg blamed himself. He should have pulled her off the story. But he had imagined that Senator O'Neill would instruct Richmond and his heavies to cool it. And he could not understand why the

Feds had not informed him that Deborah had gone off on her own.

Maybe Donovan was right. Maybe he had assigned Deborah the Craig interview because he felt something for her. Maybe his heart had been ruling his head.

There was a knock at the door, and Frank Callaghan, the national news editor and a close confidant of Goldberg's, came in. 'Sam, I've got William Craig on the line. I tried to stall him, but he says he wants to speak to the man in charge.'

'How did he find out about this?'

'I've no idea. I filled him in on what we know.'

'And he's phoning from death row?'

'Yeah. Able to make social calls, apparently.'

'Put him through.'

Callaghan left the room and Goldberg stared at his phone, waiting for it to ring. When he picked up, Craig's voice was low, as if he was afraid of being overheard by the guards.

'I believe you're the man responsible for this—is that correct?'

'I guess so,' Goldberg replied.

'Your colleague Mr Callaghan has informed me that Deborah Jones was kidnapped late last night. Is that true?'

Goldberg's heart was pounding. 'I regret—'

'What the hell happened?'

Goldberg decided he had to be straight with Craig. 'She's been in protective custody for the last week, following threats made to her. Unfortunately, she left that protective custody yesterday and hasn't been seen since she arrived at the Naples home of Senator O'Neill, where she managed to gain an interview with O'Neill's wife.'

'And she was kidnapped from there?'

'Yes.'

'So what are you doing about it?'

'We're using all our resources to track her down. So are the FBI and the Naples police.'

'How long has she been missing?'

'Nine, perhaps twelve hours.' Goldberg winced as he said it.

'Christ, they could've done anything to her. That girl's put her life on the line for me and your paper.'

Goldberg gave a nervous cough.

'How did the men enter the house and leave?' Craig asked.

'Police believe through some French doors which opened out onto a deck beside the water. They left in some kind of speedboat.'

'And they did this without any camera catching them?'

'Apparently.'

'This has all the hallmarks of an inside job. Had to be. Someone within that community . . . Tell me, are there other houses which overlook O'Neill's place?'

'I believe one house is in the line of sight, but that's more than half a mile away. Unless someone's got great eyesight.'

'Or high-specification binoculars.'

Goldberg felt like a complete amateur. He hadn't thought of that.

'They could've spotted Deborah as soon as she set foot in that house or at the entrance to the community. Maybe the security guards alerted them. I think Deborah Jones is being held there. It's perfect. No one can enter or leave, apart from the residents, right?'

'Mr Craig, I don't want to rain on your ideas, but the homes are occupied by some of Florida's richest people.'

'I don't give a damn. She's there somewhere. And the police should be conducting house-to-house searches.'

'They won't want to upset the residents.'

'What sort of police force do you have here in Florida, Mr Goldberg? When I was heading up missing-person investigations, your chief of police was probably still in nappies. I know what I'm talking about.'

Goldberg didn't doubt it.

32

Deborah awoke to a blinding white light shining right in her face. As her eyes slowly adjusted, she found herself staring back at her reflection in a huge rectangular mirror. She was tied to a wooden chair by ropes, hands behind her back, feet and legs restrained by duct tape.

Was it a one-way mirror she was staring at?

She heard the slow drip of water. She counted. Once every ten seconds. The air was damp and she remembered coming to briefly, before being led down a flight of wooden stairs.

How long ago had that been?

She tried to move her hands and legs, but the tape held her tight. She examined her surroundings—industrial white-painted walls, like a loft-style apartment. The odd rust-colored patch on the white floor made her wonder if it could be blood splatter.

Deborah faced the mirror and squinted into the light. 'Where am I?' Her voice echoed. 'Please tell me what you want.'

An electronically distorted man's voice replied, 'All in good time.'

Deborah closed her eyes. The light was too painful. Her mouth felt dry. The room was sticky and warm. No air conditioning. She felt herself drifting into sleep when a door creaked open.

Deborah's blood ran cold.

A small black silhouette of a figure emerged from the far corner of the room, and walked towards her in a slow and deliberate manner.

She looked up through her heavy eyes and recognized the thin-faced features of John Richmond. He wore the same shades he'd worn at the Ritz. He stopped in front of her, illuminated from behind by the powerful lights.

'You've crossed the line once too often.' His voice was as tight as piano wire.

Deborah's head dropped and she began to sob. She could never have envisioned her life would end like this. Pitiful. Crying in front of a madman.

Richmond signaled through the glass and a couple of men emerged. One taped up Deborah's mouth.

She screamed, but only a gurgling sound came out. She wondered how her daddy would cope with her death. She wanted to say so much to him, now that they'd made up. Her thoughts turned to Craig. And waves of sadness washed over her. Despite all the revelations, nothing had changed.

Richmond pulled a gun from his waistband. 'I

think we're gonna stop your suffering right here and now.' He pulled out a penknife from his back pocket. It glittered in a fierce spotlight. 'Just wanted you to know that I'll meet you in the next life. You'll never be able to escape me.'

The Lord is my Shepherd, Deborah recited in her head. *The Lord is my Shepherd*.

There was the sound of a door opening.

She squinted against the light, tears running down her face. Standing, hands behind his back, at the far end of the room was the silhouette of another man. He watched Deborah in silence for a few moments. Then Richmond stepped aside . . .

The man moved closer to her and she closed her eyes.

33

Sam Goldberg paced his office as the national desk editor, Frank Callaghan, sat and watched him in silence. Sometimes, at a paper like the *Herald*, the difference between a friend and a colleague was a chasm. Every organization had its share of yes-men prepared to agree that every move the man in charge made was a good idea.

Callaghan was different. Not only a good sounding board, but someone whose views Goldberg could trust implicitly.

Goldberg slumped back down in his seat, running over in his head what he'd done. He had followed Craig's instructions and called the Naples police and the FBI. Both were less than enthusiastic about barging into the gated community, especially after a tip-off from a convicted killer. They had promised to keep in touch if there were any developments.

To try and alleviate the burning sensation in his stomach, Goldberg popped a couple of Zantac and washed them down with a swig from a bottle of water that was lying on his desk.

'Sam, calm down,' Frank said. 'You're gonna give yourself a heart attack over this. Let's just sit back and hope for the best.'

Goldberg looked at Frank who took everything in his stride. He was a man who ate healthily, drank moderately and even found time to tend his garden or do jobs around the house. By contrast, Goldberg was tied in knots—thinking of stories, thinking of deadlines, thinking of his dead wife, and now thinking of a girl he'd allowed to pursue a most dangerous story. He wasn't good at relaxing, unless a drink was at hand.

There was a knock at the door and Larry Coen walked in, his face like stone. He handed Goldberg a picture. 'Thought you'd want to see this . . .' It was a ten-by-twelve-inch color photo of Senator Jack O'Neill and Governor Wilkinson looking relaxed on a sandy beach, palm trees and turquoise sea in the background.

Goldberg said, 'What's the significance?'

'It was taken on the Fourth of July 1998 and appeared in the *Miami Herald* the following day.' He showed the photograph to Callaghan as well. 'It shows the governor and the senator in Puerto Vallarta, Mexico, as part of a trade delegation.' Coen then produced another photo that looked almost identical, except that there was a third man in it.

Goldberg leaned closer and screwed up his eyes. ‘Dennis Morrison? What’s the head of the Miami Beach police doing in Puerto Vallarta on a trade delegation?’

‘Absolutely.’

‘Where did this come from?’

‘It was taken by a photo agency in Fort Lauderdale, hired especially by the governor’s people. I asked to see the original, just as a matter of routine, and what do you know, the whole picture emerges.’

‘The three of them on holiday?’

‘It was a fact-finding trade mission. Tony Marino, the owner of the agency, was told to keep the police chief out of the official photo. So it was cropped before it was sent down the wire to us.’

‘How come?’

‘Apparently the real photo, showing the three of them together, was a memento. They each ordered several copies.’

Goldberg leaned back in his seat. ‘Good work, Larry.’

‘Something else we’re working on—when Deborah was in Arkansas with the FBI she e-mailed me, asking for the details of how much Senator O’Neill had paid for the house, that kind of thing.’

‘And?’

‘We started doing some checks. Turns out the O’Neill house is not owned by the senator.’

‘You’ve lost me, Larry.’

‘The house is owned by Bensonhurst Inc. Wanna know the majority shareholder?’ Coen paused for a moment. ‘John Richmond, alias Paulie Fachetti.’

‘The Mob owns a senator’s house?’ Goldberg

was incredulous.

'It doesn't end there. Guess what else Bensonhurst Inc owns?'

Goldberg shrugged. 'I don't know. The golf course?'

'Every goddamn mansion within that community. Sixty-three huge houses, whose combined worth is conservatively estimated at one and a half billion dollars.'

'Frank, get on the phone to the Naples police and the Feds.' Goldberg looked at Coen. 'Write it up, Larry. All you've got. This could be the breakthrough we've been waiting for.'

The phone rang and Goldberg picked up as Coen left the room.

'Mr Goldberg?' It was a man's voice. 'Lance Armstrong, FBI headquarters.'

'Any word on our girl?'

'She's been found.' Goldberg felt the tension knots in his neck begin to subside.

'Is she okay? Is she alive?'

'Thank God, yes. But she's in deep shock, otherwise just a few cuts and bruises. We found her in a basement cell at the house of one of the senator's neighbors.'

Craig had been right after all. 'You wanna tell me who?'

'Sorry, Mr Goldberg, I can't disclose that at this stage.'

'Where is she now?'

'Receiving medical attention at a military hospital. She's also helping us with our inquiries. We'll be in touch again soon.' And Armstrong hung up.

Callaghan got up and patted Goldberg on the

shoulder. 'We got lucky, Sam.'

34

The days that followed took Deborah into the darkest recesses of her mind. She had been picked up by four FBI agents—including Brett—in an SUV that had powered away from the front lawn of the huge home where she'd been kept. She had then been driven at high speed to Naples airport where she had boarded a Cessna aircraft. Sedated, she was flown up to the Quantico marine base in Virginia.

A functional dormitory room within the main training complex at the FBI Academy was her home as a procession of military psychiatrists and psychologists got to work on her. She was quickly diagnosed as suffering from post-traumatic stress disorder, primarily caused by her rape but compounded by her recent imprisonment.

On the first night Deborah lay awake on her single bed, dressed in her FBI tracksuit, listening to the bedside clock ticking like a time bomb towards the execution deadline . . . Images of John Richmond's gaunt features flooded her mind along with other frightening memories. The sickening aroma of chloroform. And the sound of breaking glass as a SWAT team had smashed their way into the basement.

She wanted to switch off time, leaving herself in a timeless void, unable and unwilling to deal with the anxiety that was swamping her.

She kept the light on all night, terrified that the

darkness and the nightmares would return.

The sound of laughter echoed in the corridor. Rookie FBI girls, she guessed, returning from the shooting range. Her eyes were growing heavy and, as she felt herself falling into a bottomless pit, she thought she heard the guffaws of men.

Deborah awoke screaming in the dead of night, imagining that someone was turning the handle of her locked door. Two female FBI agents were assigned to stay with her thereafter.

Stress-inoculation training, a behavioral treatment to tackle her fear and anxiety symptoms, was given to her by a Georgetown professor of psychiatry who taught at the Academy. She was told how fear develops as a learned response to trauma. And she was instructed on how to identify cues in the environment—all-male environments—that triggered the fear. Cognitive relaxation exercises helped her to relax her muscles. Cognitive Processing Therapy, where she had to write about what the rape meant to her, was the hardest to endure. As she wrote down her thoughts, she had to relive the dreadful memories of San Francisco again.

*   *   *

The first thing I remember was being aware that I was being carried out of that bar against my will but unable to do anything about it. I tried to struggle, but I couldn't move. The Rohypnol had paralyzed me, if indeed that was what they'd used to spike my Long Island Iced Tea. Faces of the boys next door became the faces of evil. It was their very ordinariness and boy-next-door quality that was so scary. They didn't look evil.

When I came to, watching the spectacle on a small TV, it was like I'd gone mad. Entering me from behind, one after the other, they screamed and laughed. They wanted to degrade me. Why? They had obviously planned it. Was I their victim all along? Were there others? Humiliation and carnal gratification were their goal. And they succeeded. It was all a power trip. Their power over a defenseless young woman. The flashbacks over the coming months were as bad. I wish I had had the guts to confront them in court, rather than doing what my father wanted and hushing things up. I wish I had had the guts to track them down and kill them. I wish Brett hadn't left. But most of all, I wish I was someone else.

* * *

Daytime was okay. People were around her, kind faces. But when the sun set on the autumn foliage encircling Quantico, Deborah felt herself regressing. The lights stayed on, the seconds ticked by. When morning came, the demons were banished again until darkness fell. She had to endure six more terrible nights, seeing shadows in the corner of her room, hearing sounds under her bed.

Deborah knew that the experts were trying to piece her back together again. They encouraged her to take long walks in the acres of woodland around the base, accompanied at all times by the two female FBI agents—Suzie and Pam. But she didn't want to confront demons any more. She would have preferred to be back at work, or back in her condo, trying to help Craig.

By the end of the first week Deborah was sleeping better, although she did suffer an embarrassing anxiety attack in the middle of one day. She freaked out when watching DEA agents training in Hogan's Alley, a mock city on site with façades replicating a typical small town. She thought she saw Richmond watching her from a window, but it was only an old instructor, wearing shades.

Towards the end of the second week she was feeling stronger. Her mind was sharper and her body more relaxed. When she told her handlers within the Behavioral Science Unit of her need to get back, they seemed dismayed. This would be the second time she'd walked out on the Feds, despite their protection and help. The Quantico psychiatrists wanted her to take a whole year off, if possible, to recover. They said her mind was in a fragile state and she could relapse at any time. Medication and rest should be the order of the day. But they also admitted that one of the reasons they were keen for her to stay was that they wanted her recollections of her ordeal at the hands of John Richmond to help them build a case against him.

She was more concerned about the fate of William Craig.

Thirteen days after she'd been rescued, Deborah caught a train to Miami and returned to work.

*   *   *

Deborah sat at her desk and read the short handwritten note. It said simply:

Glad you are okay and unharmed. Love, Brett.

She felt teary as she looked out of her window, glad to see the waters of Biscayne, even the thick clouds overhead. Despite everything that had happened between them, part of her still cared for Brett Pottinger.

He had helped her into the Cessna at Naples, and had held her hand throughout the journey, occasionally squeezing it to comfort her, knowing that she had become terrified of flying since her rape. He couldn't look her in the eye, not wanting her to see the tears streaking his face.

Deborah picked up her cell phone and called Raiford, where she waited to be put through to William Craig's Death Watch cell. He had three days left to live.

She felt edgy and imagined people were following her back to her condo. And she still couldn't understand the intervention of the man in the shadows. Who was he? Had he been the one who'd spared her? But then again, maybe she'd imagined the man in the cellar. Perhaps she was hallucinating.

Most of her colleagues were shocked that Deborah had returned to the office so soon. She found it uncomfortable to talk about what had happened to her, without therapists there to hold her hand. But it felt good to be back, although everyone was caught up with the upcoming elections. Kathleen Klein, in all her blonde glory, was in her element, barking orders to the Washington bureau on her cell phone as she stalked the newsroom floor like a panther. Deborah felt as though she had been away for a lifetime. Whose numbers were going up? Whose going down? It was Chutes and Ladders for political anoraks.

Larry Coen's stories had rocked O'Neill's bandwagon, but still he rolled on. Pressing the flesh, meeting the minorities, the defense workers and the Jewish snowbirds. Even under the cloud of an FBI investigation, O'Neill talked the talk and walked the walk. It seemed as if he was on every talk show, where he portrayed himself as the victim. It was bizarre and worrying. His numbers were respectable, putting O'Neill on course to re-enter the Senate.

Deborah pulled a loose thread off her black trousers. Eventually, she was put through to Craig. She pictured him in an airless cell, guards monitoring everything he did.

'How are you keeping, my dear?' he said. 'Heard about your father. I'm so sorry.'

Deborah had put that to the back of her mind.

'I was speaking to your boss, Sam Goldberg,' Craig went on.

Curious, Sam hadn't mentioned that when she'd seen him first thing that morning.

'Told me about the FBI protection and what happened to you at O'Neill's home.'

Deborah shifted in her seat. 'He might've exaggerated a little.'

'They kidnapped you—that's not an exaggeration. Look, Deborah, can I talk straight?'

'Sure.'

'You think putting your neck on the line is smart? It's not. It's bloody stupid.'

'I don't want you worrying about me.'

'I want you to promise me that you'll drop your investigation. I appreciate all your efforts. Christ knows I do. But you must not push these people too far.' Craig paused for a moment. 'Are you still there?'

Deborah sighed. 'Mr Craig, if you honestly think I'm gonna walk away at this time, you're crazy. There's a whole team working here for you, not just me.'

'I don't want any more blood on my hands.'

'You're not to blame for what happened to Rachel Turner or my father.'

'If you hadn't investigated my case it could've been avoided.'

'Mr Craig, I care what happens to you. My father might be in the hospital because of them, but I wasn't brought up to run away at the first sign of trouble.'

There was no reply.

'Look, we're finding out things all the time. I don't want to say too much but, from what I'm hearing, the senator, Richmond and the police chief may be involved in something. Problem is, we don't know what it is.'

Craig gave a weary sigh. 'I hope I don't come across as an ungrateful old bastard. For what it's worth, your stories are going down a storm here on death row. Even the guards are talking about the investigation. Everyone is talking about Deborah Jones. Now they all want to be interviewed by you.'

Deborah spotted Frank Callaghan holding up his phone. 'Mr Craig, I've gotta go. I'll call back. Someone's on the other line. We'll talk again soon.'

The new call was diverted through to her desk phone.

'Where the hell y'been?' It was Manhart, her mystery detective. 'Been tryin' to reach you.'

'Been tied up with the Feds. You got something for me?'

'Not now.'

'Time's running out, mister, or don't you realize that?'

'The story about Dennis Morrison's trip to Mexico is raising a few eyebrows at HQ. Things are startin' to loosen up. I've had my suspicions for a long time that he mixes with the wrong kind.'

'Isn't that an occupational hazard?'

'Kind of. But not playing golf with the fuckers. Or staying on their yachts.'

'You got proof of that?'

'Not yet.'

'Oh come on, Manhart.' Deborah didn't mean to sound so ungrateful. After all, he had pointed her in the direction of Jimmy Brown, which had kick-started the investigation at a very low point.

'I have a friend at Fort Meade.' Manhart was talking about US intelligence's biggest agency, the global eavesdropping facility of the National Security Agency. 'He's their top computer geek. He's got an inside track on everything, and I mean everything.'

'I need you to come through for me. Gimme something.'

'Not on the phone.'

'Things are getting desperate. I need information now. I thought you were in on the original investigation?'

A beat. 'Look, I'm trying to get it to you. But things are tricky. I think I'm being watched.'

Deborah remembered the previous afternoon, when she was escorted back to her condo by some Feds. She had received a steely glance from a man in the underground parking bay. Not to mention this morning, when she'd seen a middle-aged woman across the street who spoke into a cell phone and stared at Deborah as though she was relaying information to others. Deborah mentioned her suspicions to the FBI special agent in charge, but he said that she was being paranoid. 'You wanna gimme a clue?'

'It's another piece of the jigsaw.' The line went dead.

35

Sam Goldberg sat in his office with Frank Callaghan as they watched live Fox News pictures of the senator being greeted as a conquering hero in his old Brooklyn neighborhood. The whole spectacle was surreal. The guy was being humiliated in the press every day—cartoonists, political commentators and radio shock jocks, all unable to make up their minds whether O'Neill was in the pocket of the Mob, or just a crazy grieving father.

Out of the corner of his eye, Sam caught sight through his office's wooden blinds of Deborah walking through the newsroom. He had tried to speak to her about what had happened, but all she'd said was that she was 'coping'. It didn't fill him with optimism.

As for his own well-being, he hadn't had much time to think about it as William Craig's execution day got closer. He knew he was drinking too much, staying up too late, reluctant to return to his empty home with all its painful memories. The office had become his real home, the place where he spent nearly all his waking hours, apart from his drinks after work when he liked to listen to the blues and jazz standards being belted out at Tobacco Road until early in the morning.

And all the time he was running his paper, making sure that the stories were solid. That day the *Miami Herald* was packed with good material. Cuban exiles alleged to have blown up a Cuban plane in 1976; a German plane with faulty gear landing safely at Miami International; predictions of a record number of hurricanes by an amateur weatherman; two thirteen-year-old black kids shot dead by police in Liberty City; and a small story by Deborah about how William Craig had refused to choose a final meal.

Goldberg swiveled on his chair and stared out over Biscayne. He felt as low as the encroaching dark clouds.

'I don't get it,' he said to Callaghan. 'Why hasn't Craig been released or clemency offered? After all Deborah's uncovered, it's unbelievable.'

'She's still making the calls out there. The kid's not giving up. Unlike Harry Donovan who seems hell-bent on reaching a settlement with O'Neill.'

That was a sore point that Goldberg didn't want to contemplate. At the end of the day, Donovan was the top guy. 'When lawyers are involved it's always messy. Frank, we're leading this story nationwide.' He picked up that day's *Herald* and pointed at the front page. 'Feds are saying on the record that they're investigating O'Neill. What more do they need?'

'Who the hell knows?' Callaghan answered. 'The

senator's team is playing this real cute. You read Kevin Skerl's column today? Interesting how he said the PR offensive is turning O'Neill into a cult celebrity across the networks. Everyone wants a piece of him.'

At that moment on TV, O'Neill was being hugged by a small Italian-American woman. 'He's a cool bastard. What's the latest bulletin on the hunt for Richmond?'

'Zilch.'

'Craig's got ratings politicians would kill their mother for, right . . . ?'

'What're you saying?'

'I'm saying, why's the governor going ahead with this execution?'

'He's a twenty-four-carat knucklehead. By the way, you see O'Neill on *Good Morning, America*?'

Goldberg loosened his tie with his right hand. 'Guy deserves a fucking Oscar.'

He stared out of the window. It would be nice, he thought, to disappear up north for a few weeks to escape the Miami madhouse. The bitter cold of Wyoming where his sister had a ranch would be the perfect place to blow away the cobwebs. Horseback riding, doing ordinary, simple things, watching his hot breath turn to steam, that would be heaven.

His doctor wanted to prescribe Prozac. But Goldberg declined, preferring the buzz of Jim Beam any day.

'Y'know, Frank,' Goldberg said, 'there's something more to all this. I can't put my finger on it. But I think we're real close. But I can't figure what the governor's playing at. He's not listening to anyone.'

'Why don't you give him a call? We could turn it around into a "Governor justifies execution" angle.'

Callaghan had a crafty news brain. He saw angles. Goldberg flipped through his Rolodex and punched in the number for the governor's press secretary. He had to endure some maudlin country song for nearly ten seconds.

Then a cheery voice answered. 'Hi, Tania Beckwith, governor's office.' He knew all about Tania Beckwith. A former Playmate of the Month, bizarrely she'd been taken under the wing of straight-laced Wilkinson for her photogenic qualities, among other things. Secret liaisons with fundraisers, bed-hopping with oil billionaires and summers in St Tropez were an integral part of her job description, according to informed gossip in Tallahassee.

'Tania, Sam Goldberg here. Looking to speak to my favorite governor.'

She groaned like he'd asked her to do his shopping. 'Not a great moment, Sam. Election's taking up all our time.'

'That's not why I'm calling.' The sound of phones and faxes could be heard in the background.

'Don't tell me, you're still trying to get that crazy old man off the hook?'

'You're a quick learner, Tania.' Goldberg pictured her curling her hair cutely behind her ears.

'I'll check and see if he's got a spare moment,' she said. 'He's due to go walkabout any moment.'

'Just a couple of minutes of his valuable time. I'm sure the readers of this fine paper will be interested in his views.' He tried to keep the sarcasm to a minimum.

The line clicked twice. After a brief pause, on came the man himself, his voice expansive and commanding like that of a Shakespearean actor.

'Sam, good to hear from you,' he said.

Insincere bastard. 'How's the weather in the Fort, governor?'

'Not much blue, but pleasant. Receptive crowds. You see my Town Hall meeting on C-Span?'

'Sorry, gov, a million and one other things.'

'Surprised you missed my little soirée in Clematis Street for the press last week. Everyone was there.'

'Kinda busy time, y'know.'

'Tell me about it.'

'Governor, I'll come straight to the point. It's about William Craig.'

Wilkinson paused for a moment. Then he let out a long sigh. 'That's old hat, Sam. Look, I'm gonna have to dash, some cable channel's wanting five minutes—'

'With respect, governor, it's not old hat. Our polls show your numbers are heading south over this issue.'

'We've got our own numbers people and we're doing real well, thank you. If you ask me, Craig's lucky to have enjoyed nearly a dozen extra years of life on this earth. Something denied to Joe O'Neill.'

'Governor, can I be frank?' Goldberg glanced at Callaghan who was listening in to the conversation on the speakerphone.

'Sam, y'know I like straight talking.'

'I'm curious. Does your dismissal of Craig's case have anything to do with your relationship with Senator O'Neill? He's treated you to more junkets around the world than anyone I know.'

The line went quiet. Had Goldberg hit a nerve?

'Now you listen to me.' Wilkinson's voice was harder. 'Since when were fact-finding missions at trouble spots around the world considered a junket?'

'Are you telling me that all those trips were necessary to help the people of Florida?' Goldberg winked at Callaghan.

'Foreign policy's an integral part of good government. Whether it's inward investment we're trying to attract from the Far East or just keeping our ear to the ground in developing countries.' Wilkinson sounded weary that he had to explain the fundamentals of economics and politics to a newspaper editor. 'Sam, the world's moved on. This is a global village we're living in. Not some shit-kicker media world. We need to keep abreast of developments and, frankly, your tone offends me.' When Goldberg didn't reply, Wilkinson continued, 'Are you seriously telling me that as a young politician I shouldn't have hooked up with a respected, experienced senator, no matter what our political differences were? Know something? I think you've been taken in by this crazy old killer.'

'William Craig may be old and he may be a killer, but can you imagine how many other women Joe O'Neill would've raped if Craig hadn't got to him?'

'You suggesting we build statues in his honor?'

'What's that supposed to mean? Did you know that my young reporter, Deborah Jones, was kidnapped from the senator's house? And did you know that this involved John Richmond, long-time associate of O'Neill?'

Wilkinson went quiet.

'Just move the guy off death row,' Goldberg said. 'I'm begging you, please think again. The guy's got a heart condition. I've got mail from all over the States. From all over the world. Our Internet site crashed yesterday because of the number of hits.'

'And what about the victim's family?'

'Check today's paper. O'Neill's up to his neck in a conspiracy and you, as governor, should be taking control of the situation.'

'I ain't got time for this bleeding-heart bullshit. You're the one who's been discredited. Your paper's been made to look foolish. A fifty-million-dollar lawsuit? That could cripple you. And that reporter of yours, Deborah Jones, she's just—'

The line went dead. Wilkinson had hung up.

Goldberg slammed down the phone and buried his head in his hands. Maybe he'd played that all wrong.

The governor's rise in politics hadn't surprised anyone. Goldberg could see how he had done so well. He was photogenic, only in his late forties, had a mediocre business management degree from Yale, became a McKinsey consultant in New York and downsized everything in sight throughout the 1980s. But he got his big move into politics in the early 1990s when he got hooked up with the movers and shakers in Florida. Big money, real-estate brokers and billionaire fruit growers bankrolled his campaign in the mid-1990s, and he took up residence in the governor's mansion in Tallahassee . . .

Wilkinson quickly forged links with right-wing Democrats, including O'Neill. But there was nothing new in that. The illusion of confrontational ideological politics was for the electorate at large.

There had to be a catch somewhere.

The governor seemed to be a happily married man. He had seven children, and was vehemently against abortion. He was signed up to the Christian Right agenda and was a devout Roman Catholic.

Callaghan said, 'If you ask me, Deborah's opened up a real can of worms.'

'She's still hoping this mystery detective's gonna come through for her.'

'Maybe the governor has some skeletons in his closet?'

He was clutching at straws.

'Frank, the guy's Mr Family Values personified. Fundraising for disabled charities, disadvantaged kids. He's . . .' Goldberg paused. It was so obvious. It had been staring him in the face all along. 'He's too good to be fucking true.'

36

Just before eleven that night, Senator O'Neill padded along the corridors' exquisite carpeting back to his suite on the fourteenth floor of the Plaza Hotel in New York. He was preoccupied as he thought of his appearance the following morning on NBC. Even a great meal, which he ate alone, a bottle of the finest burgundy and some whiskey could not lift his mood after that day's headlines.

The successful tour of his old haunts in Bensonhurst, accompanied by camera crews, had been overshadowed by other matters. No doubt

NBC would ask about the latest *Miami Herald* revelations.

The exposure of the senator's part in covering up his son Joe's excesses and mistakes was a nightmare. Richmond's Mob connections did him no favors and the picture of him on holiday with Morrison and Wilkinson looked downright strange.

O'Neill swiped his room card and pushed open the door. His suite was cloaked in darkness. He could have sworn he had left the lights on when he went down to dinner.

He shut the door and wondered if the maids had been in. This definitely wasn't how he'd left it. The curtains were now open.

Had the two double Scotches blurred his memory?

He fumbled for a switch and the chandeliers and wall lamps bathed the room in a soft glow.

There was someone in a chair by the huge windows, watching him. His heart nearly seized up.

'Hello, Jack,' Rose said, brandy in hand.

'How the hell did you get in here?'

She smiled. 'Thought you'd be pleased to see me, now that I'm out of the hospital.'

'Of course I am.'

O'Neill pecked her on the cheek. 'How are you, honey? You should've phoned.'

'You should've visited me in hospital.' She leaned back in her seat and sipped her drink. 'You look exhausted.' Her green eyes were as beautiful as they'd been the day they'd first met at Harvard Law School—the bright carpenter's daughter from Baton Rouge and the rough-and-ready son of a Brooklyn bum.

He sat down and undid his tie. 'I didn't realize you'd got out. I'm so sorry. I should have come.'

'The doctors advised me against leaving. Said I was still depressed. In shock.'

'Rose, I swear I never knew anything about it.'

'That comes as a great comfort.'

'Rose, I'm fighting for my life, don't you see that?'

'And I'm not? They kidnap a girl from our house, in front of my eyes. Are you insane?'

O'Neill bowed his head. But his wife was not finished with him yet.

'I had another reporter from the *Herald* on the phone. Larry Coen. The crime reporter, if you didn't know. Told me we don't even own our house. Jack, is that true?'

'The house was a present from Richmond. It's a technicality for tax purposes.'

'A present? Is that what they call it these days? Sounds more like a bribe, Jack. What did you have to do for that?'

'Rose, please.'

O'Neill went over to the bar and fixed himself a double Scotch. He walked across to the windows and looked down on Fifth Avenue, crystal glass in his hand. The taxis and people and movement never stopped. 'It was a thank you for all my consultancy work over the years.'

'All your *con*-sultancy work.' She emphasized the first syllable. 'My, sounds like you've had the most fruitful relationship with Mr Fachetti. Or should I say, Mr Richmond.'

'I need your help, Rose. Two days and they're gonna finish Craig. Just hang in there with me until this is over.'

O'Neill knocked back his whisky and felt it burn his stomach.

'You're so over your head, Jack. Why don't you cut all ties with Richmond and sort things out?'

'I've tried. Believe me.'

Rose got up and slipped her arm around his waist. 'You've come a long way, Jack, haven't you . . . ?'

'Bensonhurst was never enough for me, you know that.'

'Jack, I know why you stayed with him all these years. You both grew up there. You both knew the streets. He's from your backyard. And if it wasn't thanks to him, you might not have gone to Harvard. You'd still be back on 18th Avenue now, right? Working in a two-bit legal practice, nickel-and-dime clients?'

'Possibly.'

'Jack, I've never doubted your love for Joe. I felt the same about him. But you've got to let go now.'

'That's what my father would've done. I'm not like him.'

'I know that. But we have to face the facts. Joe attacked all those women, and you covered it up. This madness has to stop.'

O'Neill's mind flashed blood-red images of his son lying naked on the mortuary slab. 'It'll stop only when Craig is strapped down and executed.'

Rose sighed. 'I didn't want to do this, Jack, but you've left me with no option.'

He extricated himself from her arm. 'What're you talking about?'

'You haven't told me everything about this case, have you? About how far you'd gone.'

O'Neill looked down again on the yellow cabs,

the neon lights and the general hustle below. 'Know something? Me and the boys from the neighborhood used to head up to Fifth Avenue, hustling for dimes.'

'I decided to go through your papers and all the things in your room. Find out what else you were hiding from me. About time, I reckon.'

O'Neill was dumbfounded.

'I saw more than papers. I saw pictures.'

'What pictures?'

'Us. In Paris, Rome and all over. Pictures of us and Joe.'

He felt his muscles relax. She was talking about the photos he kept in a shoebox in a cupboard in his study. When he felt low, he brought them out.

'I took them from our albums. Hope you don't mind. Just sentimental, I guess. Nice memories, though.'

Rose touched the nape of his neck. 'You were a different person then, Jack. We were a family, always laughing and joking.'

'It was the 1960s. Everyone was laughing and joking.'

'Can't remember the last time we laughed together.'

'I'm under pressure, Rose. Pressure I cannot even explain. I'm so tired, Rose. So, so tired of it all.'

'You used to have such a nice warm laugh. Now you just seem angry and bitter. I want to help you.'

'We've moved on, Rose. I've changed.'

'I haven't. I still love you, despite everything.'

'I love you too.'

'Do you? Do you really? Do you trust me?'

'What kind of question is that?'

Rose paused. 'Why didn't you tell me about the video?'

'What?'

'I saw it, Jack. The video. The one you tried to conceal. Now I know why.'

O'Neill's mind flashed back to his study after his return from the secret trip to Saudi Arabia. The video from Richmond had been waiting for him. How could Rose have stumbled on it?

'What video?'

Rose stepped forward and slapped his face. 'You know perfectly well what video. The one lying among all the photos, hidden under the loose carpeting in the cupboard.'

O'Neill felt his face sting and his neck flush. 'I told you never to snoop in my study.'

'Well, I did.'

'So where's the video now? You got it here?'

'No.'

'Don't play games, Rose. I need the tape. Hand it over.'

'I'm sorry, Jack. I don't think I know you.'

'What've you done with it?'

Just then, there was a sharp *rat-tat-tat* at the door. 'Open up!' a man's voice shouted.

O'Neill looked at his wife. 'Wait there.'

He opened the door and his heart sank. Three men wearing dark suits stood staring at him, their eyes dead.

37

The following morning, as an ominous gray dawn broke across Miami, Deborah headed over the windswept causeway to the *Herald*'s office in her convertible. A Latino FM music station played, but she struggled to hear the songs as the tail end of an offshore hurricane whipped across the bay.

Her cell phone rang. It was Sam Goldberg.

'Deborah, you're never gonna believe this.'

Deborah scrunched up her face to hear as the crosswinds blew her hair in her eyes. She was forced to shout. 'Believe what?'

'O'Neill's just blown out NBC in New York. Night editor's just called to tell me we've got a press release from his people saying that his schedule's been changed.'

'So what's he doing instead?'

'That's just the thing—they won't tell us. Kinda strange, huh?'

'Absolutely.'

'Where are you?'

'Crossing MacArthur. Gimme ten minutes.'

'I'm running late.' Goldberg sounded as though he had not slept. 'I'll see you around seven.'

Deborah put her foot on the gas and screeched round the quiet downtown streets. A few minutes later, she pulled up at the *Herald*'s near-empty staff parking lot, under the shadow of the towering cranes that were working on the new Performing Arts Center.

She walked briskly past the huge concrete pillars and was glad to get inside the lobby, having discarded her FBI protection.

She picked up a coffee at a vending machine and was at her desk by six-fifteen. The only other person in the office was Kathleen Klein. The veteran reporter did not look up or even acknowledge her younger colleague.

Nothing new there.

Klein strummed her red nails against her keyboard as if contemplating a good sentence. Deborah wondered if she should tell her about O'Neill withdrawing from the NBC program. She was a politics reporter, after all. But she decided not to bother. Klein would have seen it on the wires. Anyway, she wouldn't thank her because she was always cranky in the morning.

Deborah switched on her computer and scrolled through the newswires. Sure enough, AP had the story. She leaned back in her seat and tried to figure out what had happened.

It didn't seem plausible. Why would O'Neill pull out of a TV show forty-eight hours before Craig was due to be executed and on the day of the election? The guy was being fêted and had grown wings. Why change things? Was he ill? If he was, that would've been stated in the press release.

She scanned the latest wire reports. Bombs in Israel, Palestinian incursions, earthquakes in Italy and Al-Qaeda formally linked to a nightclub massacre in Bali. It was deeply depressing.

Deborah started to read that day's *Herald*. The front page was powerful, provocative even. In essence, the paper had asked its readers why the Miami Beach police chief had taken a holiday in Mexico with the tainted senator and the governor. It was probing journalism of the kind she loved.

The mysterious photo of the three of them together in Puerto Vallarta was being published for the first time and had sparked, as the *Herald* pointed out, more questions than answers.

Larry Coen had done excellent work.

Out of the corner of her eye, Deborah noticed a white envelope in her in-tray.

Mail wasn't delivered until mid-morning to editorial staff. She wondered if it was internal mail. Her eyes scanned the writing on the front. Her name was written in bold letters in black felt pen. Hand-delivered?

Deborah and Klein were the only people in the office. Deborah ran her index finger along the seal. It seemed intact. Using her thumbnail, she opened the envelope. Two pieces of paper were inside.

The first was lined paper, a scrawl of handwriting in red pen. It said:

Deborah, here's a bank statement attached. Don't ask how I got it. Checked it out. It's legit.

Deborah's stomach knotted as she unfolded a Bank of Zurich statement—with rows and rows of withdrawals and deposits. A name at the top left of the statement leapt out at her. Dennis Morrison . . .

Further down, highlighted in yellow, was an amount of one hundred thousand dollars, paid into his account on July 6, 1991. The company that deposited the money—Bensonhurst Inc.

That was exactly three days after Craig had been sentenced. They couldn't have been more blatant if they had tried. Was this payback for a botched police inquiry into the activities of Joe O'Neill?

Deborah rechecked the figures. It was as clear as day. Joe O'Neill's trial had been sewn up before it had begun. And now she had the evidence to prove it, hidden away in what they assumed was a secret Swiss bank account.

The fact that the highest echelons of the police in Miami Beach were caught up in the scandal made the situation all the more frightening. Who could you trust?

Having locked the statement in her top drawer, Deborah began to wonder again who had delivered the envelope in the first place.

Kathleen Klein was the only other person in the office. She was wearing a pinstriped suit, yellow blouse, three buttons opened, part of her fleshy bronzed breasts exposed. Her heavily made-up face was still and composed as she worked at her keyboard.

Kathleen Klein was the detective's ex. Could *she* have delivered the document? If so, why? Wasn't she supposed to be the senator's pet journalist?

Deborah popped her head above her monitor and Klein suddenly looked up.

'Thanks,' Deborah said, smiling.

Klein nodded, poker-faced, as if acknowledging that she knew what Deborah was thanking her for. And that was that.

* * *

An hour later, Deborah handed over the Swiss bank statement to Goldberg.

'Reckon this'll take some explaining, don't you?'

Goldberg didn't seem interested in the figures. He was miles away.

‘Are you all right?’

Goldberg shook his head. ‘A year ago today my wife died.’ He shrugged. ‘Believe it or not, it’s completely escaped my mind in recent weeks. Never smoked, drank only moderately and didn’t eat junk food in her life. Go figure.’

Truth was, Sam Goldberg needed a few weeks off. Maybe even a few months. The pressure of the job, coupled with his heavy drinking, had put years on him. He bore a heavy responsibility. But Deborah admired him more than ever.

‘Self-pity hasn’t got a lot going for it, has it?’ Goldberg said.

‘I know the feeling. It’ll pass. I promise.’

‘Okay.’ He cleared his throat. ‘Where were we?’

He focused on the figures in front of him. ‘Jesus. Unbelievable. Money going into a top cop’s account from the Mob?’

‘That’s what it looks like.’

‘It doesn’t get much more blatant than this. How did you get your hands on this?’

‘I never reveal my sources. You know that.’

Sam grinned and shook his head. ‘You’re starting to worry me, Deborah. What is it with you and exclusives?’

She laughed, enjoying the compliment.

His phone rang and he picked up on the first ring. ‘Goldberg.’ He frowned as he listened. Then he barked into the receiver, ‘Get in here right away. This story’s going nuclear.’

He hung up and looked across at Deborah, his face flushed. ‘That was Larry Coen. Just been woken up by one of his top FBI sources. Apparently, Senator Jack O’Neill is under arrest and has been taken to a secure location for questioning.'

'When did this happen?'

'Last night in New York. At the Plaza.'

'That's got to be a good thing for Mr Craig, right?'

Goldberg leaned back in his seat and rubbed his eyes. 'Maybe. But I wouldn't count on it.'

'Why not? Surely this peels away any semblance of credibility that the senator might've had. The governor has got to move Craig off death row.'

'Larry said he'd phoned them five minutes ago. Said the execution was still on.'

'That's insane.'

'We've a mountain of evidence piling up, O'Neill's in custody and Craig is still gonna be executed. What's that say to you?'

'Perhaps there's more to this case than money,' Deborah said.

Goldberg got up and walked across to the window, his hands in his pockets, and stared out over the city. 'Work on the Dennis Morrison story. Have it on my desk by three this afternoon.'

'They're gonna kill Craig whatever I write.'

Goldberg said nothing.

'What else can we do?'

Goldberg gazed at her with sad eyes. 'Pray.'

38

The Gulfstream was cruising at forty-one thousand feet over Virginia. Five FBI special agents, three crew members and Senator Jack O'Neill were on board.

'You're in deep shit, Jack,' Special Agent Joachim Vanquez said as he sat opposite him. 'Your friend John Richmond is crazy. What's a nice guy like you getting messed up in this for?'

O'Neill leaned back in the luxury seat, restrained at the waist. He had to speak to Rose. Secure the video. 'Why can't I see my lawyer?'

'You can, but first we're making sure that nothing's gonna happen to you. We're taking you to a secure location. Look, Jack, you better play ball, otherwise you're facing federal charges of conspiracy to commit bribery and taking illegal gratuities.'

O'Neill stared at Vanquez, one of the team that'd arrested him at the Plaza. 'I want to make a phone call.'

Vanquez shrugged as if enjoying O'Neill's discomfort. 'Depends who it is.'

'I need to speak to my wife. She's worried about me.'

Vanquez looked at him long and hard. 'Guess there's no harm in that, right?'

'Appreciate that.'

Vanquez pulled out a phone, hooked up to the side of his seat, and handed it over. 'Go ahead, it's all yours.'

'I need to tell her where you're taking me.'

'Then it won't be a secret, will it? Just say you're safe and well and helping us with our inquiries.'

O'Neill pulled the tangled phone cord nearer and punched in his home number in Naples. Rose picked up immediately.

He tried to keep his voice measured. 'Rose, it's me. Glad you got back okay.'

'Where are you, Jack? I've had Lomax and all

those advisers wondering what the hell's happening. The phone's never stopped.'

'Listen Rose, it's important that—'

'The press keeps calling, you gotta help me!'

'Rose, this is all a misunderstanding.' Vanquez arched his eyebrows as if he knew better. 'I'll be back home before you know it. Don't worry, please. Tony Stone will sort things out.'

'Jack, please do the right thing. This has gone too far.'

O'Neill glanced at Vanquez who was being served some pretzels and a can of Diet Coke. 'What did you do with the video?'

'It's still here.'

'Listen to me, Rose. Let's remember what we're doing this for. It's for Joe, no one else.'

Rose was silent. 'Never in my wildest dreams did I think you'd turn out like this, Jack. Sad, immoral and corrupt.'

O'Neill closed his eyes and sighed. 'You could be right.'

'We used to laugh at guys like that.'

'Are you laughing at me now?'

'No, Jack, I'm not laughing. I'm crying. Crying over what you've done. I'm ashamed of you.'

'We need the video, Rose.'

'Who's "we"?'

'Us. We need it to help Joe. Are you going to help me to help Joe?'

The line went quiet.

'You still there, Rose?'

'Yeah.'

'So, what do you think?'

'I think it's over.' There was a click as she put the phone down.

Vanquez couldn't keep the smirk off his face. 'Your wife pissed at you, Jack?'

'I need to make another call.'

Vanquez shook his head and crunched some pretzels. He smiled and seemed to be having the time of his life. 'Come on, Jack,' he said, his hand outstretched.

O'Neill handed over the phone and Vanquez clicked it back into its slot.

39

Deborah was still sitting at her desk in a near-deserted newsroom as another rainstorm lashed Miami. Clearly there was going to be no last-minute stay of execution for Craig. She had lost.

She checked her computer clock. It was 11:59 p.m. on November 4, 2002—the eve of the midterms and seven hours from William Craig's execution.

Suddenly, on her screen, an advance wire feature on 'The Life and Times of a Death Row Hero' came in from Associated Press.

The rest of the newsroom, including Sam and Larry Coen, were drowning their sorrows at a nearby bar. It seemed like a reasonable thing to do in the circumstances. But watching her colleagues down Tequila slammers as Craig faced his lethal injection didn't appeal to Deborah.

She stared blankly at the beige phone on her desk. Beside it was a yellow Post-It with a number scrawled on it. Deborah thought for a moment, then decided to call.

'It's Deborah,' she said.

There was no reply.

Deborah felt choked. She watched the car lights on the glistening MacArthur Causeway heading down to the beach. 'I'm so sorry, Mr Craig. I didn't want it to end like this. I've failed you.'

'You've not failed me, my dear. You showed guts and you took it to the wire. I admire you more than ever.'

'But we lost.'

'*I* lost. You just ran out of time.'

'I so wanted you to live.'

'I've lived in a tomb for nearly a dozen years. Where I'm going, it's got to be better than that, right?'

'Do you regret what you did?' She'd been wanting to ask that for a long time.

Craig sighed. 'I've let my family down and I'll die alone. I can't even say sorry to them, face to face, that's my chief regret. Sorry for the hurt I've caused.'

'Have you heard from them?'

'My sister Annie phoned half an hour before you. It's hard on her. We were very close.'

'I just want to say it's been a privilege and an honor to know you, sir,' Deborah said. 'I don't know what else to say.'

'Deborah, listen to me. I'm an old man with my life behind me. You have the world at your feet. Learn to move on.'

Deborah wiped her nose with a tissue. 'Please remember that I'll be thinking of you. And you'll also be in the thoughts of many good people here in Florida, and all across America.'

'What about Jenny? Do you think . . .'

'More than anyone. You didn't just save her that night. You undoubtedly saved many other women. We all owe you a huge debt of gratitude.'

Craig cleared his throat. 'I've got to go. It's time.'

Deborah felt a shiver run down her spine. She sat motionless. 'God bless you.'

Craig said nothing.

A timeless void opened up between them. Deborah wanted it to stay like that forever. She wanted to postpone the future. Then Craig hung up.

40

Staring at the TV in the newsroom only made things worse. Deborah couldn't bear to watch as protesters sang hymns and joined hands in a candlelit vigil outside Florida State Prison.

The newsroom door opened and Deborah looked up. It was a young guy from the mailroom.

'This is for you, Miss Jones,' he said, handing her a parcel. 'Came in earlier this morning.'

Her name was written in thick red ink on the brown wrapping paper. 'Are you serious? You know what time it is?'

'We had to put it through a couple of checks—X-ray, chemical scans. Just in case . . .'

Deborah waited until the young man had gone before she opened the parcel. It contained a TDK cassette. But there was no accompanying note or letter. Was this another way for Richmond and his men to frighten her? Was it video footage of her undressing?

She went over to Kathleen Klein's desk—she had a TV and VCR—and loaded the tape. The video started after several seconds—a shot of a bed, a white bedspread on top of it. It looked like high-quality amateur footage as the camera panned round the room. In came a man wearing nothing more than a white fluffy towel around his waist.

It was the governor.

He had a great Florida tan and was smiling broadly. He pulled out a bag of white powder from a bedside cabinet and, using a razor blade, started cutting it up into raggedy lines on a small vanity mirror. Then, using a rolled twenty-dollar note, he took a large snort.

'Oh my God,' Deborah said, covering her mouth with her hand.

Then a lithe, blond-haired young man, also with a towel round his waist, came into frame. He kissed the governor on the cheek before he bent down to snort a couple of lines. His eyes were glassy as he looked into the camera, wiping the white powder off the tip of his nose.

Deborah was transfixed but felt deeply uncomfortable. Then things got even worse.

The governor lay back on the bed and the young man used his teeth to pull off the governor's towel. He started to perform fellatio on the older man.

Deborah turned away, unable to watch any longer. At the other end of the newsroom the night editor was preoccupied on the phone. Deborah heard the governor moan and her gaze returned briefly to the screen. She believed that sex should be a deeply private and personal thing, not a spectator sport.

Suddenly she made the connection. How could

she have been so blind? Through this incriminating video, O'Neill had been able to blackmail the governor. He could ensure that his son's killer would be executed, no matter what.

Deborah forced herself to watch as Wilkinson flipped the boy over, pulled down the towel around his narrow waist, and entered him from behind.

41

Deborah stared bleakly through the rain-streaked windows to the lights of the beach in the distance. In the background—on one of the newsroom TVs—she heard the somber tones of an NBC reporter describe the growing anti-death-penalty vigil outside Raiford.

Who had most to gain from sending the video? It obviously wasn't the senator. Did his wife get hold of the tape inadvertently? That was a possibility. Had she discovered it hidden in her own house? She had seemed very ill at ease, knowing that Craig's life and her husband's were in her hands.

If only the tape had arrived twenty-four hours earlier, William Craig might have been saved.

Deborah drank a cool glass of water and fought with her conscience. She could call Sam Goldberg and secure herself a scoop. She could call the FBI . . . She remembered how Brett used to chide her about her 'ethical' approach to journalism, even as a student. He found her 'playing by the rules' attitude mildly amusing, as though she was naive, not streetwise. But the germ of an idea had formed in her head.

Heart pounding, she made up her mind. Checking her PDA organizer she punched in a number.

The phone at the other end rang, and rang and rang. No answer. She kept on holding. *Someone please pick up. Someone has to be in*.

She waited nearly a minute before a syrupy voice answered. It was Tania Beckwith, the governor's secretary.

Deborah hesitated for a split second. 'Sorry to disturb you. I've an urgent call for Governor Wilkinson . . . Can you put me through?'

'Who's calling?'

'I need to speak in confidence.'

'Are you a member of the press?'

'Yes. And please, it's critical.'

'There's not been any last-minute stay, if that's what you're angling for.'

'I'm well aware of that, but I need to speak to the governor right now.' Deborah heard Wilkinson curse as his secretary called him to the phone.

'I have a proposition for you, sir,' Deborah said.

'Is that you, Janine, yanking my chain?' He let out a long, dirty laugh.

'My name is Deborah Jones. A video has come into my possession within the last hour. An incriminating video.'

'What the hell's this got to do with me? I've got better things to do, Miss Jones, than glad-hand the press, y'understand?'

'The video shows you having sex with a young man, while taking narcotics.' Deborah heard a sharp intake of breath at the other end of the line. Had she just made the biggest mistake of her career? Of her life?

‘Who else knows about this?’

Deborah took another gulp of water. ‘I can’t be sure. Me and whoever sent it, I guess.’

‘Can we talk about this?’

‘No.’ Deborah’s heart thumped harder. ‘The time for talking’s over. I want William Craig to be freed.’

Wilkinson snorted in derision. ‘Are you hustling me, Miss Jones?’

‘I guess so. If you reprieve Craig, I swear that the tape will be destroyed. No one will be any the wiser. Your secret will be safe.’

‘And if you’re lying?’

‘I’m not.’

‘I’ll need some time to think things through.’

‘Like I said, the time for talking’s over. Goodnight, governor.’

Deborah hung up and buried her head in her hands.

42

Sam Goldberg was back in his office with Frank Callaghan, waiting for the inevitable. For the last six hours they’d drowned their sorrows in Tobacco Road, but copious quantities of beer, Scotch and red wine had failed to lift the mood.

Goldberg shook his head at the media circus on TV. A blonde CNN reporter lapped up the drama in a concerned Mary Tyler-Moore-type voice. Hundreds of people were lined up along the chain-link fence, chanting and singing civil-rights songs of love and joining hands in solidarity. Some even managed to hold candles in the wet.

'Damned vultures,' Goldberg muttered to Callaghan, pointing at a blow-dried TV anchorman on CNN. 'Be honest, Frank, I mean brutally honest. Could we have done any more?'

'Sam, we took this baby to the wire.' Callaghan peeled the label from his bottle of Bud. 'There ain't nothing more we could've done. The leads we produced, right up until this morning. Deborah's revelation about the chief of police's bribe was sensational. Absolutely first-rate investigative work. Christ, she'll probably get a Pulitzer for the whole thing.'

'I'm sure she'd rather have Craig off death row.'

There was a knock at the door and Larry Coen popped his head in, his face flushed. 'We've got a development. Wilkinson's called a press conference for six.'

'He's what?'

'They're going live at six. We'll pick up the copy from AP and Reuters who're already there.'

'Has this come across the wires?'

Coen shook his head. 'No, expecting that around five-thirty.'

Goldberg looked at Callaghan and rolled his eyes. 'Fucking politicians. Always want to be the center of the universe.'

'One more thing,' Coen said. 'Deborah's disappeared. She left the building around four.'

43

Deborah sat in her bathroom, lights off, door locked, phone pressed to her ear. She was waiting for Faith to answer. The sweet smells of her bath salts and perfumes were making her feel sick.

Eventually Faith picked up, her voice a bit woozy as if she'd been drinking. A TV was on in the background.

Deborah sniffed and wiped the tears from her cheeks. 'Hi, it's me.'

The TV volume was turned down immediately.

'Honey, I know this must be a bad time, but—'

'Faith, I think I've done something bad.'

'Deborah honey, you're worrying me now. What the hell is it? You taken some pills?'

'No.'

'What, then?'

'I've just blackmailed the governor of Florida.'

'You did *what*?'

'I got hold of some incriminating video footage. He's a closet homosexual and drug user, and I blackmailed him to free—'

'Honey, that is not good.'

'You don't have to tell me that.'

'Look, I know how much that old guy means to you, but . . .'

'I wanted him to get a break for once.'

'You ain't the law, honey.'

Deborah started to cry again. 'I just couldn't live with myself if I'd let him die.'

'Where are you? I'll come round.'

'It doesn't matter.'

'Like hell it doesn't. You're my friend. And we stick together.'

'Faith, I'm so scared, I can't breathe. What if the governor is talking to the police right now about me trying to blackmail him, and goes ahead and kills Craig anyway?'

'Honey, just slow down. Now, we're gonna just sit and wait this out. What's done is done, okay?'

Deborah blew her nose.

'Goddamn, girl, you sure like to do things the hard way.'

'I'm a fool, Faith.'

'You ain't no fool, honey. You're just too close to the story. Much too close. Hell, you've *become* the story . . .'

'They're gonna crucify me for this, aren't they?'

'We don't know anything yet. No use worrying about something that might never happen.'

'Faith, I just want to say I love you and all the girls. And I've loved being part of your group. Just wanted to say thanks for everything.'

Deborah hung up, unable to talk anymore.

She left her tub to cool and went back to the living room. She switched on her TV and went out onto her balcony T-shirt sticking to her back in the pre-dawn humidity. The black sky was already turning a pale gold.

She heard an ABC anchor describe the group outside the fence singing hymns. And Craig was being prepared for his slow journey to the execution chamber, a Presbyterian minister by his side.

Gazing out over the still waters of the Atlantic, the sound of drunken laughter drifting up from the neon-lit drag below, car horns still blaring,

Deborah reflected that the hedonistic world of South Beach was quite oblivious to the endgame that was being played out in north Florida.

She leaned forward on the balcony and stared all the way down to Collins below. Two hundred feet. Three hundred feet . . .

Loitering tourists and partiers wandered unaware of her torment high above.

For a brief moment, Deborah wondered if she had the guts to jump. What had gone through Rachel Turner's head at the Mandarin Oriental before she fell?

Inside her apartment, the ABC anchor spoke in stentorian tones. 'In five minutes, we're being told to expect an announcement from Tallahassee. We don't know what to expect, but our correspondent, a witness to the forthcoming execution of William Craig, says he is being led, as we speak, to the execution room. I repeat, he's being led to the execution room.'

Deborah blinked away the tears and stared up at the millions of faint stars in the sky above.

44

The small windowless room was hot, the fluorescent lighting harsh. Senator Jack O'Neill sat hunched over a scalding coffee and watched the TV pictures in the FBI's field office in North Miami Beach. Alongside him were five special agents, all stares focused on Tallahassee. The smell of stale sweat and cologne was overpowering.

'Why am I still waiting for my lawyer?' O'Neill

asked the man in charge, Special Agent Frank Alonzo. 'I'm entitled to see him.'

Alonzo just shrugged, as if it wasn't his problem.

'So that's it then, huh? Whatever happened to my constitutional rights?'

Alonzo didn't answer.

There was a close-up on TV of Governor Wilkinson—tanned, immaculately groomed in a dark three-piece suit, matching tie and white shirt. He stepped forward through the huge whitewashed columns of his Tallahassee mansion into a blizzard of flashbulbs, a light drizzle overhead.

O'Neill felt his blood boil.

The eyes of the world were upon the governor as he walked to the lectern. And didn't he know it. He adjusted his tie and glanced around the assembled throng like the old pro he was.

Then he lowered one of the phalanx of microphones and gripped the side of the lectern. A lackey held a golf umbrella over him.

Wilkinson cleared his throat before speaking, an affectation that his media minders had advised him to persevere with, as it made him seem vulnerable and hence likeable to women.

'Ladies and gentlemen of the media,' he said. His voice boomed out over the ghost-like faces of the journalists. 'Appreciate you turning up at such short notice. I'm here speaking not only to the people of Florida, but indeed to the people of America about a case which has attracted a lot of publicity in recent weeks.'

O'Neill felt his insides burn and longed for the humiliation of his situation to be over, for his son to be avenged.

Wilkinson paused and cleared his throat again.

'It is, of course, concerning William Craig,' Wilkinson said. 'Now, as you all know, I am zero tolerance when it comes to crime. I was elected on a mandate to keep the streets of Florida safe. Recently I've been inundated with requests to move this man off death row. It is worth remembering that this man killed the only son of Senator Jack O'Neill in cold blood in South Beach nearly a dozen years ago.'

Out of the corner of his eye, O'Neill noticed Alonzo watching him. Probably wanting to see a reaction. Well, he wouldn't be getting one.

Wilkinson continued, 'The senator has been at the center of newspaper allegations which I cannot comment on as they are subject to legal action. However, I believe that the serious allegations in the press against the senator's son, Joe O'Neill, naming him as a serial sex attacker, merit further investigation.'

O'Neill's throat felt dry.

'My job is not to take the easy option. My job is to uphold the great traditions of men who have held this post in the past. Men who have fought for democracy and had the courage to stand against those who try to wreck our society. As a Christian, my own faith has been tested to the limit. "Thou Shalt Not Kill" is something I learned as a child.'

Wilkinson paused and gazed around at the cameras and journalists, milking the situation for all it was worth.

'However, as a Christian, I was also taught "an eye for an eye". Ultimately, I listen to the wishes of the victims of crime. The people who don't make the headlines. The ordinary people. The good people of the world who have e-mailed and written in their thousands to my office, demanding clemency.'

O'Neill fiddled with the American flag pin on his lapel.

'The good people of Florida put me where I am today because of my views on crime, criminals and criminality. And their unanimity of voice can't be ignored.' His left eye twitched and he gazed straight at the camera. 'I've thought long and hard about this case. I would, undoubtedly, be well within my rights to give the go-ahead to this execution, ignoring all protests to the contrary.'

A shiver ran down the senator's spine. The bastard was caving in.

'But it would be remiss of me to ignore the persuasive and passionate arguments any longer. What has become apparent is that there are huge doubts about the integrity of Joe O'Neill's original trial. In addition, the *Miami Herald* has campaigned tirelessly on this issue. They have discovered that William Craig served with distinction in the Second World War. In fact, his bravery was deemed worthy of the UK's highest military honor, the Victoria Cross. After more than a decade on death row, I believe this man has suffered enough.'

Wilkinson made intimate eye contact with the camera. 'I'm sorry I left it so late in the day, but such a momentous decision could not be taken lightly. It required a lot of prayer and soul-searching on my part.'

O'Neill felt unable to breathe.

'I believe the suffering has gone on too long,' Wilkinson said. 'That's why I have some important news for the world. Let it be known that within the last fifteen minutes, I have contacted the Department of Corrections and the Florida State Prison. With immediate effect, William Craig is a free man.'

As his mind struggled to come to terms with the double-cross, O'Neill knew Richmond would make sure that someone would pay for this. There would be no warning. And no reprieves.

This time someone would die.

45

Sam Goldberg wondered if he was dreaming. Outside his office, he heard the cheers and whoops of joy from the reporters in the newsroom.

On the TV, as dawn broke in northern Florida, there were scenes of bizarre celebration among gum-chewing kluckers, anti-death-penalty activists and Christians holding candles outside Raiford.

Never in his life had he witnessed anything like that.

'You believe this shit?' he asked Callaghan.

Callaghan clenched a fist and grinned. 'Who cares, Sam? We did it.' He reached across the desk to shake Goldberg's hand. 'They'll talk about this day in journalism schools across America for generations. This is a great day for the *Miami Herald*. We did this.'

'First things first. We have a new special edition to get ready.'

'You got it, Sam.'

*　　*　　*

Deborah sat on her sofa, knees tucked up to her chin, and hugged her legs. The curtains were drawn against the morning light in her ocean-front condo. How could she live with what she'd done? It was the pinnacle of her career in journalism, yet she felt like a criminal.

Her phone rang but she did not feel like answering. After eight rings it switched over to her answering machine.

'Hope you're okay, Deborah.' It was Sam. 'Gimme a call ASAP. I'm gonna need a thousand words from the reporter who started the whole thing. You did it, kid. Gotta go.'

On her TV screen she scanned the joyous crowds outside the huge Raiford fence. They were ecstatic that a war hero wasn't going to be put to death in their name. Just then, a face appeared among the throng. An old black face, creased with delight. She scrunched up her eyes as her father's twisted mouth sang. *I was lost, but now I'm found. I was blind, but now I see*.

His eyes sparkled like they used to before his stroke. Beside her father stood her brother. Both supporting the freedom of an old white man.

The fire was back, just like the old days.

'I love you, Daddy,' Deborah said out loud.

* * *

Within ten minutes, a reporter was talking in excited tones.

'I think we have him, folks,' he said. The TV pictures from Raiford showed a gray-haired old man walk out in a gray suit. His back was straight, his head held high. He was surrounded by guards, reporters and well-wishers. And was that the large frame of Warden Erhert, looking smug and self-satisfied as if he had made the decision himself?

'God bless you, Mr Craig. God bless you, sir.' The reporter could not get near enough with his microphone, and the cameraman was clearly being jostled by the crowd.

William Craig's eyes shone clear blue, and his face was alabaster white. He seemed frail as he walked slowly towards the archway. Then he smiled.

'I don't think I can ever remember this many people cel-ebrating a man walking off death row,' the TV reporter said, his voice husky with emotion. 'Never in my life.'

46

Just after nine a.m. Deborah, drained of emotion, scanned through the words on her computer screen. Thirty minutes earlier, she'd e-mailed the copy—a thousand-word piece giving vent to her feelings about the case—to Sam Goldberg. She explained for the first time how her father's heart attack after a visit from unidentified goons had nearly derailed her investigation. She reiterated that her investigation had come at a high price. Lives had been lost and ruined because the legal system, the Miami Beach police, and the DA's office hadn't done their job. And she ended her article by saying that Craig's release was the right thing for the governor to do, but she didn't think an old man should have had to resort to the law of the jungle to ensure his granddaughter's safety.

Goldberg had just got off the phone. He sounded like he was speeding as he babbled his congratulations. They meant a lot to Deborah. Champagne corks were popping in the background. He asked why she wasn't in the newsroom enjoying her finest hour. She mumbled about being exhausted and needing time to recover. But she said that if he needed to contact her she'd be hanging out at the beach.

Family and colleagues had called to say how wonderful it was about Craig's release. Klein even invited her out for lunch at a fashionable new South Beach restaurant, part-owned by Ricky Martin. She respectfully declined.

Deborah leaned back in her seat, arms outstretched, and gave a huge yawn. She needed to get out of her condo. She craved fresh air, the sun on her skin. Her mind was buzzing too fast for sleep.

She changed into some faded Levis, a blue Berkeley T-shirt, black leather sandals and shades.

Grabbing a bottle of water from the cooler, she put on a Dolphins baseball cap, stuck her cell phone in her back pocket and stepped out into the hazy morning sunshine, desperate for some solitude. On the coral-pink sands the heat and humidity hit her, like a Turkish bath.

The beach was nearly deserted as Deborah headed towards the huge condos of North Miami Beach. Seagulls swooped low for scraps left by revelers or tourists who'd dropped the odd burger or half-eaten pizza. She never did understand what possessed some people to litter, but those minor misdemeanors paled into insignificance compared with her crime.

Deborah took a deep breath, feeling waves of anxiety sweep over her. Ordinarily, she'd be loving the exercise, but her mood didn't match the blue skies and brilliant sun, which had just broken through the clouds.

Up ahead, maybe a couple of hundred yards, some Hispanic kids were using their T-shirts as goal posts. The laughs and fun they were having, slapping high-fives after a goal, was what the game meant to her. It seemed like she'd forgotten what a good time was.

'Hey, miss,' one shouted as the ball crossed her path.

They all looked surprised at the accuracy of her kick. She walked down to the ocean's edge, skirting their game, and wondered what William Craig was doing now.

Deborah passed by a few families on the beach, laughing and joking, exhibitionists playing volleyball, everyone smiling, just getting on with their lives. Kids were building sand castles, carefully digging moats, happily filling them with plastic buckets of water scooped from the crashing surf.

She thought of her own childhood, visiting Biloxi to play in the sand, and those great picnics at Bienville, paddling in the tannin waters that ran through the forest.

Innocent times. So long ago.

An attractive young girl wearing a blue bikini ran towards her alongside an equally attractive young man. She handed Deborah a camera. 'I'm sorry to bother you,' she said, half apologetically. 'Do you mind taking a picture of us? We're from Salt Lake City. We're on our honeymoon.'

Deborah smiled and took the camera. 'Sure.'

The couple kissed each other, and beamed as Deborah clicked the shutter.

'Well, thank you,' the girl said, and the couple ran off again, hand in hand.

They seemed so relaxed and natural with each other. The way it had been with Deborah and Brett, before the rape. Now she was like ice when a man even held her hand, or pecked her on the cheek, no matter how innocently. Except for Sam. He had been there for her all down the line. Was there more to it than that?

For the next couple of hours Deborah walked. Further and further away from the place she now called home, the citadel in the sky where no one ever visited, where there was no laughter anymore. Despite the fact that her condo had been swept regularly for bugs, she still couldn't get it out of her head that someone was watching her.

Was someone maybe watching her now? Photographing her every move, ready to take her out. Since she'd got back from Quantico, she'd never felt so uneasy.

Innocent smiles from bystanders on the street indicated possible traps. Men crossing the street, headed in her direction, brought on cold sweats.

Deborah got off the beach, hailed a cab and headed back to her condo. She made herself a coffee and switched on the TV. Political commentators were still trying to understand what had changed the governor's mind at the last minute. He was being hailed by both liberal and conservatives as ‘visionary’, ‘compassionate’ and—what really annoyed her—‘a man of total integrity’.

Deborah could not sit still and went out to enjoy some brunch in the sun. She hadn’t realized how starving she was after the crazy last twenty-four hours.

She gazed at the pastel pinks, yellows and turquoises of the art-deco hotels and bars along Ocean Drive. Latin music pulsated from a neighboring café. She enjoyed a Brie sandwich and some sparkling water. Absent-mindedly, she paid her check and wandered off to the beach. Suddenly she felt absolutely exhausted and lay down on the sand. Huge gulls squawked overhead, but Deborah did not hear them. As soon as she closed her eyes she fell asleep.

She heard a woman’s voice call her. Was she dreaming?

A woman, her face partly hidden in the shadows of the late afternoon, gazed down at her. It was Jenny Forbes.

Deborah thought that her heart would explode. She jumped to her feet immediately and hugged the other woman as tight as she could. A small girl appeared from around the back of Jenny Forbes’s legs. She had long wheat-colored hair and blue eyes, and she wore a pink dress. A yellow ribbon was tied in her hair. She looked around seven, maybe eight, and she seemed excited.

‘Thank you, Miss Jones.’ She spoke in a sing-song voice, as if she were reciting a nursery rhyme.

Deborah kneeled down and held her tiny soft hands. ‘My, you’re pretty.’ She smiled and brushed her hand against the girl’s soft cheek. ‘What’s your name?’

The child seemed coy. 'Annie. My mom named me after one of great-granddaddy's sisters. She lives in Scotland. Do you know where that is?'

'Yes, I do.'

Jenny Forbes smiled and hugged herself as if in shock. She seemed like a different woman. 'She was born while he was inside,' Jenny said. 'If it weren't for my grandfather, she wouldn't be here.'

'Has he met her?'

'Earlier this morning. We flew up to Gainesville. I still feel in a complete daze. All those people, the press—'

'How did you manage to escape?'

'Your paper kindly laid on a helicopter which brought us straight here. Got a doctor to examine my grandfather first, and here we are.'

'How did you know where to find me?'

'Blame Mr Goldberg. Said you were chilling out on the beach. Hope you don't mind.'

'It's a big beach,' Deborah said.

Jenny Forbes motioned for Deborah to turn around. Walking towards her was a tall man, silhouetted against the towering condos.

Tears spilled down Deborah's face as he leaned forward and kissed the side of her cheek. 'How can I ever thank you, Miss Jones?' His Scots accent was as crisp as ever, but he seemed formal, as if he was unsure of his surroundings.

'I'm not the only one,' she said. 'There were a lot of people at the *Herald* who worked real hard on your behalf.'

He smiled and looked down at Annie, then ruffled her hair with a huge hand. 'Thanks to this young lady, Annie, I've met you. We've got a lot of catching-up to do.'

Tears in her eyes, Jenny Forbes hugged her grandfather, who wrapped his huge arms around her and held her close.

'That's all in the past, my dear.' Gently, he disengaged himself and then walked slowly down to the ocean's edge as the breakers crashed onto the sand.

He took off his shoes and socks and paddled ankle-deep like a child would. He looked out across the waters and tilted his white face back, enjoying the last remnants of the crimson sun.

* * *

An hour later, as Deborah, Craig, Forbes and little Annie sat together chatting in the gathering gloom, the silhouettes of two men appeared. They were wearing chinos, sandals and loose-fitting shirts.

A familiar New York accent croaked, 'Well, ain't this something. It's the hotshot reporter and her tough-guy friend.'

John Richmond was wearing his shades—even though it was getting dark. He had been on the run since Deborah's kidnapping.

Craig moved towards the two men as if to stop their advance. 'Who the hell are you?'

The sidekick pulled a gun and Craig froze.

The little girl let out a terrible cry, hiding behind her mother and clinging to her skirt. Richmond was grinning like a mental patient.

Deborah stood up. Jenny and her daughter followed suit.

Richmond's face was thinner than Deborah remembered it. His cheekbones poked through his scaly skin like those of a famine victim. He ignored

Deborah completely and fixed Craig with a long stare.

Craig didn't flinch. 'What do you want?'

'You.' He turned to Deborah. 'And you.'

Deborah didn't know what to do. Should she grab Annie and try and run for her condo? Should she scream for help? No one would come. Screams were heard all the time around here from revelers, drunks and college kids having a good time.

'Why did you let me go in Naples?' Deborah asked.

Richmond gave a dark chuckle. 'That's because the senator was so kind-hearted.' So it was O'Neill who'd entered that basement where she had been held. It had been his silhouette. 'He's a gentle man. Me, well, I just whack anyone who gets in my way.'

Without warning, Craig lunged at Richmond, his huge hands gripping his throat. But with surprising speed the goon stepped forward and smashed the barrel of his gun into the side of Craig's face.

Craig fell to the ground, blood pouring from the side of his head.

Jenny dropped to her knees beside her grandfather and held a white handkerchief against the wound. She looked up beseechingly at Richmond. 'He needs a doctor.'

Richmond grimaced as he tried to swallow, holding his throat, obviously still struggling to breathe. Then he started laughing, the sound carrying down the beach. It was the sound of the asylum. 'He needs a doctor!' he rasped.

The goon laughed too, before launching a vicious kick into Jenny's stomach. She squealed and curled into the fetal position. Annie ran to her side. The goon then leaned over and pressed his gun against

Craig's bleeding temple.

Richmond kneeled down to lift up Craig's chin. 'Not so tough now, hard man, huh?'

A single shot shattered the dark stillness. And the goon dropped with a grunt to the sand. He'd been hit in the right eye.

Deborah spun around. Further down the beach, two hundred yards away, she saw a man aiming a scoped rifle at them. He wore what looked like virtual-reality goggles.

'Go ahead!' Richmond shouted. And he laughed like a screwball again and started walking towards the gunman. 'Know something? You're fucked. Have you any idea who you're dealing with?'

A split second later, one side of Richmond's face was ripped apart, just like John F. Kennedy in the grainy, color footage from Dallas. His face hung off his skull, a crimson mess of skin and bone.

Deborah pulled Annie and her mother close as they quivered in fear.

Another shot rang out. A bullet struck Richmond in the chest and he fell to the ground.

Deborah covered Annie's eyes as Craig groaned and blood seeped into the sand. They would be next.

But the rifleman had disappeared.

Deborah scrambled for her cell phone and called 911. There was a screech of burning rubber as a car sped away along the ocean front, past her condo. She narrowed her eyes and tried to make out what sort of vehicle was being driven.

It looked like a red Chevy.

47

In the weeks that followed, Deborah began enjoying life again. For the first time since San Francisco the sadness and guilt receded. Soft drinks at the Hard Rock Café and clubbing on Washington with some of the girls from the office, not to mention Faith and the Overtown crew. It was fun to let go, after all. The obsession with Craig was over.

She redecorated her condo in pastel pinks and yellows to match her more optimistic mood. Only the lingering guilt about her devil's pact with the governor gnawed away at her.

Senator O'Neill cut a deal with the FBI after a couple of weeks of negotiation. By late November, he had divulged everything on Wilkinson in return for a five-year stretch at the white- collar Federal Prison Camp at Eglin in the Florida panhandle. FBI sources told the *Miami Herald* that he had turned informer as soon as the governor released Craig.

He wrote to his wife who didn't reply to his letters. It was reported that he enjoyed yoga, bocce ball and tennis with computer hackers half his age. Rose was never seen outside the gated community.

O'Neill was signed up to write his memoirs. He became one of the most famous inmates—including Watergate conspirators H. R. Haldeman and E. Howard Hunt, Medellín cartel boss Jorge Valdes, and former Florida House Speaker and well-known tax evader Bolley 'Bo' Johnson—to grace Eglin.

Like most of the eight hundred and fifty Eglin jailbirds, the ex-senator alternated between pulling laundry or kitchen duty. He preferred to stay inside and not join one of the groups who volunteered to tend the grounds.

A month after Craig was freed, Tallahassee police received an anonymous tip-off that Governor Wilkinson did drugs. After a dawn raid at his mansion at 700 Adams Street, a five-gram bag of cocaine was found in the desk drawer of his study. The maximum sentence for possession was one year in jail, but he managed to escape with probation. He quit office in disgrace. But he never raised the question of blackmail, possibly feeling more comfortable with the public's acceptance of recreational drug use than with coming out of the closet as a homosexual. And he made a comeback. He started appearing on talk shows, televangelist programs and the college lecture circuit as a staunch anti-drug campaigner. Deborah lost count of the number of times he broke down on TV, claiming that the stresses of the job had made him 'weak'. The public lapped it up.

Dennis Morrison, the Miami Police Chief, committed suicide after his wife took her children to live with her mother in Key Largo. He had faced charges ranging from accepting bribes to perverting the course of justice.

The William Craig story became part of history. As 2002 drew to a close, the preparations for a war against Iraq took center stage. Deborah was promoted and headed up investigations at the *Herald*. She was the youngest journalist ever to lead that team. She found her confidence again and was no longer racked by guilt and self-doubt. She had moved on.

Sam Goldberg had awarded her the assignment and they had grown closer. She discovered that he was not the distant man she had thought he was. And she admired the fact that he was a hard-working, dedicated journalist who encouraged all his staff. And she really enjoyed his company.

In her spare time she wrote a book about her experiences after receiving a six-figure advance from a New York publisher. By December, no one was paying any attention to the red Chevy that parked opposite her condo.

* * *

It was December twenty-second, and South Beach was hosting a rap-athon fronted by Will Smith down on the sand. The music throbbed as people in Santa masks strolled along Ocean Drive. Tourists from Iowa and Buffalo laughed as they took snapshots.

Deborah was packing the last of her clothes into a tan suitcase. She had completed her Christmas shopping. In twenty-four hours she'd be going back to Jackson to spend Christmas in Farish Street with her father, mother, brother and sister-in-law.

She smiled as she glanced out of her window. Midwinter in South Beach was hot, in the high nineties.

Her cell phone rang. She picked it up, expecting to hear Goldberg. But it was Manhart, the mystery detective.

Deborah said, 'I've been wanting to speak to you. You haven't phoned for nearly two weeks.'

'This is the last time you'll hear from me.'

'Why?'

'I have two bits of information about Richmond which you might find interesting.'

Deborah grabbed a notepad and pen from a table.

'I know who killed him.'

'You do?'

'Yeah.'

'So, you gonna tell me?'

'There wasn't a single person responsible. It was an organization.' His voice was low, as if he was afraid that he would be overheard.

'Cosa Nostra?'

'Bigger than that. Far more powerful.'

'What's more powerful than the Mob?'

'The federal government.'

Deborah felt the old familiar shudder.

'Richmond had iced four Feds. They'd had enough.'

'Are you telling me the American government had him killed?'

'In a roundabout way.' It was something that was perfected by undercover operatives in Latin America in the 1970s and 1980s.

'Which agency?'

'Look, I ain't goin' there.'

'Are we talking covert ops?'

'Could be.'

'Authorized by whom?'

'You don't wanna know.'

'I see.' Deborah wanted to keep him talking but sensed that he was going to stop the conversation ASAP. 'Is it over? Their work, I mean.'

'On this occasion, yeah, it's over.'

'What's the second thing you had for me?'

'Richmond and Senator O'Neill are connected. And I don't mean Mob-connected.'

'You lost me.'

'The Feds took DNA samples from Richmond's body during the autopsy and also some from O'Neill. Richmond was O'Neill's father. Turns out that old Mrs O'Neill had a brief fling with Paulie Fachetti when he was a young man. She provided sexual favors in return for money. That way she fed and clothed her family, and put Jack through Harvard.'

'Can you get me proof?'

'The report'll be on your desk in the New Year.'

'Was this your NSA guy?'

Silence. Manhart had said enough.

'One final thing. Have I anything to worry about?'

'With regard to what, exactly?'

'The special-ops guys.'

The line went dead.

Nicaragua, Guatemala, El Salvador, Honduras: the list of atrocities committed by US-backed death squads—at the instruction of the CIA—was well known. This was something else. Or was it? Wasn't the assassination of President Kennedy in Dallas rolled up in some Mafia/CIA/FBI cover-up? Wasn't the forthcoming ousting of Saddam Hussein part of the same hypocrisy? A US-backed psychopath who eventually had to be chased down, but not before the torture and wholesale murder of his own people.

Had Richmond's putrid world of corruption and killing been tolerated while it suited the establishment? Then, as his links to so-called mainstream society were exposed, the powers-that-be decided that enough was enough.

The red Chevy outside Raiford had followed Deborah down I-95. Had the driver been assigned to look after her interests, knowing the danger she was in?

*   *   *

Deborah rode the elevator to the lobby and froze when the doors opened. Sam Goldberg was staring back at her, jacket slung over his shoulder.

'Sam, what's going on?'

He smiled, eyes tired as always. 'You wanna take a walk?'

She followed him out into the brilliant Miami sunshine, blue skies overhead, and headed along Washington.

'There's something I need to tell you,' he said. 'Something I've not mentioned before.'

Deborah smiled, her insides churning. 'I'm listening.'

'I've stopped drinking. And I'm getting my life into gear again. I'm looking forward, you know, instead of living in the past.'

She smiled at him. 'I'm pleased.'

Sam scratched the back of his head, sweat beading down his forehead. He couldn't have looked more awkward if he'd tried. 'I guess what I'm trying to say is that I've made a reservation for my two sisters and their partners at Tequila Blue. It's a great Mexican restaurant. Anyway, I was wondering if you'd like to join us.' The words seemed to hang in the air forever. Was this his clunky way of inviting her out on a date? 'They're dying to meet you.'

Deborah thought her legs were going to give way. 'Are you sure they won't mind?'

'Not at all.'

She didn't have to give it much thought. 'Okay, I'd love to.'

And that was that.

Deborah and Sam walked on for a while in silence. Then stopped for a coffee at the News Café where they went over the Craig story yet again.

Deborah felt at home in South Beach. Even the slightly rougher edges to the area—the tattoo parlors, scruffy twenty-four-hour convenience stores and screwed-up veterans begging on Ocean Drive—appealed to her, along with the beautiful art-deco hotels.

They strolled back slowly to her condo. Sam pecked her on the cheek and said he'd pick her up at seven.

Deborah seemed to float through the silver and gold tinsel-decorated lobby of her condo tower, suddenly at peace with herself and life.

She took off her sunglasses. The song playing on the small radio behind the desk was John Lennon's 'Happy Christmas (War is Over)'.

She picked up her mail.

Only one card.

She smiled at the concierge. 'You finished your shopping, Steve?'

He shrugged. 'I leave that to my wife.'

Deborah pulled a face in mock indignation. 'Shame on you,' she said. 'I thought you were a new man.'

'Believe me, Miss Jones, she's the one who wears

the trousers in our house.'

Inside her condo she triple-locked her door. *Old habits die hard*, she thought.

A gentle Atlantic breeze blew through the curtains, making them sway slightly. The card had a postmark from Scotland.

Craig had sent one every week from a different part of the country. Said he was rediscovering his homeland.

The picture on the front showed a wide expanse of golden sand, fringed by cool blue waters. It was Belhaven Bay, Dunbar—his hometown.

Happy Christmas from a free man. Would be honoured if you and your family could come and visit.

Fondest regards,
William Craig

Deborah put the postcard in her bag. She walked out to her balcony and gazed across the blue waters of the Atlantic.

Thousands of miles away, William Craig had been reborn.

She closed her eyes for a moment and smiled. So had she.

Acknowledgements

I would like to thank the following people for their help and support:

Many thanks to my agent, Caradoc King, and to my editor, Paul Sidey, for all their hard work, enthusiasm, and belief in this book.

Also, thanks to Alice Peck, of Brooklyn, New York, who looked over an early draft. I also want to acknowledge the help of the *Miami Herald*, especially Elissa Vanaver and Dave Wilson, the current managing editor/news. They both gave me an insight into how the paper works, but for the sake of drama, I put my own spin on things. And Nick Austin, a fine copyeditor.

Last, I would like to thank my family and friends for their encouragement and support. And, most of all, my wife, Susan, who was with me every step of the way, as each draft developed, offering brilliant advice and displaying the fortitude and patience of a saint, all down the line.

FRIDAY
ollie
2.40PM.